THE NOTORIOUS MAN

(Book 3 of The Anonymous Man Series)

by

VINCENT L. SCARSELLA

Also by Vincent L. Scarsella

Novels

The Anonymous Man (Book 1: The Anonymous Man Series)
Still Anonymous (Book 2: The Anonymous Man Series)
Lawyers Gone Bad (Book 1: Lawyers Gone Bad Series)
Personal Injuries (Book 2: Lawyers Gone Bad Series)
Winning Is Everything (Book 3: Lawyers Gone Bad Series)
Pardon Me (Book 4: Lawyers Gone Bad Series)
The Messiah
Mind Plague
Escape From The Psi Academy (Book 1: Psi Wars Series)
Return To The Psi Academy (Book 2: Psi Wars Series)
Within A Dream
InHumane: A Novel of Extraterrestrial Invasion
The Walrus Was Paul: A Novella Of Paul McCartney's Death and Replacement

Story Collections

Unusual Suspects
Spectacular Fictions
Time Travelers

Non-Fiction

The Human Manifesto
Beyond The Lie
The Bad Lawyers Primer

The Notorious Man
(Book 3 of The Anonymous Man Series)

Copyright © 2023 by Vincent L. Scarsella

Walrus Productions, LLC

All Rights Reserved

Printed in the United States of America

No part of this book may be used or reproduced in any manner

whatsoever without the written permission of the publisher

All Rights Reserved. First Edition

This is a work of fiction.

Names, characters, places, and events are the product of the author's imagination or are used fictitiously.

Any resemblance to actual persons, living or dead,

events or locales is entirely coincidental.

ISBN: 9798389284845

Contents

Chapter One: The Award 1
Chapter Two: Holly Then Jade 7
Chapter Three: The Real Anonymous Man 14
Chapter Four: Holly 24
Chapter Five: Jade 33
Chapter Six: King Midas 39
Chapter Seven: The Decision 49
Chapter Eight: A Visitor 54
Chapter Nine: Wesley Chandler 64
Chapter Ten: Holly's Plan 72
Chapter Eleven: A New Wardrobe 80
Chapter Twelve: Getting The Ball Rolling 86
Chapter Thirteen: Jack Fox 92
Chapter Fourteen: Holly's Gambit 97
Chapter Fifteen: Dean Alessi 104
Chapter Sixteen: Alessi and Fox 112
Chapter Seventeen: Jerry Shaw Lives! 117
Chapter Eighteen: Cat Out Of The Bag 124
Chapter Nineteen: Hardball 132
Chapter Twenty: A Real Solid 140
Chapter Twenty-One: Billy Ray Blacksnake 145
Chapter Twenty-Two: The Call 153
Chapter Twenty-Three: Jack Brewster 159
Chapter Twenty-Four: Doppelgänger 165

Chapter Twenty-Five: 1215 Manasota Beach Road 173
Chapter Twenty-Six: The Credit Card 178
Chapter Twenty-Seven: Florida Bound 185
Chapter Twenty-Eight: A Real Person 190
Chapter Twenty-Nine: Rest Stop. 196
Chapter Thirty: North Port 201
Chapter Thirty-One: Lawyers Gone Bad 208
Chapter Thirty-Two: The Stake-Out 214
Chapter Thirty-Three: Outfoxed 221
Chapter Thirty-Four: Jerry-Rigged 229
Chapter Thirty-Five: Kidnapped 238
Chapter Thirty-Six: Swingers. 245
Chapter Thirty-Seven: Gone 253
Chapter Thirty-Eight: Go F--- Yourself 258
Chapter Thirty-Nine: Holly's Mom. 263
Chapter Forty: Break In The Case 268
Chapter Forty-One: Rescue. 275
Chapter Forty-Two: Another Kidnapping 281
Chapter Forty-Three: Ransom. 286
Chapter Forty-Four: A Triple-Cross. 291
Chapter Forty-Five: Chief Reynolds 297
Chapter Forty-Six: Jade's Visit 302
Chapter Forty-Seven: Jack Fox's Visit 309
Chapter Forty-Eight: Dean Alessi's Visit 314
Chapter Forty-Nine: Big Pete 319
Chapter Fifty: A New Ending 325
Chapter Fifty-One: Nuptials. 333
Chapter Fifty-Two: The Premiere 338
Chapter Fifty-Three: The Notorious Man 343
About the Author 350

Chapter One

The Award

It's my award! Jerry Shaw thought after the darkly handsome actor, Chad Helton, one of the presenters for the Comic-Con International Will Eisner Comic Industry Awards, who'd played the Black Bee in Marvel Entertainment's latest blockbuster smash hit, "The Sting of the Black Bee," had ripped open a red envelope, cleared his throat and stated, "And the winner of the Wil Eisner Award from the Best Continuing Series is..."

He held back a moment as he looked out at the crowded ballroom with a knowing smile and then, finally, announced, "The Anonymous Man, written and illustrated, appropriately enough, by   The Anonymous Man."

Jerry pumped his right arm straight up, leapt out of his recliner and shouted, "Yes!" He pranced around the room for a few moments before plopping back down on the chair. His heart raced as he continued watching his fellow comic book and graphic novel writers and illustrators, including those nominated with him for the award, as well as the various comic book superhero celebrities and fans sitting at round tables in the vast, packed ballroom, break out into grateful applause as the dark figure of Jerry's enigmatic superhero, and alter-ego, "The Anonymous Man," flashed up on a large screen at the back of the stage.

The annual Wil Eisner awards ceremony was being broadcast live, as it had been the last fifteen years, from the spacious ballroom of the Bayfront Hotel in San Diego, California by the streaming service, CON-TV+ Comics. For the last hour, Jerry had been nervously watching the broadcast on the 80-inch, top-of-the-line flat screen television hung on a wall in the gathering room of a four-bedroom house on Manasoto Beach Road three-thousand miles away in Englewood, Florida, the home that he shared with his lover and front, Jade Martin.

"Accepting the award for the author and illustrator of The Anonymous Man series is Jade Martin," Chad Helton informed the audience. He then added, "Though we were hoping that Mister Anonymous himself would at long last surprise us tonight and reveal his, or her, true identity, and accept the award in person."

If only I could, thought Jerry.

All eyes were on the pretty lady, Jade, the mysterious front for the doubly mysterious anonymous author and illustrator of the popular comic series, as she stood up from her table with a wide grin and, to the continuing gentle applause of the attendees, made her way up to the stage. She wore a stunning ocean-colored, one-shoulder, pleated cape-sleeve satin gown by Alex Perry Marnel that she'd purchased (with Jerry's approval) from Neiman Marcus a month ago for three-thousand dollars shortly after they'd been notified that The Anonymous Man comic had been nominated for the prestigious Will Eisner Award.

"It better be worth it," Jade had told Jerry after she'd given the slinky Neiman Marcus retail clerk with the prince haircut her credit card. "If you lose, we just dropped three grand for nothing."

"Hell, even if I lose," he replied, "it'll be worth seeing your body wrapped in that thing prancing around the house every now and then." He winked at her and added, "And even more worth it when I get to take it off that body. And anyway, who says we're gonna lose?"

After clopping up the steps along the side of the stage in her pitch black, nine-hundred dollar Christian Louboutin high heel shoes, Jade was greeted with a smile and brief hug by Chad Helton. After stepping back, he handed Jade the

Eisner Award – a golden globe inscribed with the name, "Wil Eisner," set upon a thick, square wooden base. Then, arm-in-arm, he escorted her formally to an ornate glass podium.

Smiling, Jade faced the audience waiting for their applause to die down. Finally, she said, "Thank you, thank you." When the ballroom fell silent, she cleared her throat and took a deep breath, mindful of the nomination committee's admonition, in its email announcing The Anonymous Man's nomination several weeks ago, that acceptance speeches were limited to no more than two minutes. From then until tonight, she'd practiced the speech written for her by Jerry at least a hundred times.

"C'mon, darling, get to it," Jerry whispered to himself. "Like we practiced - be brief, be humble, be proud."

In her practiced, sultry voice perfected years earlier while an escort working in Binghamton, New York, Jade began, "I want to thank the selection committee and members of the board of comic book professionals for this great honor. I can tell you that the author is greatly humbled and gratified by your recognition of his work."

It was at that point when someone in the audience shouted out, "Well, who is he? And where is he?"

"Or she?" someone else yelled.

Jade turned to the direction of the voices, squinting in the glare of the stage lights. In her most sultry tone, she laughed and replied, "I'll never tell."

There came a smattering of laughter and applause. The guy who'd called up the question, and several others, booed her answer.

Jerry's identity had become the notorious, unsolved mystery of the comic book industry. Was he real, or could it be that this lovely Jade lady was the actual author of the adventures of the odd superhero, The Anonymous Man, whose "superpower" was his ability - because he himself had become anonymous after faking his immolation when the North Tower of the World Trade Center's Twin Towers came tumbling down on 9/11 – to help people escape their difficult lives by using his anonymity to hide from their former lives for as long as it took for them to embrace a new identify and undertake a new life. For some reason, that ability, or the idea of being able to shelf one's life and embark upon another, appealed to a fairly diverse and wide audience of varying ages and pedigrees that had made The Anonymous Man series wildly popular and, now, finally, award-winning.

But Jerry knew it was the relationship of his two superheroes – The Anonymous Man and King Midas – that had brought his series to new heights of critical and popular acclaim propelling his comic creation to win this year's coveted Wil Eisner Award.

Thrown off balance by the heckler, Jade completely

forgot the rest of her brief speech and instead, simply bowed her head, mumbled another thank you to everyone, turned to her right and somewhat embarrassedly, strode off the stage arm-in-arm with Chad Helton.

Chapter Two

Holly Then Jade

~~~

As Jade was being led off stage, Jerry's cell phone chimed. Looking down at the screen and seeing that it was from an "unknown caller," Jerry frowned. He suspected the caller was none other than his actual wife, Holly Shaw.

"Hello?"

"So, how'd it go?" Indeed, it was Holly.

Jerry was again surprised, and equally disappointed with himself for having felt that twinge of excitement every time Holly called.

"Did you, did you... win?" she asked.

"Yeah, I did," he said. "I won." Then he laughed and

blurted, "I fucking won!"

"Hey, that's great," Holly said. "Congratulations!" She waited a moment before asking, "And, and Jade's out there, collecting the award for you?"

"Yeah, she's there. Just gave the acceptance speech on my behalf."

At that moment, Jerry's cell phone beeped. He was getting another call. He pulled the phone back, looked down at the screen and saw that it was Jade.

"Look, Holly, I gotta go. Jade's calling."

"Oh, yeah, okay, okay. But, hey, can you call me back – tonight? I, I really, really need to talk to you."

"Yeah, sure. I'll call you back. Gotta go."

Jerry clicked off the call and them fumbled a moment before tapping on the incoming call icon. But it was too late. He'd lost Jade.

"Damn-it." Jerry cursed himself for allowing Holly to come between him and Jade – again. "Double damn-it."

But then his cell was ringing again and seeing that it was indeed Jade, he quickly clicked on the call.

"Jade?"

"Yeah, what happened? Where were you?"

"Oh, ah, checking on Seius."

"He okay?"

"Yeah, sure. He, he woke up for a minute – bad dream or something. Or maybe he knew his Daddy had just won the Eisner and his Mommy looked beautiful collecting it for him. Which you did, by the way, look beautiful, ravishing, in fact. Anyway, he's back asleep and all's well. No worries."

"And you gave him a bath?"

"Yes, he's clean as a whistle." Jerry drew in a breath. It was a small lie. Seius' bath had not been in the cards that evening – but, tomorrow morning, after breakfast, he'd definitely get to it.

"So, how was it?" he asked. "I mean, it looked fantastic watching it from here. I only wish...well, you know."

"Yeah, I know. Had to be killing you not to be here." She sighed and let out a short laugh. "See that stupid heckler. He ruined my speech."

"No, it was fine," Jerry said. "Funny actually, and you know, it kinda captured the essence of The Anonymous Man, I think."

"Yeah, maybe," Jade said. "But, Jer, I couldn't wait to tell you this – I have some extra, extra good news. Some guy from Marvel Entertainment approached me back stage. His name's Dan Maxwell. Anyway, he gave me his card and wants me to call him first thing in the morning to set up a meeting sometime tomorrow with him and some other Marvel producers." She sucked in a breath. "Marvel wants to turn The Anonymous Man into a movie."

Jerry swallowed and leaning forward in his chair, his heart racing, he laughed and said, "What? A movie. Holy shit!"

"Yeah, babe, holy shit," Jade said, her voice edged with glee. "Can you believe it?"

"What's Gabe say?"

"I haven't told her yet. I'm still backstage waiting for an usher to come escort me back to my table."

Gabe was Gabriela Tivoli, his, or actually, their agent. Of course, even Gabe didn't know the real anonymous man's identity, or, for that matter, if he actually existed.

Jerry let out another laugh and said, "Marvel Entertainment! This is a dream come true. A movie? A goddamned movie?"

"Yeah, Mr. Anonymous Man," Jade said. "A movie. Maybe you'll get to use that screenplay you wrote after all. I still think it's damned good." She let out a sigh. "Ah, here he is. The usher.

"I'll call you later, okay," she promised. "After I talk with Gabe. There's still a bunch more awards to be handed out, and then the after-parties." She laughed and added, "Can you stay awake til then?"

With a laugh, he told her, "Actually, the real question is - can I get to sleep? Do I have your permission to have a celebratory cocktail?"

"Sure, but only one, my anonymous man. You have a child to take care of." Then, she added, "And don't open that expensive champagne we bought – we're drinking that together."

***

As Jerry looked in on Seius, he felt a pang of guilt for having used the boy as his cover for Holly's call. Satisfied that the two-and-a-half year old was still sound asleep, Jerry closed the door to his bedroom and walked down the hallway back to the gathering room.

At a sideboard against a wall that he and Jade used to store their booze, Jerry fixed himself a celebratory whiskey and ginger ale. Standing there, he raised his drink and toasted, "To my Eisner!" After taking a sip, he winced and thought – too much whiskey. Still, he raised his glass again and made a second toast to seeing The Anonymous Man on the silver screen. But, then, it hit him –his name, "Jerry Shaw," would not be among the movie's credits, either as creator or writer.

He wondered then if only he'd kept on working at writing and illustrating comics and honing his talent and skills, instead of wasting all those years after college giving up on himself and becoming like the song says, *comfortably numb*, in the life that he and Holly had languished into, he would never have had to fake his death and become an actual anonymous man. He would have been in San Diego tonight, with Jade on his arm, accepting his award.

Then he had the weird thought - had he not faked his death, he would have never met Jade and it would have been Holly sitting at his side in the ballroom of the Bayfront Hotel tonight when The Anonymous Man was announced as the winner of the Eisner.

But all of that was nonsense. The truth was - it was *because* he'd become anonymous by faking his death that had enabled him to drastically change his life and become the man capable of writing The Anonymous Man. And it had been Jade, not Holly, who had helped him to effectuate that drastic change and realize his dream. In fact, Holly had held him back during their marriage and then ultimately betrayed him by becoming a willing participant in a plot to have him murdered.

Accepting this, Jerry wondered why he risked his relationship with Jade by keeping tabs on Holly's life through their occasional phone calls. It also worried him that he'd felt a twinge of jealousy after Holly had told him a couple months ago during one of those calls that she was finally seeing someone, a guy named Eddie, a mechanic for a local car dealership. He felt even worse when she confessed to Jerry a couple weeks later that she had moved in with him.

At some point, Jerry feared that there'd be a final reckoning. He'd have to jettison Holly once and for all, cut her off completely and forever, if he was to keep Jade. Of course, a dark part of his soul whispered that the opposite was equally possible.

Chapter Three

The Real Anonymous Man

After silencing the disturbing Jade/Holly love-triangle thoughts swirling around his brain, with drink in hand, Jerry strolled down a short hallway to his work studio – a bedroom at the front of the house that had been converted into his creative inner sanctum. For the past two years, he'd spent at least three hours every morning in that room, weekends included, (even when sick with Covid a year ago), and often later in the day, either at his drawing table or laptop, depending on how his creative juices were flowing, jotting notes and outlines, drafting story-boards and panels, illustrating and finalizing issues of The Anonymous Man or working on some other comic book or graphic novel project.

Whenever Jerry finished a project, he'd let Jade review it to help him correct his typos and mistakes of grammar and even to make substantive suggestions. Once it got her seal of approval, she'd email the much revised product to their agent, Gabriela "Gabe" Tivoli, who'd then submit it to his publisher and arrange the contract and payment details.

After tonight, Jerry had become a star in the madcap world of comic books. The only problem was that he was the invisible man behind the creative curtain. Jade was his representative and mouthpiece, appearing as his spokesperson for YouTube interviews, podcasts, and other social media presentations. But she wasn't the author, the mind behind the characters and adventures of The Anonymous Man, King Midas, and Jerry's other superhero and villainous creations. Because of this, to his fans and fellow comic book artists, there always seemed something missing or, worse, something amiss. There were even rumors that perhaps the anonymous author of "The Anonymous Man" didn't exist, that it was Jade who was the true genius behind the works attributed to the alleged mystery author, and that the whole "by anonymous" thing was simply a ruse, a clever publicity stunt. Jade seemed to revel in such speculation while Jerry brooded over it. Like anyone else, he craved recognition and fame that his anonymity denied him. That was the wicked curse, he'd long ago accepted, of his having become an actual anonymous man.

Not too long ago, when one of those, "Is it really Jade," speculations was brought up during a comic book podcast, Jerry had brought his fist down on the arm of the living room couch and, to Jade's surprise, shouted, "I'm sick of this shit! I'm sick of being anonymous!"

***

After entering his work studio that night, Jerry placed his drink on the desk and nosed about the room for a time. Finally, from the top shelf of the tall bookcase along the far wall, he plucked out a binder containing Issue #1 of The Anonymous Man. Turning it over in his hands, Jerry was overcome by a wave of nostalgia. He had a private laugh, too, realizing that because the series had won an Eisner, this very first issue had instantly become a high-priced collectors' item.

It had taken Jerry six months to crank out Issue #1 following his graduation in May 2006 from the State University of New York at Binghamton. Holding it now, sixteen years later, he smiled at the ominously hooded figure on the front cover. Though he'd done much better work since then, honed his illustrating skills substantially beyond what he was capable of back in 2006, he was nevertheless proud of his ability even then to reflect, through this illustration, the character of his budding superhero.

Opening the comic to page one, Jerry examined his drawing of the nameless man in his thirties, who was to become The Anonymous Man, as he stood at the site of the 9/11 World Trade Center Memorial some five years later reading the names of the thousands of poor souls who lives had been extinguished that murderous, tragic day – including his own.

Of course, the fictional anonymous man's life had not been extinguished. He'd survived due to pure dumb luck by showing up late for work. Panel by panel, Issue #1 told the fantastic tale. By the time he'd arrived for work at around nine-thirty that fateful morning for his job as an investment analyst for a medium-sized firm, with offices on the ninety-third floor of the North Tower, the Tower had already been struck by the hijacked jet at 8:46 and was destined to collapse at 10:28. Thus, his tardiness that morning had prevented Jerry from being at his cubicle waiting for the market to open and thus he'd miraculously avoided being among the hundreds killed, including each and every one of his co-workers.

The fictional anonymous man had been late that morning because of a bitter argument with his wife, Cynthia, that had continued from the night before. As revealed in subsequent issues of the comic, the mess of their lives had finally boiled into a raging feud caused by living above their means and their mutual infidelities after marrying far too

17

young. The anonymous man's money problems were caused by his overwhelming desire to become filthy rich so could escape his mundane existence, and perhaps Cynthia as well, and live the life that he wanted to live free of obligation and toil. This desire led him to execute a modest Ponzi scheme that had defrauded his customers of close to three million dollars by 9/11, funds that were now hidden in offshore bank accounts. Only days before destruction of the Twin Towers, he'd learned that Securities and Exchange Commission investigators were hot on his heels and that his Ponzi gig might be up any day now.

It was this intrigue and trouble that had boiled over that fateful morning with Cynthia. Accusations flew back and forth causing him to leave a tad past his usual departure time that in turn caused him to miss his train connection into the city.

After both World Trade Center towers crumbled floor-by-floor into piles of broken concrete and twisted beams and human dust, a plume of white and gray ash was lifted upward and outward from the destruction that darkened an otherwise crisp, clear blue sky. This same plume ultimately dropped onto a horde of humanity that included the Anonymous Man and his fellow office workers, police and firemen, store owners, and tourists fleeing from the catastrophe that had inexplicably befallen lower Manhattan.

Once clear of the smoke and ash, The Anonymous Man

stopped and sat on a bench overlooking the East River and tried to come to grips with what was happening around him. After an indeterminable time sitting there and examining his life that mirrored the mayhem around him, he reached the momentous decision to use this situation to extract himself not only from a marriage gone sour, but from certain financial ruin and a stint in federal prison. He decided to extract himself from life itself – not by suicide, of course, because life was simply too dear to him, but by becoming The Anonymous Man.

Upon reaching this firm decision, Jerry's fictional character simply disappeared. He called no one, not even his wife, to announce that he was not amongst the dead. And so it was assumed that he'd sadly perished that morning with the nearly three-thousand other poor souls who'd perished in the collapsed North and South Towers.

As one of the panels of Issue #1 depicted, The Anonymous Man ignored the frantic calls from his wife and refused to return her teary voicemails left on his cell phone pleading with him to pick up or call her whenever he could. Her expression of worry and grief over his silence surprised him, and would haunt him over the years. Had she really loved him after all? Had he been mistaken that she was cheating on him with his best friend? Had all the troubles in his life when he disappeared on 9/11 - financial and emotional and otherwise - been solely his doing and she'd been a mere innocent bystander. By the time these thoughts occurred to him, it was too late. He'd already become The Anonymous Man.

The remaining panels of that first issue depicted how after escaping the chaos of lower Manhattan that afternoon, the Anonymous Man made his way to the obscure and sleepy town of Endicott, New York, roughly three hours west of New York City on State Route 17. After a month-long stay in a cheap motel, he purchased a house using cash withdrawn from one of his secret, off-shore bank accounts, funded over the last year with the over three million dollars he'd embezzled from his investor clients.

As Issue #1 further explained, the offshore account had been opened under the name of a limited liability company formed under New Mexico's unique incorporation laws that hid the identity of the owners of such companies. Not that it mattered. Presumed dead, the SEC was no longer investigating The Anonymous Man's suspected multi-million dollar misappropriations.

Skimming those panels, Jerry presently smiled, recalling that it had been his research into New Mexico's laws for Issue #1 that had provided the means for he, Holly and Jeff to hide the four million dollars of life insurance proceeds stolen from Global Life and Casualty Insurance after they'd faked Jerry's death.

Jerry let out a satisfied chuckle at the clever ending of Issue #1 he'd concocted that depicted his overwrought sister believing that she'd spotted him on TV that evening running amongst the masses fleeing down some Manhattan street engulfed by the smoke and ash descending upon them from the collapsed towers. Jerry remembers drawing her sitting forward from the couch in her living room with a arm jutting toward the TV exclaiming in a cloud above her, "There's Jerry. He's ALIVE!"

Even after her brother failed to turn up, and was presumed dead, his sister persisted in her belief that he was still alive, though disturbed that he had chosen, for whatever reason, to fake his death and disappear. Though no one was convinced she's actually seen him that morning, she would not be dissuaded from her certainty that he was alive, and she subsequently convinced her family to hire a highly respected private investigator, Oscar Plato, to find him.

Issue #2, written and illustrated after Jerry had himself become an anonymous man, chronicled Oscar Plato's pursuit of the fictional Anonymous Man. The story of that fictional pursuit spanned the many subsequent issues of the comic book series ending, of course, with a final confrontation as the series came to an end.

Through Issue #1 of the series, Jerry also went at some length trying to convincingly explain The Anonymous Man's rather prosaic and obscure superpower — that is, using his anonymity as a cloak to help a person hide, and then escape from, an unhappy life only to emerge as a new person reborn into a new life. As demonstrated in that inaugural issue, The Anonymous Man's first case involved him in assisting a physically and emotional scared woman, Karen Smith, to escape from an abusive husband.

While finishing his drink, and then fixing himself another, Jerry dug out more binders containing subsequent issues chronicling the exploits of The Anonymous Man that he'd written and drawn over the next weeks, months and years. Sitting on the floor of his work studio, he flipped through these issues, gratified, and even a bit surprised, by the cleverness of plot and development of characters he'd fashioned in tale after tale spun about his strange, fictional superhero without an actual superpower. He couldn't fly, couldn't bend metal pipes, couldn't stretch himself out, couldn't run fast as the wind...he could only transform a person's dreadful life into a better one. Somehow, he'd manage to make such a superpower interesting and believable, culminating in being recognized for his efforts by the iconic Wil Eisner Award.

It also struck Jerry as odd, proving that truth sometimes is stranger than fiction, that since becoming an actual anonymous man, like his fictional anonymous alter ego, he had also helped people escape from their failed lives and hide behind the cloak of his real-life anonymity. First there was Jade's best friend, Rachel, whom he'd helped escape from a vicious pimp. After that, he'd helped a Latino boy escape from a drug gang and a crime-infested neighborhood. After a suitable time hidden by Jerry's "cloak of anonymity," both Rachel and Marco had stepped from behind that cloak to assume new and better lives.

But what had ultimately turned The Anonymous Man into an award winner and possible feature film, Jerry felt, was Issue #26, in which he'd used his fictional creation's cloak of anonymity superpower to help an actual superhero – "King Midas" – to escape from the US government and sinister villains seeking to either use his superpowers for evil purposes or to subdue them.

The chiming of Jerry's cell phone broke his concentration and revelry. With a sigh, he pushed himself off the floor and stood. Grabbing his cell phone from the desk and seeing it was already almost midnight, he thought, it must be Jade. But it wasn't. The screen told him the caller was "unknown," and so he knew instantly that it must be Holly calling him again.

Chapter Four

Holly

"You don't care anything about me, do you?" Holly whined. "Not a thing."

"Of course, I do," Jerry replied. "I've cared about you from the first day we met."

How could he forget the first day they'd met? It'd be forever etched in his brain. He'd been a frumpy college guy back then, a junior at Binghamton University in southern New York, about a three hours' drive west of New York City along State Route 17.

Jerry was without much in the way of romantic prospects at the time when out of the blue that night drinking with a couple equally unappealing pals in an off-campus bar in

Johnson City, this hot-looking blonde co-ed walked over to his side of the bar and started coming on to him. Why she'd done so, and then stayed with him and eventually married him, were questions no one was ever quite able to answer – not her friends or her family, and not even Jerry. He later surmised that Holly's romantic attraction was perhaps akin to the Florence Nightingale effect – she saw Jerry not as a frumpy, unattractive guy, but as someone vulnerable and therefore in need of her attention and, yes, love.

That was a long time ago in a galaxy far, far away. Jerry was no longer an overweight, unattractive guy. Indeed, it was the excess blubber he'd carried back in college that had obscured a rather ruggedly handsome face – the face he'd sculpted with Jade's help in the weeks and months after he and Holly and Jeff Flaherty had faked his death. Of course, ridding himself of the blubber around his mid-section had also earned Jerry a hard, athletic body and dramatically increased his libido.

"I'm still talking to you, aren't I?" Jerry added. "If I didn't care, would I be?"

"Yeah, you are, but just barely," Holly said.

"What do you expect of me, Holly? I shouldn't be talking with you at all. Do you realize what I'm risking with these phone calls."

"Then don't bother if you're worried so much," she said sulkily, then fell silent.

Jerry couldn't think of anything further to say. Perhaps, the next step was to finally end these calls. To break their bond completely. Then, he heard Holly sniffling at the other end of the call.

"I just feel so alone," she panted. "So completely alone. And then, you didn't call me back like you said."

"I got distracted," he explained.

"Jade." She said the name like it was poison.

"No," he said. "I mean, we talked, yeah, but only briefly. She's still at the awards ceremony, and after that, there're afterparties." He sighed, then snapped, "All shit I'm missing."

"What?"

"Nothing."

Checking his watch and seeing that it was almost midnight, Jerry started pacing his studio with the phone to his ear. Looking down, he saw the binders of past issues of The Anonymous Man cluttering the floor.

"Anyway, it's only nine out there," he said. Then, he remembered about the possible movie deal. "And you know what else?"

"No, what?'

"Jade was approached by someone from Marvel Entertainment," Jerry told her, feeling the need to celebrate the news with someone. "They might want to make a movie out of The Anonymous Man."

"What, a blockbuster likeSpider Man or something?" Holly asked with a laugh.

"I don't know," Jerry said. "We'll find out more tomorrow."

"Holy crap, Jerry," Holly said. "That's great, fantastic. You'll end up being a millionaire."

"Yeah, a millionaire," he said. But then, he thought gloomily, no one would know about his success except him and Jade and Holly.

Holly thought of mentioning that it'd be nice, once he became a millionaire, if he'd help out financially more than he'd been doing over the last couple of years. He'd sent her money every now and then, but she seemed always to be broke, on the verge of homelessness. After a moment, Holly decided against bringing up the subject of financial aid. After all, she was no longer his responsibility. She given that up when she'd stupidly hitched her wagon to Jeff Flaherty.

After a moment, Jerry asked, "Holly?"

"So, ah, you still watching the ceremonies?" Holly asked.

"Nah," he said. "Got bored with it." He laughed. "Too many damned awards."

"So whatcha been doing?"

He glanced down at binders of The Anonymous Man issues spread out on the floor.

"Reminiscing," he said. "Flipping through past issues of The Anonymous Man. Having a couple drinks to celebrate."

"Yeah, celebrate. Wish I had something to celebrate."

"What's wrong, Holly? You sound so down."

"What's wrong? Everything's wrong," she whined. "My life's a total fucking mess."

"No, it's not."

"Yes, it is. Eddie and I broke up." She sighed. "I'm fucking back living with my parents."

For some reason, Jerry was happy to hear that. She was free again. But why should that matter? He quickly banished the thought from his brain.

"It's fucking humiliating having to move in with them again," Holly went on. "I'm nearly forty fucking years old. And even worse, I have no money. I quit my shitty job at Walmart."

"You quit? Why?"

"Why? Because the asshole manager of the produce department was coming on to me, that's why. Said he'd get me better hours if I went out with him. And the old bastard's married. So I quit."

"Well, there's other jobs."

"Like where? McDonald's?"

"What about a legal secretary job?"

"I won't do that anymore," she said. "Typing up motions and bullshit letters all day for arrogant pricks like Jeff Flaherty." She fell silent and Jerry wondered if saying his name had called up within her feelings of grief over his death two years ago. With a bitter laugh, she added, "Plus, I doubt any law firm would hire me. I'm somewhat notorious around these parts you know. Soon as I go in for an interview, they'll be asking, aren't you the lady who murdered your husband and stole four million bucks from that insurance company then spent some time in state prison and was released on a technicality?"

"Holly, it'll work out. You'll get a better job, meet someone. You'll fall in love." He laughed. "It was something you told me after we first met. Remember? Love is like a butterfly, when you least expect it, it lands on your shoulder."

"I said that?" She let out a bitter sigh. "Well, it was bullshit then and it's bullshit now. And all that's easy for you to say – you've got Jade. And a son." She held her breath a moment. "A son."

The obvious bitterness in Holly's voice told Jerry that she

was thinking again of her inability to get pregnant during their eight years together. The doctor had told her there was nothing wrong with either of them to prevent that. But no matter how much they tried, especially during the first couple years after they were married, Holly had remained barren. Sometime around year three, they'd both given up and decided to remain forever childless. She went on the pill and they never talked about having a baby again.

"I've got fucking nothing and no one," Holly lamented and seemed to suck in a breath as if to stop from crying. "And, and I – love you."

This sudden, stark admission stopped Jerry cold. He'd once loved Holly, very much. But she'd betrayed him with Jeff Flaherty, more than once. She'd even stood by and let Jeff try to murder him. It was Jade who'd saved him from death by Jeff's hand with Holly standing in the motel room in Kissimmee right behind him. It was Jade that had constantly demonstrated her love for him. So, Jerry wondered, why was he still talking to Holly.

"Did, did you hear me, Jerry?" Her voice became soft, sweet, enticing. "I love you."

"No," was Jerry's flat reply. "You don't. It's only because right now, you think I'm your only option."

She didn't respond right away. Finally, in a soft, repentant voice, she said, "No, you're wrong. Totally wrong. I do love you. I've always loved you. And I always will. I just...went astray for a little while. I..."

Holly's voice cracked and she started crying. It was a soft cry, barely audible and Jerry could think of nothing to say to make her feel better. A part of him was thrilled that she'd declared her love for him. But another part was doubtful, worried, even frightened by the intensity of her declaration. That he was listening, and wondering, perhaps hoping, it was true, suddenly disgusted him. They'd been down this road before. And there was Jade lurking in the back of his mind. His failure to tell Holly to go to hell two years ago and allow her calls, and his connection to her to continue, seemed a betrayal of the highest magnitude, as bad as if he'd slept with her again – like that time two years ago in the Holliday Inn across the street from the Buffalo airport. What the fuck was wrong with him?

Finally, he said, "You have to stop this, Holly. We maybe should stop these calls."

A period of silence passed between them. Then, out of nowhere, she started sobbing and said, "No! Please. No."

Then, another call was beeping Jerry's cell. He glanced down at the screen and saw that it was Jade. "I have to go, Holly," Jerry said. "It's Jade. We'll talk, we'll talk in the morning. Okay?"

"Go," Holly said.

Her whimpering was the last sound Jerry heard as he thumbed the icon to answer Jade's call.

Chapter Five

Jade

"Hi, darlin'," Jerry said.

"Hi, hon," she said. "Well, it's over. What a night."

"You back at the room already?"

"Yep. In bed, in my pajamas, sipping wine."

"So, what did Gabe have to say?"

"She made a call and the studio's interest is definitely legit. Gabe's already set up the meeting for tomorrow morning, around eleven or so. But I had to switch my flight. I won't be coming home until the day after tomorrow. Can you handle Seius another day all by yourself."

"Of course, I can't," Jerry said with a laughed. "No, I'll manage it. So you think this could really be a dream come true - The Anonymous Man on the big screen."

"Sounds real, hon," Jade said. "So dust off that screenplay. I told Gabe about it and she thinks you should email it to us before our meeting. Might come in handy."

"Yeah, sure," Jerry said. "I'll get right on it. Spruce it up a bit. I've been meaning to do that for a while now anyway."

"Well, don't stay up too late," Jade said. "You still do have our child to take care of."

"I know." He let out a sigh. "You know, this gets me to thinking."

"Yeah? What?"

"Should this actually happen, the movie deal I mean," Jerry said, "I – I don't know if I'd want to be an anonymous man anymore. Maybe it's time to come out of the closet -well, in a different sense. You know, reveal myself – turn myself in. I mean, we get a movie deal, we'll have all the money we'll ever need. And we've been doing quite well with my sales as it is, and winning the Eisner is certainly gonna help with that." He laughed and added, "Maybe rather than anonymous, I need to become the notorious man."

Jade kept silent. It was not something Jerry had ever brought up before. Jerry wondered if she was prepared for it.

Perhaps she liked being the front for the anonymous man. It kept him under wraps, hidden in her shadows.

"I think we need to really think about that, hon," she finally said. "I mean, you could end up going to prison. Plus, it might scare off the studio. Would they want to make a deal with a felon?"

"Or it might enhance the deal," he said. "Make the story even more interesting. And maybe I'm getting sick and tired of hiding behind the cloak of my own anonymity. Maybe I'm jealous that you're in a swank hotel and I'm not."

Again, Jade fell silent. Finally, she said, "Well, just don't do anything rash, okay. We need to think this through. Talk it out. See what Gabe says. Okay?"

Jerry shrugged.

"Jerry? Okay?"

"Yeah, sure. Okay. I'll think about it. What I need is for you to be one-hundred percent behind me."

"Alright."

They fell silent again.

"So you didn't attend any of the after parties?" Jerry asked.

"No, not for me," she said. "It's been a long couple of days and I wanted to chill."

"Okay. Can't blame you."

"Gabe said she'd represent us. She knew I'm beat." After a pause, Jade asked, "Hey look, could you take a picture of Seius sleeping in his bed and send it to me? I miss him so much."

"Yeah, sure.," he said. "But we could do one better than that - do a Facetime and have you whisper in his ear. But not too loud, I don't want you waking him up."

Jade laughed. "Great idea. And don't worry, daddy, it'll be like the quiet whisper of an angel."

They hung up and Jerry placed the Facetime call as he walked from his studio to Seius' bedroom on the other side of the house.

At the doorway, Jerry whispered, "See him?"

The small bed against the far wall held the tiny body of their toddler son. He was turned on his side, clearly in a deep sleep, his chest gently rising and falling.

"He's so darling," Jade whispered and seemed about ready to cry.

"Sh!" Jerry whispered as he walked into the room and stood at the edge of the bed. He looked into the screen and said, "Ready?"

Jade smiled.

Jerry lowered the phone to Seius' left ear.

Jade

"Sweet dreams, my darling baby boy," Jade whispered. "Mommy loves you."

Seius stirred momentarily, let out a peep, sighed and fell back into a deep sleep.

Jerry crept back from the bed. He closed the door but left it a crack open. Then, he strolled to the master bedroom a few feet down the hall. He brought up the phone to eye level and asked, "That make you feel better?"

"No, it just made me miss him more."

"Just him," Jerry said with a pout. "Not me?"

"Of course you," Jade said.

Jerry hopped onto their wide, King bed and looked into the phone. "Well, if you miss me so much, prove it."

"How?" She laughed.

"You can Facetime it."

"Facetime what?"

Jerry swallowed. "Ah, well…"

"Ah, well, what darling?"

"Facetime sex," he blurted.

"Jerry," she laughed. "Facetime sex? What's that?"

"You know," he said. "You talk dirty to me – just like

that first time we met and made love, in Binghamton. And well, we let nature take its course."

"You mean you masturbate to my dirty words?" She laughed. "Jerry, you pervert."

"Alright, never mind. Just the thought of you alone in bed in a hotel room makes me horny."

"Typical man." Jade laughed again and said, "I didn't say I wouldn't do it." She sighed and then in that favorite sultry voice she'd used on him so many years ago when they'd first met in Binghamton, she said, "So, Mister Anonymous Man, are you ready for me?"

Chapter Six

King Midas

After ending his call with Jade, he checked in on Seius and smiled seeing that the boy was fast asleep, looking like an angel safe and sound in his bed. Jerry then returned to his studio, sat at his desk and powered up his laptop. He clicked on his screenplay formatting software icon and after it loaded, he opened the file for "The Anonymous Man."

Reading through it, he made a few minor changes while sipping the last of his drink. After a time, his eyes grew heavy and he found himself nodding off sitting there before the laptop screen. Minutes later, he woke with a start and decided to get to bed and finish polishing the screenplay in the morning, then email it to Jade and Gabe. After all, he had three hours on them, more than enough time to perfect his script.

Jerry saved the revised screenplay, shut off his laptop and ambled to the master bedroom. After brushing his teeth, he took off his shorts, climbed into bed and quickly fell into a deep dreamless sleep. But it was a sleep that didn't last. Two hours later, at three in the morning, Jerry woke and found himself tossing and turning thinking about a new and seemingly improved plot twist for the screenplay. After fifteen minutes of even more tossing and turning, he threw off the sheet covering him and jumped out of bed. It was no use – he had to work on that screenplay.

It was not unusual for Jerry to wake up in the middle of the night and scamper down to his work studio to write a flash of something about the latest issue of a comic book or other creation that had percolated up from somewhere deep within his subconscious and awakened him. From experience, he knew it was fruitless to try and get back to sleep once that happened. During the few times he'd resisted, Jerry had regretted not getting up and padding off to his studio because the following morning he'd often lost the idea or the inspiration that had come with it. It was forgotten or obscured like a dream.

After his laptop powered up, Jerry started the formatting program and then opened the latest version of "The Anonymous Man" screenplay. Once it flashed up on the screen, he strolled down to the place where he felt that his change in the plotline that had come to him while sleeping needed to go – at the point where Oscar Plato, the private investigator hired by his sister to find the fictional Anonymous Man, had after many long months finally done just that.

Up until this point in the story – similar to the issues in the comic book series upon which the screenplay was based – Plato had been like the detective in the old TV series and later movie, "The Fugitive," who was always just a step behind apprehending the actor playing the fugitive, Dr. Richard Kimble – David Janson in the TV series and Harrison Ford in the movie.

"Here goes," Jerry whispered as he began typing.

```
Ext.  Driveway of House - Night
The Anonymous Man and King Midas are exiting
The Anonymous Man's SUV. As they stroll
toward the front of The Anonymous Man's
house, Oscar Plato bolts from behind bushes
along the front of the house and points a
pistol at them.

          PLATO
    Stop! Hold it right there!
The Anonymous Man and King Midas turn to Plato
with surprised and concerned expressions.
```

```
                PLATO
      That's right.    Got you.   Took me five
      long years, but I finally did it.
           (laughs)
      Longest chase of my career.
```

Jerry had previously informed his readers of Plato's background as a seasoned and now retired federal marshal. In the process of drafting Plato's role in the comic, Jerry had modeled him after the character played by Tommy Lee Jones in the movie version of "The Fugitive."

Though not as sinister, Plato also reminded Jerry of Pete Sharkey, the retired federal marshal turned investigator and bounty hunter that Jeff Flaherty and Holly had hired to find him down in Florida just a little more than two years ago. Along with Jeff Flaherty and Chuck Bruno, Sharkey had met a justifiable death in the motel room where he'd kidnapped Jerry and Jade.

Looking at the laptop screen, Jerry drew in a breath and got back to the screenplay.

```
      Plato lifts a cell phone out of the front
      pocket of his jeans.

                THE ANONYMOUS MAN
      Who you calling?
```

                    PLATO

    (pause, frowning)
    Who'dya think? Nine, one, one.
    I told ya, Gigs up, Jerry.
    Cops'll be here any minute.

    (smiling)

    Followed by a squad of SEC investigators.

                 KING MIDAS

    Why don't you put that phone down,
    Mister Plato.

                    PLATO

    (to King Midas)

    And who the hell are you?

                 KING MIDAS

    Nick Hollister's my name – though
    you'll never remember it. Some
    people call me, King Midas.

    (smiling, nods)

    I turn people into gold.

                    PLATO

    Look, I got no time for riddles.

Plato looks at his cell phone screen in
this right hand while holding the pistol in
his left, then uses the thumb of his right
hand to tap the number, 9.

CLOSE-UP: Plato's thumb tapping "9"

          KING MIDAS
    You don't want to make that call.

We see Plato scowling as he looks up at King Midas.

          KING MIDAS
    I don't want you to tap another number on that phone.

          PLATO
    Wha?

Plato looks down at his cell phone screen, lifts his thumb as if about to tap in the number, "1."

CLOSE-UP: Plato's thumb stuck, shaking, unable to move forward. Then his whole hand begins to shake.

          PLATO (CONT'D)
    (grunting)
    Why...can't...I...
    (shaking his head, squinting)
    What's...wrong with me?

KING MIDAS

Now, you can put the pistol on the ground.

The Anonymous Man steps forward into King Midas' line of sight and turns to him.

THE ANONYMOUS MAN

No, Nick. I've had enough of hiding. It's time to end the charade.

(turns to Plato)

You don't need to call the police. I'm turning myself in.

KING MIDAS

But, but, Jerry - you're my front. There are people - bad people - still, still after me.

THE ANONYMOUS MAN

You're safe from them for now. They don't know where you are. You'll just have to be careful. From now on, you'll have to use your powers wisely... sparingly. And always, of course, to help people in need. And to help yourself.

                    PLATO

          (thrusting out the pistol)
          Okay, I've had just about enough of
          this small talk. If you're coming,
          Jerry, let's go. Now!

The Anonymous Man nods, turns and walks
over to King Midas. They embrace.

                    PLATO (CONT'D)
          Come on, Jerry. Let's go.

The Anonymous Man backs away from King
Midas. With a nod, he strolls over to Plato
and he and the investigator walk off into
the darkness.

                     THE END

"That's it," Jerry whispered to himself. "Done. The perfect ending."

There goes The Anonymous Man, finally revealed as someone named "Jerry," strolling off into the darkness with his fugitive hunting nemesis, Oscar Plato - off to reveal his true identity and face the consequences of his prior indiscretions. Off to become The Notorious Man.

Jerry was already imagining the possibilities for the sequel. After all, The Anonymous Man's readers and the movie audience would be dying to know what happened to Jerry following his capture. Did he end up going to prison? How did his sister whose sighting of him the morning of 9/11 after the Towers went down and his wife (and her lover – who, Jerry learns existed even before he faked his immolation in the North Tower collapse) treat him when Jerry was brought back to life by Oscar Plato. And even more intriguing – what happened to King Midas. Do he and the now Notorious Man hook up again to save people from themselves?

Jerry re-read this new ending in the screenplay that had replaced the previous one in which King Midas had used his powers to simply compel Plato to let The Anonymous Man go. In Jerry's rewrite, The Anonymous Man was, in a sense, killed off, and King Midas would take his place in the realm of comic book superherodom. With a nod of certainty, Jerry sighed and felt that this ending was much better. This one surprised where the other was predictable.

The many readers of Jerry's comic book series, "The Anonymous Man," had already been introduced to King Midas. His real name was Nick Hollister, a guy with the power to influence the thoughts and actions of those who came near him through the emission of his brain waves in a phenomenon known as the Zurich Effect, named after a renowned neurologist who had discovered it during experiments some years earlier conducted at Harvard Medical School.

After making some minor revisions to the last scene, Jerry sighed and said, "It's done." There was nothing left to say. Then, he decided – as he'd let go of the fictional Anonymous Man, he must let go of the real life anonymous man that he'd become. He must turn himself in and become the notorious man.

Chapter Seven

The Decision

Jerry went back to bed around five and woke up at seven. He re-read the screenplay and, still satisfied with the new ending, emailed it to Jade and Gabe. As it was nearly eight, his time, and only five a.m. in San Diego, they'd have it waiting for them when they woke up.

Despite the early hour out west, Jerry was desperate to tell Jade about his momentous decision to become the notorious man. Seius usually didn't wake up before nine and once that happened, he'd be fixing him breakfast and giving him a bath and he might not get to talk to Jade until after her meeting with the Marvel Entertainment people.

Then, his cell phone rang. As if feeling his distress from

three thousand miles away, it was Jade.

"You're up early," he said with a laugh.

"Couldn't sleep," she said. "Hey, I got your email, the screenplay."

"I changed the ending," he told her.

"Yeah?"

"I – I had The Anonymous Man give himself up to Oscar Plato," he said.

"Really."

"Yeah, I think it works," Jerry said. "It even sets up a sequel - what happens to The Anonymous Man after he becomes The Notorious Man. And, for that matter, what happens to King Midas." He laughed and went on, "Maybe I'll have King Midas help The Anonymous Man by making the Judge give him a light sentence." He sighed and added, "I don't know. If nothing else, it finally passes the baton to King Midas, a superhero with a real superpower. I think I've finally grown tired of The Anonymous Man."

"Just like in real life?" Jade asked, an obvious question.

"Yeah, just like in real life," Jerry relented. He drew in a breath and blurted, "Jade, I'm tired of being what I've become. I – I want and need to resurrect Jerry Shaw."

Jade fell silent, as if considering the implication of what

Jerry was saying, where Jerry's resurrection would lead them. To good, or bad – she wasn't certain.

"I still think you should give it some time," she said. "Resurrecting Jerry Shaw may end up badly for you, and for all of us, including Seius. You don't have a real life King Midas to convince a judge to go light on you. And like I said last night, this might not go down so well with the Marvel Entertainment people. And don't forget, I'd be a criminal, too, for being your front and harboring you all these years."

"All that should be able to be worked out through negotiations," Jerry reasoned. "I mean, I'm not just gonna walk out of the closet with my hands stretched out for the handcuffs to be put on as they send me off to prison. What I'm thinking - I'll start by calling Jack Fox, tell him what I want to do. See if he can help me swing a deal. I mean, I'll be paying back the rest of what Holly, Jeff and I took from Global." He sighed and added, "Of course, everything depends on us getting a movie deal."

"So, bottom line," Jade said, "your turning yourself in is contingent on a movie deal."

"Has to be," Jerry said. "Right? That's what I'm talking about. And, you know, I figured an angle in the story that the Marvel Entertainment guys might like."

"Yeah, like what?"

"I wait until the premiere of the movie to turn myself

in," he told her. "It'd be a perfect way to gin up interest and ticket sales. The creator of The Anonymous Man becomes the Notorious Man just like his fictional creation. I think they might like the marketing potential of that outcome. "

Jade sighed, thinking it over. "Yeah, maybe," she said. "Of course, I need to run all this by Gabe."

"I really want to do this, Jade, end the charade," Jerry said. "I'll finally be able sleep at night without worrying about someone crashing the party, catching me – catching us."

After a deep sigh, Jade relented, "Alright. Let's see about the movie deal, and if they're as serious as they seem to be, you go ahead and call Jack Fox, feel him out. Get the ball rolling."

"Yeah, sounds like a plan," Jerry said. "So we're on the same page?"

"Yes, I think so."

"Man, now I'm really nervous about how your meeting will go," Jerry said.

"Gabe feels real good about it. She even called me after we spoke last night – or, did our Facetime thingy together."

"Hey, that was hot," Jerry said. "Have to try that again real soon."

"Well, I think what we did on the phone is way better in person," Jade said with a laugh. After a breath, she added, "Hey, look at the time. It's almost nine back there. Our son should be waking up."

"Yeah, great. Guess I won't be napping anytime too soon."

"No, sorry, lover," Jade said. "Welcome to motherhood."

Chapter Eight

A Visitor

When Holly called Jerry and he didn't pick up at nine that morning, she laid back down on her narrow bed in the guest bedroom of her parents' house, pulled the covers over her head and started sobbing.

"I should just kill myself," she whispered bitterly.

Her life seemed to have spiraled down to as low as it could get. She was living with her parents and there seemed few prospects for moving out any time soon. She had never lived up to her promise and accomplished nothing special since college. She hadn't even given a man a baby.

Perhaps the worst of it was that there seemed little hope that she'd ever achieve her dream of becoming a famous

Hollywood actress. She still attended acting classes run by a local never-was shrill actress who'd appeared years and years ago in a minor role on Broadway. Driving home from these weekly sessions, Holly often cried thinking of all the time she'd wasted since college. She envied her classmates - the young girls, budding starlets, who had a million per cent chance more of making it big on Broadway or in Hollywood or even in community theatre than she could ever hope for.

And on top of all that, she presently lacked a man in her life and there seemed little hope of finding one.

"Love is like a butterfly," she'd once told Jerry. "When you least expect it, it lands on your shoulder." Well, she accepted now that was utter bullshit.

"My life's a fucking waste," she moaned to herself, still under the covers.

After tossing and turning for another five minutes, she tried Jerry's cell number again, and again, he didn't answer.

"Damn him!" she growled.

Then someone was knocking at her door.

"Holly?" It was her mother's soft voice. "Holly, dear."

"Yeah? What?"

"There's someone here to see you," her mother said.

She sat up and called out, "See me? Who?"

She had no friends, and no lover again, so who could it be?

"Can I come in?' her mother asked.

"Yeah, sure," Holly said.

Upon her mother's timid entry, Holly pulled herself up and sat against the headboard. "Are you okay?" her mother asked.

Holly shrugged and in a deadpan tone, said, "Yeah, ma, sure. I'm okay. I'm great."

"You're off today? I thought..."

"Yes, I'm off," Holly snapped. "So who's at the door for me?"

"A young man," said her mother. "Said his name – oh, I forgot already." She frowned and thought a moment before saying, "Wesley something. Says he went to school with you."

Holly frowned and asked, "School with me? What school?" Unable to attach a person to the name, she said, "I don't know any Wesley."

"Well, he says he knows you," her mother said. "And he's waiting for you on the porch."

"Jesus Christ," Holly hissed, then looked at her mother and said, "Give me a minute. Tell him I'll be right down."

After her mother left the room, Holly rolled out of bed and scampered to a small guest bathroom across the hall. After splashing water on her face, she looked at herself in the mirror. There were bags under hey eyes and without make-up, she looked horrible, an aging skank, though she was only thirty-eight. The only thing she'd retained from her youth was her shape. At least, she hadn't developed any flab and become a wide body like so many women her age. Still, the reflection staring back at her that morning didn't inspire much confidence. Her eyes were sunken and lacked life. She was awfully pale.

"Jesus H. Christ," she muttered to herself. "What the fuck's happened to me?"

After a sigh, she splashed more water on her face, then spread some lipstick across her lips and blushed her cheeks. There was no time to do anything with her eyes. As she was making herself somewhat presentable, she wondered, who the fuck is this Wesley guy who'd come calling for her that morning? From Binghamton?

She sipped and gargled some mouthwash, then spit it out into the sink and crossed back into her bedroom. After slipping into a pair of jeans and throwing on a Buffalo Bills tee shirt that highlighted her ample enough breasts – just in case Wesley turned out to be someone worth pursuing – she strode out of her bedroom and scuttled downstairs. Her mother was sitting in her usual armchair reading the morning paper with a cup of old coffee on the table next to her.

As Holly passed by her mother on the way to the short foyer leading to the front door, she asked, "He still out there?"

"Should be," her mother said. "He didn't look to be going nowhere."

Holly brushed a hand through her dyed brown hair that curled down to her shoulders, furrowed her brow, then strode to the front door. After a breath, she opened it.

A lanky man about forty had his back to her. He had sandy blonde hair down to his shoulders that looked like it needed a good washing. There was an worn, thick backpack at his feet as he stood there against the front porch railing staring out at something across the street.

Holly coughed and said, "Excuse me?"

When the man turned around, Holly was immediately drawn to his sharp blue bedroom eyes and sharp edged good looks.

"Do I know you?" she asked.

He flashed a smile and said, "Name's Wesley Chandler. Wes for short. And no, you don't know me. But I know a lot about you."

"My mother said you knew me from school?"

"I lied." Then he smiled and added, "I had to tell her something."

"Well, what's this about then?"

"I knew Jeff Flaherty."

That stopped Holly cold. She drew in a breath and told him, "Jeff's dead."

"Yeah, I know."

"So, you knew him." Her eyes narrowed. "From prison?"

"Yeah, prison."

"So what'dya want from me?"

Wesley Chandler broke out into a wide grin. "Ya know, you're just about how Jeff described you."

Holly frowned and gave him a curious look, then asked, "You gonna tell me what you want?"

"I want to talk to you about Jerry Shaw."

Holly did a double-take. "Jerry Shaw?" she asked. "What about him?"

"Maybe you know where he is."

"Jerry's dead. Died in a garage fire five years ago."

Wes Chandler stepped toward Holly. He raised then propped his arms against the door frame above her and leaned forward, intentionally looming over Holly.

With a sneer, he said, "Look, sister, I know all that's bullshit. Jeff told me the whole sad, sorry story – how you and he and Jerry Shaw faked Jerry's death for the insurance money. Four million dollars, right?"

Holly cursed Jeff for revealing that to this stranger who looked more trouble than he was worth. She took a step forward, ducked under Wes's arms and away from him out onto the porch.

She turned to him and said, "Look, bud, you can get the fuck out of here before I call your parole officer. I got nothing to say to you about anything Jeff told you. It was all bullshit."

Wes flashed a devious smile. "No, sister," he said. "I don't think so. Jeff was pretty sure about it. In fact, he asked me to help him get his hands on whatever was left of all that money – at least a million bucks, he thought - if we ever got out of prison. Well, he got out of prison before I did, and you did, too, on some kind of technicality. Right?"

"Yeah, a technicality," Holly confirmed. "So what's your point?"

"Well, I'm out now, too, finally been paroled," Wes said. "And, when I heard Jeff was dead, that he'd been murdered, I figured, maybe that pretty little lady he told me about might still want to get her hands on what was hers. What this Jerry fella took from her."

"Look, that's all behind me now," she said. "I did some bad things, but I've turned over a new leaf." She furrowed her brow. "I'm trying to be good."

Wes laughed. "Trying to be good?" He let out another laugh. "Like now?"

"Yeah, like now," Holly replied. "Could be worse. I could be out on parole with an old backpack full of my belongings – and probably no place to sleep."

Wes eyes narrowed. He took a step toward Holly and said, "And it could be a lot better. For both of us."

She gave a noncommittal shrug.

Wes walked over and sat against the porch railing, turned and glared at Holly. "Look, I got no time for this," he said. "Do you know where you ex is or not?"

Holly looked at him for a time. "First of all, he's not my ex," she said. "And second, what if I do know where he is? What's it to you?"

Wes's lips curled into a smile. "Then you can help me find him," he said. "And we help ourselves to the money he's got. Money that's just as much yours as his."

Holly sighed, shook her head and looked away from him.

"And it sure seems that money is something you could presently use," Wes added.

Holly couldn't disagree. She could use it, though it was looking more and more out of reach.

She turned around and admitted, "Yeah, I could use it. Who couldn't use a million bucks." After a sigh, Holly looked into Wes Chandler's sleepy blue eyes and said, "But look, I told you, I turned over a new leaf. I promised to leave Jerry alone and I'm gonna leave him alone."

Of course, it wasn't entirely true that she was leaving Jerry alone. There were, for instance, their semi-regular phone calls, including two from the night before. Anger rose up in Holly as she thought back to their second call. Jerry hadn't wanted to hear a goddamn thing. For him, it was always Jade and their baby boy and writing his stupid comic books. But Holly was mollified in the next moment by the thought that despite his supposedly profound commitment to Jade, Jerry still permitted her to remain in his life even if by only the thin thread of their irregular phone calls.

Wes Chandler pushed himself off the porch railing. He seemed impatient, sick of her intransigence.

"Look, sister, all I'm asking is that you think it over," he said. "Help me find Jerry and get your fair share of what remains of that insurance money. How long you wanna be living with your mommy and daddy?"

"You could care less about that," Holly snapped. "What you care about is getting your grubby hands on that insurance money."

"Yeah, no shit," he said. "Why else do you think I'm here, sister." As he reached down and lifted up his backpack,

Wes gave Holly a crooked, mischievous grin and said, "Well, there was also Jeff's bragging about what a pretty lady you were." He clicked a wink at her. "And about that, he wasn't exaggerating."

Holly frowned and shook her head, trying to disregard the compliment although it did please her a little bit. Then, she looked down and noticed Wes's worn sneakers.

"Hey, you are homeless, aren't you?" she asked. "For real."

He shrugged and said, "Yeah, I'm homeless. So what? They don't give you a pile of cash when they let you out of the can."

Holly gave Wes an appraising look. She couldn't deny the appeal of his rugged, good looks with that reckless, domineering edge, somewhat like Jeff Flaherty had. Once cleaned up, she imagined herself kissing him, or maybe even doing more. She was also lonely at the moment, and hadn't had a man in three weeks.

"Well, you look like you could use both a hot bath and decent breakfast," she said.

"Yeah, I surely could, sister," he said.

She nodded to the door. "Hey, just don't stand there," Holly snapped. "Come in before I change my mind."

Chapter Nine

Wesley Chandler

~~~~~

When Holly led Wes into the living room, her mother looked up with a frown, wary of this ruggedly good-looking, though obviously troubled and threatening young man.

"Ma, as it turns out, me and Wes did go to school together."

"Binghamton?"

"Yeah, Binghamton." Holly smiled as she looked back at Wes. "Right, Wes."

Wes turned to Holly's mom and said, "Yes, Ma'am, Bing-ham-ton. But that was a long time ago." Then, he nodded and added, "Nice to meet you, ma'am."

"And nice to meet you," Holly's mother said. "Where you from?"

"Grew up in Randolph," he said. "That's in the southern tier, near Salamanca." He gave a weak smile. "I don't live there anymore."

"Where do you live?" Holly's mother asked.

But Holly didn't let him answer. She asked her mother, "Mind if I make another pot of coffee and cook up some scrambled eggs, so I can catch up with Wes? Oh, and Wes is visiting up here for a couple days. Only the person he came to see doesn't live here anymore." Holly turned to him and with her mother unable to see her, winked at him. "Right, Wes?"

"Yep, either that or I got the wrong address," Wes said.

Holly turned to her mother again and said, "So, after I feed Wes breakfast, I'm gonna let him get cleaned up, take a shower in the guest bathroom. That okay?"

"Sure," Holly's mother said, frowning as she again appraised her daughter's guest.

"Oh, and do you mind if he stays with us a couple days until he figures out what happened to his friend? We got the room. I mean, he can stay in the extra guestroom, right?"

Holly's mother nodded doubtfully. "S-sure, we got the room," she said though without much enthusiasm. "But he's gonna hafta leave his car on the street."

"Oh, ma'am, I don't have no car," he said. "I took one of those Ubers to get here."

Holly's mother looked confused. "But, if you have no car, how…"

Again, Holly interrupted, "I thought you and dad were riding out the Falls today, go to the casino."

"Yes, we are," her mother replied. "We're gonna make a day of it."

"Okay, ma," Holly said. "When you leaving?"

"Soon as you father gets back from the dealership. He took the car in this morning for an oil change."

Wes flashed Holly a knowing smile. They'd have her house to themselves. In return, Holly shook her head, knowing full well what this hard-edged ex-con just released from prison was thinking about. But he was good looking, and after a bath, he'd be even more appealing. And she'd hadn't made love to anyone in a while.

***

As Holly showed Wes to the extra upstairs bedroom, he turned to her, held up his soiled, worn backpack and said,

"After we eat, mind doing a wash for me? The few clothes I have in here are pretty rank."

Holly frowned. Maybe taking in a paroled homeless bum who wanted to fuck her then help him betray Jerry Shaw again hadn't been such a good idea after all.

"I suppose," she said with a sigh. "What's in there?"

"Three pairs of boxers, couple tee shirts, another pair of jeans," he said. "That's about it. But, like I said, they ain't been washed in a while."

"Gimme," she said and took the backpack. "I'll put them in the wash and cook us some eggs and bacon. That sound good?"

"Yeah," Wes said, "real good. And then what?"

"And then what, what?"

Wes winked at her and Holly shook her head.

They went downstairs to the kitchen and Holly fixed a pot of coffee and poured Wes a cup. She left him at the kitchen table with it while she carried his backpack to the laundry room. Removing his grimy clothes with her fingertips, she tossed them into the washer, threw in some detergent, and set the machine, then returned to the kitchen.

"Looks like I've already become your maid," she protested with a laugh.

He grinned at her and remarked, "Pretty one, too."

After an incredulous look, Holly went about scrambling Wes three eggs with four strips of bacon on the side and two slices of white toast. Wes gobbled up the eggs and bacon and toast like he hadn't eaten a decent meal in days and washed it down with slurps of the hot, steaming black coffee.

"Slow down, fella," Holly said with a laugh. "You'll be licking the plate clean pretty soon."

"I just might," Wes said as he scarfed down another forkful of eggs.

After watching him another moment, she asked, "You really from Randolph?"

"Yeah," he said.

"Hick town, ain't it? Bunch of farmers down there, right?"

Chewing, he shrugged and said, "Yeah. Hick town."

"So, you a hick?"

"Sure," he said with a laugh. "A redneck hick."

"I could tell that," Holly said. "I bet you even used to ride steers in the rodeo."

Wes stopped chewing a moment and looked up at her. He smiled and said, "Yeah, I'm your original urban cowboy."

Holly glanced through the open archway that separated the kitchen from the living room where her mother still sat sipping her coffee while perusing the morning paper. Leaning toward Wes, Holly whispered, "So, how'd you end up in prison? What'd you do?"

He cut into the last of the eggs and lifted them to his mouth. After swallowing them down with some coffee, he laughed and said, "Look, my parents were dirt poor farmers. Raised produce, lettuce and shit. We lived in a shack. Yeah, we had indoor plumbing – one shithouse inside the house for eight of us. I had three brothers and two sisters. And yes, I did have shoes and sneakers and even a couple Buffalo Bills tee shirts and hoodies. But going to Disney World, that never happened. The local dairy festival with the traveling carny is about as good as it got.

"Anyway, in Randolph, there ain't much to do now and there wasn't back then," he went on. He pushed away his plate, took a last sip of coffee, then leaned back in his chair and continued his story, "So like most of my high school chums, I got into drugs, crystal meth, 'H', and coke, that sort of shit. Me and a coupla of my more enterprising buddies got around to selling it to other kids. Of course, we got caught by some state police task force. I was eighteen.

"So I spent a year in a minimum security pen called Lakeview Shock, down in Brocton. I went through their programs like a good little boy – substance abuse rehab,

GED classes, and other bullshit they tried to reform us with. But I also met some pretty hard characters in there, and when I got out, I teamed up with a coupla of them back around Randolph and went on to bigger and better things – burglaries, chop shops, and, of course, our favorite and most lucrative enterprise - dealing drugs.

"Anyway, we ended up with a fairly decent crew of outlaws and misfits – thieves and druggies who thought we were bad ass mother-fuckers. Only, we were still stupid kids, and careless, and this time some joint DEA and state police task force pinched me and another guy as the ringleaders of this so-called criminal enterprise." He laughed. "Can you believe it. They called what we led a criminal enterprise, like we was mafia dons or something. Anyway, they charged me under the state RICO and I got twenty years in the state pen – same place where Jeff got sent to on the murder rap.

"I served more than half my sentence, careful to stay out of trouble, and the parole board, needing the space I guess, let me out a couple weeks ago, a full two years after Jeff got let out and ended up dead."

Wes shrugged, leaned over and scooped up his last small pile of scrambled eggs. As he chewed, he muttered, "So, now I'm here, telling you my sad tale of woe while eating them eggs you cooked me. And trying like hell not to fall in love with you."

Holly gave him a crooked smile and said, "You mean, falling in lust with me, don't you cowboy?"

Wes nodded and his mouth clicked a sound that was in complete agreement with that sentiment.

Chapter Ten

Holly's Plan

By the time Wes was taking his shower, Holly's parents had left for their day-trip to the Seneca Resort & Casino on the American side of Niagara Falls. While he showered, Holly laid down on her bed. Listening to Wes bellowing out some rock song that she soon identified as "Ramblin' Gamblin' Man," by Bob Seger, she couldn't help but laugh. He was a tried and true redneck rodeo cowpoke. Still, with his rugged good looks and machismo, she just knew he'd be good in bed. With her parents out of the house, the opportunity to come on to Wes was certainly tempting.

Then, with that dirty idea swirling around her head, Holly thought of Jerry and the last time she'd made love to him, now almost two years ago in a room at the Holiday

Inn across from the airport. It was around eight in the morning. Later that evening, Jeff Flaherty had been killed by Pete Sharkey after Jeff had killed the Global Insurance fraud investigator, Chuck Bruno. It was also the same evening when Holly shot and killed Pete Sharkey saving the lives of Jerry and Jade and herself for that matter. For some reason, it seemed like all that had happened a century ago, or had never happened at all.

During one of their calls in the two years since then, she'd brought up their morning lovemaking session to Jerry. "That'll never happen again," he'd snapped. She'd laughed and said, "You sure?" Then, he hung up on her.

Holly closed her eyes and, thinking of having sex with Jerry, unclipped her jeans and slipped her hand down to her crotch and started massaging herself. She fantasized being on her knees with Jerry sitting on a chair before her, naked, his penis engorged, waiting for her mouth. She then imagined leaning forward and sucking him. Looking up, as if speaking to Jerry, she whispered, "See, Jerry, it is happening again."

But then, she thought, Jerry was right. It would never happen again. And the fantasy was ruined. She pulled up her hand, buttoned her pants, and sat up. Leaning against the headboard of her bed, Holly reached for her cell phone on the night table next to it and was about to try Jerry's cell again when Wes sauntered into her bedroom wearing only a bath towel around his waist.

"Whatcha been doing?" he asked and laughed. "Playing with yourself."

Holly shook her head.

"Hey, you got my clothes?"

"They're downstairs in the dryer," she said.

He looked down at the towel and asked, "So, what do I wear before they're done?"

She smiled up at him and said, "Nothing."

Wes returned the smile, then let the towel fall from his waist. Already hard, he stepped to the bed and laid down next to Holly. In the next moment, he moved her hand down to his crotch.

"Jerk it," he directed.

She obeyed and after a minute, he said, "Now, go down and suck it."

After five minutes of that, he watched as she took off her top, bra, jeans and panties. Then, he laid Holly on her back and straddling her, thrust his engorged penis inside her. Over and over, he slowly pushed it in and pulled it out, and all the while, she moaned, loving every second of it, hoping it would never end.

***

Afterwards, as Wes laid on his back staring up at the ceiling, he said, "Man, I needed that."

"Me, too," she whispered.

Still, the way Wes had so wantonly taken control of her during the sex act, together with his savage grunts and thrusts, had been, during the twenty minutes or so it had lasted, both a thrill and a turn-off.

"Who were you gonna call when I walked in?"

She shrugged and asked, "When?"

"When I walked in," he said in an accusatory tone, like a jealous boyfriend, and turned to her with a hard stare. "Before we fucked. You were holding the phone, about to call someone."

"I dunno," she said.

He smiled. "It was that Jerry fucker wasn't it. That's who you were about to call."

She sighed and said, "Yeah, Jerry. So?"

"So you do keep in touch with him."

"Now and then," she said. "We fell in love back in college and were married for eight years. We got history."

"Like the history there was between you and Jeff?"

"There was some."

"This Jerry fucker's still hot for you, ain't he?"

"No," Holly replied. "I don't think so. He's got a wife, and a kid."

Wes laughed "Yeah, but that don't mean shit. Two's always better than one."

It was Holly's turn to laugh. "You's men are all alike."

"Nothing wrong with that," Wes. said. "So, what about you? You still hot for him?"

Holly tried to give a noncommittal shrug. But that only made Wes laugh.

"You are, aren't you?" He reached down and grabbed his limp penis. "He got one this big?"

Holly laughed. "Don't flatter yourself."

"His bigger?"

"No."

"What about Jeff."

"Never mind about Jeff."

They stared up at the ceiling in the dark, quiet house for a time.

"So you gonna help me track this Jerry fucker down, or what?" he asked. "Find him and squeeze him out of your share of the insurance money."

Holly looked away. She was coming around to the idea that under the present circumstances, Wes was right. Jerry should share some of what was left of the insurance money with her – and Wes. Jerry was about to get a huge paycheck from his comic book sales and possibly even more from his potential movie deal. Most likely, he was about to be worth millions. And anyway, didn't she deserve some of this largess. After all, she and Jerry had been married eight years. If they'd gotten a traditional divorce, Holly reasoned, he'd have had to pay over to her a share of that largess.

"Well?"

Then it hit Holly like a lightning bolt out of a clear blue sky. She knew exactly what needed to be done.

Holly turned to Wes and said, "Yes, I'll help you. But not in the way you think."

"What's the way I think?"

"By going where he's hiding out now an kidnapping him, then force him to give us the money."

"Well, yeah, that was the plan," Wes admitted. "What other way is there?"

"Look," she explained, "I pretty much know where Jerry lives - down in Florida. I could find exactly where he's at pretty easy, I think. But I got a better idea than going down there, to where he lives, and strong-arming him for the money."

"Yeah, so I'm asking - what's your better idea?"

"It's called blackmail."

"Blackmail?" Wes shook his head. "I don't follow you."

"Jerry's comic book won a big award last night," Holly told him. "It's called the Eisner. Anyway, while his wife, or whatever she is, Jade, was out in San Diego picking it up for him — you know, as his front lady — she was approached by some Hollywood types who want to make his comic book into a movie."

"A movie? About that bullshit?"

She laughed. "Why, you read it?"

"Sure," Wes said. "In the can. Lot's of guys in there like that superhero bullshit."

"Well, Hollywood doesn't think it's bullshit. So, they want to make it into one of those blockbuster superhero movies that come out every summer. A different kind of one, I guess. Anyway, as you know, there's a ton of money to be made from those kind of movies, and as the creator and all that, Jerry stands to make a ton in royalties. But...," and Holly stopped a moment.

"But what?"

"But what if somehow it was to come out that the creator of this superhero is himself a thief, a villain who ripped off four million dollars from an insurance company and has been on the lam ever since. I doubt the Hollywood types would like that. Or his fans, for that matter. And neither would Jade or Jerry, because it'd mean he'd be arrested – they'd both be arrested - and shamed and have to watch his superhero comic and movie deal dream go up in smoke. Not to mention that they'd be facing jail time and have to watch their baby boy get sent to foster care by child protective services."

Wes let all that sink in. Then, he nodded and smiled.

"Yeah, I get it," he said. "Jerry would not only be out the money he'd stolen from the insurance company what, five years ago, but also the money he stands to make from the movie deal. Not to mention his bride and child."

"Exactly. And all we have to do is lay that out for him. Tell him that he either wires us the million he's got left from the insurance money, or we blow him in to the cops."

Wes looked at Holly, smiled and nodded.

He stroked her dark brown hair and said, "You know, it's like Jeff told me about you."

"Yeah, like what?"

"You are one deceitful bitch," he said. With a laugh, he added, "But in a good way."

Chapter Eleven

A New Wardrobe

～❖～

Once Wes's clothes dried, he put on an old, worn pair of boxers and jeans and a tee shirt with a small hole along the right shoulder. Looking at him after he walked into her bedroom, Holly laughed.

"Now, you really do look homeless," she said.

"This' the best I got, sister," he told her.

"Let me take you to Walmart and get you a new wardrobe," Holly said.

"I'd really prefer a K-Mart," he said.

She laughed again. "K-Mart? They've been out of business for years."

He shrugged and said, "What's the world coming to? No K-Marts?"

"Look, just c'mon," she said.

She drove him to the nearest Walmart about five miles away in the five-year old Ford Fiesta her father had bought her last summer. It wasn't much to look at, but it was good on gas, though terrible in the snow.

On the ride over, he asked, "So how'd you end up living with your parents at your age?"

She glanced over at him with a scowl. "You think I wanna be living with them?" She sighed and continued, "After I got out of prison, Jeff and I lived in one of my brother's beat-up apartments in Lackawanna. Raymond's a fucking slumlord though he thinks himself high and mighty. Goes to church each and every Sunday and all that bullcrap.

"Anyway, after Jeff was killed, I made the mistake of moving in with Raymond. He has a big place in in Williamsville and at the time, my parents were still down in Florida. It was a stupid idea. Me and Raymond never got along. He's a judgmental prick and to be honest, never liked the idea of me being around his teenage daughters. I was considered, you know, the artsy, flighty type. I majored in drama in college. Wanted to be an actress.

"And Raymond's wife Sarah's even more of a bitch than he is. Plus, it didn't help that she caught me smoking pot with my nieces one Saturday afternoon. He kicked me out pretty quick after that, put me up in one of his slum houses back in Lackawanna. But I was always behind in the rent, thinking, hell, he's my brother. He'll give me a break. But that wore out pretty quick, too.

"So, once my parents moved back up here about a year and a half ago, after my father got sick with heart problems, I moved in with them, where I've been pretty much ever since. And now, I've officially become the no count, black-sheep of the family who lives with her mommy and daddy."

"Gotcha," was all Wes said in response to her sad tale of woe.

After that they rode in silence down a boulevard with bumper-to-bumper traffic before turning into a busy Walmart. Holly found a space toward the rear of a massive lot and parked.

Once in the men's section of the store, Wes quickly picked out a modest wardrobe – a couple pairs of dress pants, a pair of jeans, sweatpants, three tee shirts, two polo shirts, a package of boxers and ankle socks, and a belt for the pants costing in total around a hundred fifty dollars. Holly used her Walmart card to pay for it.

"Okay, I got my top-of-the-line Walmart apparel," Wes said as Holly drove them back to her parents' house. "But where'm I gonna live after spending the next couple of days at your place."

"With me, until we blackmail Jerry," Holly said. "I'll tell my folks you needed to stay a few days longer."

"They gonna be okay with that?"

Holly shrugged and said, "My mother might bitch to me about it in private, and I'll plead that I'm just doing an old college chum down on his luck a favor. She'll give me one of her looks, shake her head, but in the end, she'll give in. She always does. And my father'll go along pretty much with anything she says. He doesn't have much energy anymore after his heart attack."

"You sure about that?"

"Yeah, I'm sure about that," Holly said. "What else they gonna do? Kick us out on the street? I'll say if you go, I go."

"So what's next on the agenda?" He smiled. "I mean after we screw around again."

"Look, bud, you had your taste of me for today. I'm not your personal whore."

He cracked his crooked, bad-boy grin. "You sure about that, sister? Because one taste of me is never enough."

She laughed and said, "Good try, pretty boy. But the answer is still no. I'll give it you again when I'm good and ready to. And, rest assured, I'm not one of those women turned off by sex, so you'll get enough of it. Maybe too much. Maybe." She turned to him, winked, then added,

"What's next on the agenda is that I call Jerry. See what's what – did the movie deal get done."

"And if it did?"

"Then, we start our blackmail campaign."

"So when you calling him?"

"Later this afternoon," Holly said. "He told me Jade and his agent are meeting with the Hollywood honchos sometime today. After that meeting, he should know more about what's what, how serious they are. I figure by five or so, I'll call him, see if he knows anything."

"Alright," Wes said. "But it's only what – like three here now, and what, noon in California. How do you propose we kill some time?"

"You do have a one-track mind, don't you." Holly laughed.

"Hey, I just got out of prison."

She shook her head and let go of a sigh. "Well, only if you promise to pamper me this time," Holly said. "You know, give the girl some pleasure."

"Hey, I'll give you all the pleasure you'll ever need."

"I bet you will," Holly said.

They'd reached her parents' house and despite what she'd told him about not becoming his personal whore, Holly felt to urge to become just that. After unlocking the front door, she squeezed Wes' hand and pulled him inside. Once in the foyer she drew him to her, stood up on her toes and kissed him. He dropped the plastic bags filled with his Walmart wardrobe, bent down and picked her up.

As he carried her through the living room to the staircase leading upstairs to her bedroom, she laughed and asked, "What're you doing?"

"Taking you to bed to pamper you," he told her.

Chapter Twelve

Getting The Ball Rolling

At one that same afternoon, Jade called Jerry and told him in a rush, "They love it. Everyone loves it. They love the everyman superhero concept that The Anonymous Man represents. I mean, he could be anyone, right? The idea of a guy with a tarnished past who becomes anonymous and does good deeds, helps people, really hit home, though I wasn't surprised, because that's what drives the comic book sales."

After a breath, Jade continued, "And they loved the idea of the anonymous author with a tarnished past like his creation's turning himself into the authorities in conjunction with the movie's premiere. Gabe loved it and told me to go ahead and sell it – so I did, explained the whole thing. And, Jerry, they really bought what I was selling. The studio execs seemed highly impressed. He, he really did that, they kept asking."

"You, you told them everything?" Jerry asked, not entirely pleased with that.

"Well, not everything," Jade said. "Just the broad strokes."

"So, it's okay. They said it's okay. It didn't sink the deal?"

"Quite the contrary," Jade said. "It made it even more appealing to them that the movie's author has of nefarious and notorious past just like his superhero creation."

Jerry drew in a breath of relief and asked, "So, now what?"

"Now, they're gonna draw up the contract," she said. "Gabe said it has to get through some kind of vetting process – you know, have all the top honchos, the studio head and advisors, agree. But since the guys we met with were so enthusiastic, Gabe didn't think there'd be a problem. Hell, she said, if they don't buy it, someone else will."

"What about the screenplay?" Jerry asked.

"Oh, yeah, I almost forgot," Jade said. "They wanted to give yours a long look, run it by some writers – showrunners, they called them – that they use. You know. To smooth out the rough edges. But, after a cursory review, the head guy, a lead producer at Marvel Entertainment, Ed Blakely, said he thought that they might be able to use a lot of what you wrote – enough at least to give you a full writer's credit, which, Gabe told me after the meeting, makes the deal sweeter money-wise. They made no promises, of course. Gabe'll have to work out the details."

"Holy shit, sounds like it went really well." Jerry thought a moment, then asked, "What about the money? What I mean is – will it be enough for me to negotiate my resurrection. You know, turn myself in. The million dollars we still have in the bank ain't chump change."

"Well, those details still need to be worked out," Jade said. "But Gabe was really optimistic when I told her what kind of money we'd need. We'll just have to see what they offer. She said it's her job to make the Marvel people understand what that aspect of the deal entails."

"Did Gabe have any idea how much of an offer? I mean, a ballpark figure."

"If it's greenlighted," Jade said, "she mentioned an advance of something like half a million to a million." Jade let out a laugh, hardly believing that a movie about The Anonymous Man could be worth that much.

"Holy shit. That much?"

"Yeah, that much," Jade replied. "And that's before a percentage of the box office. You know, residuals, or whatever they're called."

"And, honey," Jade went on, "I almost forgot. They really loved your new ending. One of them said it was much better than the comic book. I think he may end up being the director of the movie. He's done a couple of the successful Marvel films."

"What's his name?" Jerry asked.

"Ah, Jesus, I can't remember," Jade said. "What the hell was it there were like half a dozen people there and everyone had to get a word in." She drew a breath, thinking. Finally, she blurted, "Gunn. That was his name. James Gunn."

"Holy shit, James Gunn?"

"Yeah, James Gunn. Why?"

Jerry laughed and said, "Because he's only one of the most famous directors of the superhero genre in Hollywood. And I think he's head of one of the Disney studios now."

"He was real nice guy. Listened mostly. Said he really liked the King Midas character, maybe even more than The Anonymous Man. Said he saw a lot more potential for sequels with him."

"Really?"

"Yeah, that's what he said."

"Well, I'm still partial to The Anonymous Man."

Jade laughed and said, "Yeah, because you're him."

"So, what's next?"

"Next? Like I said, they're run the idea by the head of the studio and if he approves, they'll send Gabe over the standard agreement and notices, standard movie industry paperwork, approved by the Writer's Guild union or whatever. Gabe said she can review it with us over the phone. Then, you and their writers hammer out a working script, they cast it, then they start filming."

"Did they say how long – I mean, when the movie might come out?"

"They're hoping next May," Jade said.

"Holy shit," Jerry said. "That's really fast."

"Well, it's almost nine months," Jade said. "But there's not a lot of special effects they have to worry about with the kind of superhero The Anonymous Man is. No pyrotechnics, they said. So that shortened considerably the time, and expense, needed to film it."

"Nine long months of remaining anonymous," Jerry said.

"Yeah," Jade said. "Nine months."

"Well, at least that gives me plenty of time to negotiate my resurrection," Jerry said. "I'll give Jack Fox a call to get the ball rolling. See if he'll help me with it."

"Today?" Jade still seemed apprehensive.

"Why not today? I want to make sure the first day of the rest of my life next May is a good one."

Chapter Thirteen

Jack Fox

~~~

When his cell phone chimed and the phone announced, "Unknown caller," Jack Fox frowned. Not yet another junk call, he sighed. That's all he seemed to get these days. Life after retirement had begun to bore him.

Someone had given him the idea of writing a memoir to document his twenty-five years on the Philly police department first as a regular cop on patrol and then as a homicide detective, followed by his five year stint as a fraud investigator for Global Life and Casualty Insurance, and last but not least, his last three years a private detective following malingers for insurance companies and cheating spouses for lawyers. He started and stopped writing this memoir many times and was for the most part unable to transform his war stories into coherent and interesting content. First of all, he didn't have the patience or drive to sit down for long stretches and crank out a string of words, sentences, paragraphs and chapters necessary to fill a book. As a cop and later private eye, he'd written short, concise reports, giving the facts, without any flowery or unnecessary verbiage. Plus, it soon occurred to Fox that his war stories were no more interesting than the thousands of similar stories that countless other cops and privage investigators of all stripes could tell.

"What you need is a ghost writer," Mary Fox, his wife of forty-five years had suggested. "Help you tell the story."

"Who'm I gonna get to do that?" he asked with annoyance.

She shrugged and said, "What about that friend of yours – the anonymous man."

Mary was the only person on the planet he'd told about his relationship with the anonymous man. But even to her, he'd never revealed Jerry Shaw's name.

To this day, it remained his life's mystery why he'd become so close to the kid. After all, Jerry was a felon who'd avoided justice for half a decade and still held over a million dollars of money stolen from Global. But Jerry's moxie and cleverness intrigued him. And his criminal misdeeds were nothing compared to those of the scumbag guys Jerry had removed from society – the likes of Jeff Flaherty, Chuck Bruno and Pete Sharkey.

"The anonymous man?" Fox snapped at Mary. "No."

"Why not? He's a writer, isn't he? Writes those comic books."

"Yeah, and he's too busy with that." That was true. The kid was constantly putting out new editions of his comic books and writing other stuff. In fact, Fox couldn't remember the last time he'd gotten a call from Jerry. The last time he'd seen him, Fox had been in a hospital bed recovering from the nasty beating by Chuck Bruno.

"Look, I'll figure out what to write on my own sweet time. Or maybe write nothing at all."

"Well, you need to do something other than sit around all day brooding and feeling useless," Mary Fox scolded him. "That'll drive you to an early grave. Or me!"

As Fox picked up his cell to answer the call from the latest unknown caller, Fox glanced at the pile of The Anonymous Man comics that filled up almost an entire row of the tall bookcase against the far wall of his den, and said, "Hello?"

"Mr. Fox?"

Fox sat up straight and said, "J-Jerry?" Amazing, he thought, how life works sometimes. All you have to do is think of someone from your past, and in the next moment, you're on a cell phone call with them.

"Yes, it's me. Jerry."

"I was just thinking about you," Fox told him.

"Yeah? Why?"

"Never mind. What's up?"

"I, I need your help."

"What's wrong?"

"Nothing's wrong," Jerry said. "In fact, everything's great." He let out a breath and said, "Last night, I won an Eisner."

"An Eisner? What's that?"

"It's an big time award for comic books," Jerry explained. "Like an Oscar. They give it out every year for various categories at something called a Comic-Con in San Diego. 'The Anonymous Man' won for best series."

"Hey, that's great, kid," Fox said. "Congratulations. Your comic is good stuff. I love reading the latest adventures of The Anonymous Man. You deserved it."

"Problem is, I couldn't go out there and accept it," Jerry said. "Jade had to do it for me. You know, as my front. And that was a real bummer – you know, not to be there when they called my name. Not to be able to give an acceptance speech."

"Yeah, I bet," Fox said. "Bummer."

"And I even got better news." Jerry went on. "Marvel Entertainment, owned by Disney, wants to make a movie out of The Anonymous Man."

"A movie?" Fox laughed. "That's great! Wow! Congratulations again."

"Thanks," Jerry said. After a sigh, he added, "And that's why I'm calling you."

"Okay, not sure I get what you mean," Fox said. Fox laughed and said, "You want me to be in the movie?"

"That'd be great, Mr. Fox. If it was up to me, you'd having a starring role. But what I need is for you to help me, well, turn myself in. I want to end my life as The Anonymous Man." Jerry laughed to himself. "And on the flip side of that - I want you to help me become The Notorious Man."

Chapter Fourteen

Holly's Gambit

~~~

During his call with Jack Fox, Jerry ignored another incoming call from Holly. She'd called twice in a row that morning and he hadn't answered because he was too busy feeding and bathing Seius. Now, an hour later, she was calling again and this time, when Jerry didn't answer, she left him a voicemail message.

"Where are you, Jerry?" she'd said. "Why are you avoiding my calls? I really need to talk to you. Please pick up next time. Talk to me. I know Jade isn't home."

After a sigh, Jerry hit the call-back icon. Holly answered on the second ring.

"Jerry," she said with obvious relief. "Where you been?"

"What's going on, Holly," Jerry said. "We agreed a long time ago that we'd talk occasionally. Not every hour on the hour of every day."

"Well, I'm sorry," she snapped back. "I just figured, what's the harm? Jade's not there."

"That's not the point," Jerry said.

The point was talking to Holly was more and more feeling like cheating – no, it was cheating, considering Jade's view of it. If she found out, that'd be the end of their relationship.

Still, Jerry had let these calls with Holly continue with no end in sight. Though they were infrequent - until the last two days, every couple of weeks or so since he and Jade had dropped Holly off at her brother Raymond's house in Williamsville – they still were a source of potential disaster for his relationship with Jade. But for some reason Jerry couldn't quite fathom, he always took them. She'd first text him and ask if she could call and then he'd text her back a time when he could talk. He'd sneak off to bathroom or tell Jade he needed to take a walk by himself to clear his mind or wait for Jade to go out shopping to get away from the baby.

Their talks were never substantial. She'd tell him what she was doing with herself, where her head was at which over the last two years, seemed hardly ever in a good place. Jerry thought when she'd met her new lover, Eddie, and then moved in with him, that perhaps she'd settle down and the calls would finally dwindle down to nothing. But the thought of that actually happening bothered him more than a little bit.

"Anyway, what's up?" Jerry asked.

"So? Did you get the movie deal? I'm curious?"

"Looks promising," he said. "Very promising."

"Really? You gotta be super-thrilled."

"Yeah, that's the word for it – thrilled."

"You don't sound thrilled," Holly said.

"Well, this whole thing has put me into a kind of dilemma."

Jerry sighed, wondering if getting into it with Holly was such a good idea.

"What kind of dilemma?" Holly asked.

Just then, with Jerry starting to tell her, Wes walked into her bedroom. He'd been in the guest bedroom taking a nap. Wes nodded to the phone and silently asked, "Jerry?"

She nodded and put a hand up to quiet him and pointed to her bed. He shrugged and sat on the edge of it.

"Jerry? I'm sorry, what? I didn't hear what you said?"

"Somebody there with you?"

"No. Course not. Who'd be here?"

"Well, anyway, what I said was, I was thinking of turning myself in. Stop this anonymous man charade. Resurrect myself."

"Turn yourself in? You mean, to the police?"

"Yes. Give Global back the money, the million or so still in my accounts, then come back up there and face the music. You know, plead guilty to something."

"Why would you do that?"

"I don't want to be anonymous anymore," Jerry said flatly. It was as simple as that. "I no longer wish to be dead. And with this movie deal, I no longer need Global's money. Even without it, me and Jade and the baby would be just fine on what I make from the comics and the other stuff I do – plus her job."

"But, but, you'll go to prison, right?"

Wes had wiggled around and his scowl had intensified. His arms raised up questioning what was happening. Then, he whispered, "What the fuck's going on?"

Holly scowled and raised a hand to quiet him.

"Maybe, yes," he said. "Probably. But turning myself in, and giving back the money, should minimize things. You know, lessen the jail time, if I hafta serve any at all."

"I, I really don't think you should do this," Holly said. "And won't it, won't it kill the movie deal. Disney would want to deal with a criminal, a felon?"

"Jade already ran it by them," Jerry said. "And, believe it or not, they liked the idea – the anonymous author of The Anonymous Man comics and movie is himself an anonymous man superhero – or something like that. I'd turn myself in in conjunction with the premier of the movie."

"Jerry, I, I don't know what to say," Holly said.

What she wanted to say was that this had totally fucked up her plan to blackmail him.

"Well, I already put things in motion," he said.

"Yeah, how?"

"I contacted Jack Fox," he told her. "You know, the retired Global investigator. He's gonna make some inquiries. Feel Global out and the local DA. Like I said, I'd be turning myself in and help them solve a cold case, plus pay back the rest of the Global money. That should help get me a decent deal."

"Well, I think you should at least talk to a lawyer," Holly said.

"Jade suggested that, too," Jerry said. "And my agent. Right after I get off the phone with you, I'm gonna search the internet and find someone."

"Well, I still don't know what to say," Holly said. "And I still don't agree with turning yourself in. But, hey, congratulations on the movie deal."

"Thanks." He laughed. "I don't think it's hit me yet."

"When's Jade coming home."

"Tomorrow afternoon." He sighed. "And I really need her too," he said and laughed again. "Taking care of a toddler by yourself is quite the ordeal."

"I wouldn't know," Holly said, and there it was again, the old bitterness about her not being able to get pregnant during their eight years of marriage.

As if on cue, Holly heard a baby wailing through Jerry's phone.

"Hear that? He's up. And he doesn't sound happy."

"Well, thanks for taking my call and once again, congratulations."

"Thanks, gotta go," Jerry said. "Talk to you soon. But remember, Jade's home tomorrow. So let's not talk for a while. I'll text you when I think it's okay. Okay?"

"Yeah, sure," she said bitterly, then clicked off the call.

When she looked up at Wes, he asked, "What?"

"Blackmail's out," Holly told him.

"Why?"

"It wouldn't work," Holly said. "He wants to turn himself in. End being an anonymous man."

"Shit," Wes said. "Now what?"

Holly's eyes narrowed. She thought of Jade coming home and their baby crying, then looked up at Wes and said, "Now, we go back to the original plan. We go down to wherever he is in Florida and kidnap the son-of-a-bitch."

Chapter Fifteen

Dean Alessi

It didn't take long for Jerry to find an attorney he believed could help him work his way back to the living. When he googled "attorneys near me," several pages of names popped up. After clicking on a few names and reading their bios, he came upon Dean Alessi, a handsome, determined looking guy wearing a dark suit who appeared to be in his late forties with an office nearby.

What immediately struck Jerry was that Alessi also hailed from Buffalo. Jerry was also impressed by the fact that Alessi had run the state Lawyer Discipline Office up there for over eighteen years. A couple years back, Alessi had left that job and come down to Florida, passed the Florida bar and set up a small, general practice law firm, Alessi & Alessi, with his wife, Kellie, who looked considerably younger than him. Their offices were located in a strip mall along the US 41-Bypass, aka the Tamiami Trail, in Venice, Florida around fifteen minutes from Jerry's Englewood house.

He called the phone number on the Alessi & Alessi website and managed to obtain an appointment for five-fifteen that very afternoon.

"I'll have to bring along my two year old with me," Jerry told the firm's receptionist. "My wife's out of town. Is that alright?"

"That's fine," said the receptionist. "I'll look after him while you meet with Dean. We even have some toys stacked away in an extra conference room for situations like this."

Three hours later, Jerry pulled into the parking lot of the strip mall where Alessi's law office was located and found a space along the far corner of the squat cinder-block building. After exiting his black Nissan Rogue, Jerry went around and opened up the rear door and unlatched Seius from his car seat. After pulling the boy out of the vehicle and into his arms, Jerry next tossed a diaper bag around his free shoulder. As he used his hip to shut the car door, then somehow wiggled his key around to lock it, Jerry said to Seius, "Okay, little guy, let's go meet our lawyer."

Carrying Seius along his hip with the diaper bag almost

falling from his shoulder, Jerry ambled onto a wide sidewalk and approached a tinted glass entrance door with the firm name, Alessi & Alessi, stenciled prominently across the top of it. Below it were the names of the firm members - first, Kellie S. Alessi, Esq., then underneath her name, Dean V. Alessi, Esq. Jerry laughed to himself thinking who must wear the pants in this relationship.

With Seius cooing playfully and pulling at Jerry's hair, Jerry opened the glass door and stepped into a rather cramped reception room. He strode up to the firm's receptionist sitting in a constricted kiosk. Looking to be in her early twenties and fresh out of secretarial school, she was attractive, if slightly overweight, and pleasant as she'd sounded during Jerry's brief phone call with her earlier that afternoon.

Dropping the diaper bag to the floor, Jerry said, "I'm Todd Smith. I have an appointment to see Mister Alessi." Whenever he had to give a name, it was either Todd Smith or Todd Jones.

"And this must be your little guy," said the receptionist with a smile. "What a cutie."

Seius turned to her and let out a yelp. Then, he said, "I See-us."

"That's his name," Jerry said.

"Wow, he can talk? How old is he?"

"Two," Jerry said. "Well, two and a half."

"But what was it – his name?"

"Seius," Jerry said.

The receptionist frowned and said, "That's an ... interesting name." The cock of her head belied the compliment.

"Well, let's just say, it's different," Jerry said, then added, "It's Latin that means something like, the anonymous man." He wondered whether he was getting a tad too cute for his own good.

The receptionist gave Jerry an odd look. "Well, let me buzz you in and you can give...what was it, his name?"

"Seius."

"You can give Seius over to me while you speak with Mr. Alessi," the receptionist said. "And my name's Kodi by the way."

"Nice to meet you, Kodi," Jerry said. "And so nice of you to do this, watch him. I warn you, though, he can be a ball of trouble."

"I have my own ball of trouble at home," she said.

After calling back to Dean Alessi that his prospective client, Mr. Smith, had arrived, Kodi clicked a buzzer allowing Jerry to open an oak door leading into an interior hallway. She then came out of her kiosk and upon her approach, Jerry handed Seius over to her. She nodded down the hallway and said, "Dean's office is the second one on the left."

"Thanks so much," Jerry said. He kissed Seius on top of his blonde hair and said, "Now you be a good boy. Daddy'll be right back."

Jerry smiled at Kodi and thanked her again before heading down the hallway. As he reached the door with the nameplate, Dean Alessi, Esq, he looked back and saw that Seius was playfully pounding on Kodi's face with the plump palms of both hands.

He smiled and waved that way before knocking on Dean Alessi's office door.

A few moments later, Dean opened it.

"C'min, c'min," Dean said. "This way."

Dean lead Jerry to a chair facing his desk. "Sit," he said, then ambled over and sat behind his desk.

"So how can I help you, Mr. Smith?"

"Well, first – can I ask you something?" Jerry asked.

"Sure, go ahead."

"Why'd you leave your job up in Buffalo?" Jerry asked. "You were the Director of the Lawyer Discipline Office. Why'd you quit that?"

"Let's just say, politics had something to do with it," Dean replied with a shrug. Then, he smiled and added, "And, of course, to get away from the snow."

Jerry frowned and after a moment, smiled, though not quite convinced.

"Anything else you want to ask me, Mr. Smith?" Dean asked.

"Yeah, ah - what I tell you here is confidential, right?" Jerry said.

"Correct," Dean said. "Under the rules of professional conduct that apply to lawyers, and even in the criminal law codes, what a client, or even a prospective client like you tells a lawyer during a consultation is privileged. It can't be divulged to anyone. It's the same kind of rule of privilege that applies to a priest's confessional or a doctor. What you tell me, I can't tell anyone else, without your permission."

Jerry nodded. He sort of knew that already.

"Alright, then." After a sigh, he began, "First of all, my name's not Todd Smith, it's Jerry Shaw."

For the next ten minutes, Jerry launched into his story, starting with his days as a college student at the State University of New York at Binghamton, where he and Holly met, to his winning the Eisner last night, the possible movie deal, and his call to Jack Fox earlier that afternoon in the hope of ending his life as an anonymous man.

All the while, Alessi listened to Jerry's fantastic story with a deadpan frown and several nods. Afterwards, he leaned back and clasped his hands together on his chest.

"Does this Fox fellow know where you are?" Alessi asked.

"Well, he knows I'm down here in Florida."

"But your specific address? Does he know that?"

"No."

Alessi thought a moment, then said, "Look, I know some people up there. I can make some inquiries, see if they can help resolve this, well, situation. I'll work with your friend, this Jack Fox fellow, and see what he and I can work out for you. Turning yourself in and paying back Global's money should go a long way toward mitigating your ultimate punishment. Of course, there are no promises."

"What's your fee for something like this?"

"My fee?" Alessi laughed. "It's a pretty unusual case. It'll depend how much time I have to put in to obtain a fair disposition of your case. For now, how's one-hundred dollars an hour to work for you? Of course, going up to Buffalo for a court proceeding for you to enter a plea to some charge will cost an additional amount. But we can worry about that later. I can always get someone up there to handle the plea. How's that work for you?"

Jerry shrugged. "Sounds reasonable," he said.

"Well, let me get started then. What's Jack Fox's number?"

After giving the number to Alessi, Jerry said, "You know, I just want all this to be over with. After five years of being dead, I just want to live again."

Chapter Sixteen

Alessi and Fox

Around seven that evening, Dean Alessi called Jack Fox. After introducing himself, Dean told him about his meeting with Jerry and that he was now representing him.

When Fox fell silent, Alessi asked, "Sir?"

"How do I know who you are?" Fox asked.

"Look, google Alessi and Alessi, attorneys, Venice, Florida," Alessi said. "Our website should come up. It has my cell phone number on it – the cell phone I'm using now. Call me back. Alright?"

"Yeah."

They hung up and a minute later, Fox called Alessi.

"Sorry about that," Fox said. "I've been trained to be careful."

"Nothing wrong with that."

"So, you were saying, Mr. Alessi," Fox said.

"Yes, Mr. Fox. Jerry told me that he called you yesterday to get the ball rolling for turning himself in. Have you done anything in regard to that?"

"Well, I've set up a call with my old boss in Philly for tomorrow morning," Fox said. "His name's Dick Reynolds, Chief of Global's fraud unit. He's been there for a long, long time. Years. Problem is, Dick's finally retiring and breaking in a new guy, someone Global brought in from the outside, former FBI or something. I don't know this guy and can only hope he'll be reasonable. I think the key is getting Global on our side. After all, they're the victim in this."

"Yes, I most certainly agree," Dean said. "As for that, do you think there's any possibility of Global taking their money and letting Jerry walk away from this? You know, without going to the authorities?"

"No," Fox said. "At least, the policy when I was there was to always refer a pending case to the authorities no matter what. If I know Dick Reynolds, he'll feel obliged to let the DA know about this change of circumstances."

"Well, do you think if Jerry turns himself in and gives

Global back their money that they'd go along with a plea that involves little if any jail time?" Dean asked. "I know that the DA's office always figures in the victim's position in negotiating a plea."

"You can ask," Fox said. "I didn't have involvement in negotiating pleas. My job was to catch frauds and cheats. But, you ask me, Jerry'll have some pretty good arguments for a reduced sentence."

"That's the hope," Dean said. "The other thing is, Jerry wants to wait to turn himself in until a movie based on his comic book superhero, The Anonymous Man, is released. Did Jerry mention that to you?"

"Yes, something." Fox sighed. "He said doing it that way will have promotional value to the studio, help them sell more tickets. That might complicate things. The movie won't come out for months as I understand it."

"Nine months is Jerry's best guess," Dean said. "Marvel Entertainment wants to release it next May. That's the start of blockbuster season."

"What do you think he's realistically looking at, in terms of sentence?" Fox asked.

"Hard to tell," Dean said. "I mean, from Global's point of view, and the DA's office for that matter, Jerry had use of their money for five years and made them look foolish thinking he was really dead. They might take the position that the only reason he's coming forward is because he doesn't want to remain in hiding now that he doesn't need their money. He wants to enjoy the fame and fortune that'll come from the release of a movie based on his artistic creation – if you can call a superhero comic book art - something he certainly can't exactly do as an anonymous man. My fear is that Jerry's motives for wanting to turn himself in tarnishes the mitigation a bit."

Fox thought about that a moment, then said, "Yeah, I think I see your point."

"Anyway," Dean went on, "from my end, I'll start making inquiries over at the Erie County DA's office. I vaguely know the Chief of the Special Investigations and Prosecutions Bureau over there, Jack Spencer. They'd likely be handling this type of investigation. Jack and I worked on a couple cases together when I was at the Lawyer Discipline Office up there – you know, for lawyers who stole money from their clients. I'll give him a call and feel him out, give him a hypothetical."

"Can I ask you something, Mr. Alessi?"

"Dean, call me Dean. But go ahead, ask."

"Why'd you leave the Lawyer Discipline Office and move down to Florida?"

"You know, Jerry asked me the same thing," Dean said. "A lot of people do." After a sigh, he explained, "It was politics, pure and simple. Let's just say I didn't have the same sense of justice that a certain judge had. As for my move to Florida, I certainly don't miss the long cold winters up there."

Fox let out a sigh. "I definitely know what you mean," he said.

"A lot of people are moving down here," Dean said. "It's literally paradise."

"Yeah," Fox said, "except during a hurricane."

Chapter Seventeen

Jerry Shaw Lives!

~~~

At eleven the following morning, Fox called Dick Reynold's office.

"Chief, it's me, Jack Fox."

"Hey, Foxy," Reynolds said. "How ya been? How's retirement treating you."

"Not so great," Fox said with a laugh. "Writing my boring memoirs. But I spend most of my time doing Mary's honey-do list mostly. Same thing you'll be doing when you call it quits. That's in a couple weeks, right?"

"Yup, two weeks from today and then every day'll be Saturday." After a sigh, the Chief asked, "So what can I do you for - or did you just call to harass me?"

"Actually, it's a business call," Fox said. "It involves an old case – Jerry Shaw was the insured."

"Shaw?" Chief Reynolds thought for a moment, then said, "Oh, yeah – the poor guy who was murdered in a garage fire."

"Yep, him."

"What about him?" The Chief then quickly added, "Hey, as its business related, I'm gonna put you on speaker. I'm with Neal Barrett who'll be replacing me in a couple weeks."

"I guess," Fox said with a frown, not entirely pleased about that. He was hoping to reveal Jerry's desire to turn himself in solely to Chief Reynolds.

After a moment, Reynolds said, "Okay, Jack, you're on speaker."

The other guy sitting in a chair facing Reynolds desk chimed in, "Hello, Jack. I've heard a lot about you. Sure you don't want to come out of retirement?"

"Yeah, I'm sure," Fox said. "I'm actually glad to be out of Philly. Place seems to be really going to seed."

"Well, it may very well be going to seed," Barrett said, "but we still got the Eagles, Sixers, Phillies, and Flyers."

"So Jack," Reynolds said, "you said you're calling about

the Jerry Shaw claim. But first, let me bring Neal up to speed."

Chief Reynolds looked at Barrett and explained, "About five years ago, this Jerry Shaw fellow was killed in a garage fire. Afterwards, his wife, Holly Shaw, put in a claim on his four million dollar life policy. I mean, four million bucks on a life policy bought by the guy about a year and a half earlier – a guy still in the prime of his life with no kids. Seemed excessive, you know, and so it made me suspicious."

"Chief, everything makes you suspicious," Fox chimed in with a laugh. "You like that Edgar G. Robinson character in that old movie, 'Double Indemnity.'"

"Yeah, great movie," the Chief said. "My favorite. And damn right, I was suspicious. I smelled a rat – two rats, actually – Mrs. Shaw and the lawyer she worked for, Jeff Flaherty. And as it turns out, I was right, because it seems that Mrs. Shaw and Jeff Flaherty had set up old Jerry for murder. They apparently spilled, then ignited, a pool of gasoline on the garage floor while he was under the car looking for a fuel leak.

"Then, a few weeks after Global paid the claim - against my recommendation, I might add," Chief Reynolds went on, "we received evidence – email messages back and forth between Jerry's widow and Jeff Flaherty implicating them in Jerry's murder. They were eventually charged and brought to trial. During that trial, they changed their pleas to guilty to voluntary manslaughter and insurance fraud – after they turned in about two and half million to Global that they claimed was their share of the insurance money."

"What they'd say happened to the rest?" Barrett asked. "The other third. Roughly, one point three million dollars.

"They claimed that Jerry had it. That they faked his death. That Jerry Shaw was alive and well and living somewhere down in Florida and that he had the rest of Global's money."

"You mean the guy they killed?" Barrett asked. "I'm not following you, Dick. How in the world..."

"I'm getting to that," Chief Reynolds interrupted. "As I said, they claimed that they'd faked Jerry's death – the three of them, Holly Shaw, Jeff Flaherty, and Jerry Shaw himself. For two years, they'd planned the caper. According to Holly and Jeff Flaherty, what the cops believed was Jerry's body burnt to a crisp on the garage floor was actually the crispy remnants of a research cadaver they'd paid some worker at the University of Buffalo Medical School ten grand to produce for them. But none of it could be verified. The worker from the medical school had been murdered weeks earlier and there was no record of a cadaver being lost by the school. DA didn't buy it. By then, the body found in the burnt out garage had been cremated and its ashes scattered by his wife, Holly. So there was no way of checking for DNA."

Chief Reynolds sighed and added, "With the DA not

buying their claim, they eventually figured it was either enter a plea to a lesser charge and get less jail time or face life in prison without the possibility of parol if they continued on with the trial and were found guilty. Holly ended up getting... what was it... oh, yeah, seven years, and Flaherty got, let's see...fifteen. Right Jack?"

"Yeah, something like that," he replied.

The Chief laughed and added, "And then, something even more bizarre happened."

"What?" Barrett asked.

"Well, after about six months, Holly and Jeff were released from prison on a technicality," Reynolds said. "Speedy trial issue, I think it was. But not long after their release, Jeff was found shot to death in a cheap motel room up in Buffalo near the football stadium. And shot to death with him was one of Global's fraud investigators, Chuck Bruno, and a former federal marshal, Pete Sharkey. The cops are still trying to figure out what happened. You were in the middle of all that, right Jack?"

"Well, ah, yeah," Fox said, not quite ready with this story. "Ah, you see, ah, Flaherty had come to me with this convoluted tale about Sharkey blackmailing him for what was left of the Global money. So I contacted Dan Miller, an inspector with the state police, with whom I'd worked with before on well, the original Holly Shaw, Jeff Flaherty murder prosecution, and we, well, set up a sting. Flaherty thought Sharkey was gonna kidnap him, but, see, Sharkey never showed up and instead was hiding out in the room next door. Anyway, after Dan Miller and his SWAT team left the motel parking lot, Jeff Flaherty, Chuck Bruno and Pete Sharkey ended up shooting themselves to death." Fox laughed. "The police are still trying to figure the logistics of that."

Everyone fell silent, trying to figure out what Fox had just told them.

"Whatever happened to the insured's wife?" Barrett asked. "I mean, when she got out of prison?"

"Nothing," Chief Reynolds said, "right Jack?"

"Yeah, nothing. I think she, ah, well, moved in with her brother."

"You didn't think to tail her?" Barrett asked, more to Reynolds than to Fox.

"No," the Chief said. "We moved on to bigger and better things."

"Bigger and better than one point three million dollars?" Barrett asked, somewhat like an accusation of incompetence.

"Yeah, bigger and better than one point three million dollars," Reynolds shot back. "This happens to be a multi-billion dollar business, Neal."

"Okay," was Barrett's response.

"Anyway, that's the whole sordid, crazy case," Reynolds chimed int. "Right, Jack?"

"Yep, that about sums it up," Fox agreed.

"So what's the point of your call, Jack?" Reynolds asked. "Why'd you need to call us about the Jerry Shaw case?"

Fox swallowed and hesitated a moment before blurting out, "Because I, ah, just found out that, well, it's true, what Holly Shaw and Jeff Flaherty claimed - Jerry Shaw never died." He drew a breath and added, "Jerry Shaw lives!"

Chapter Eighteen

Cat Out Of The Bag

~~~~~

After a long, silent moment, Chief Reynolds said, "What'd you just say?"

"Jerry Shaw lives - he, he never died," Fox replied. "Holly Shaw and Jeff Flaherty were telling the truth. They did use a medical school cadaver for Jerry's body. Jerry then became, well, anonymous, and he's remained anonymous the past five years. And he's still got the rest of Global's money. Well, most of it. And he wants to turn himself in and give it back."

"How the hell do you know this, Jack?" Reynolds asked.

"Because Jerry Shaw called me today," Fox said.

"He called you?" Reynolds asked dubiously. "Out of the blue. Just like that?"

Before calling Chief Reynolds, Fox had decided to follow Jerry's advice and not reveal that he's known Jerry for over four years. Thus, he'd protect himself from any claim by Global, or the prosecution, that he was guilty of being an accessory-after-the-fact.

"Yes, out of the clear blue," Fox said with a laugh. "Gave me quite a shock."

"I bet," Reynolds said.

"Why'd he call you?" Neal Barrett asked.

"He knew me from Holly and Jeff Flaherty's murder trial," Fox explained. "I testified."

"He was there?" Barrett asked while Reynolds let out a laugh.

"Yeah," Fox said. "Right in the courtroom, watching his own murder trial. What the hell – he told me he watched his own funeral, too."

"And nobody recognized him?" Barrett asked.

"He changed his appearance," Fox said. He wondered if he was revealing too much. "Or must've."

"How do you know it was him, this caller?" Reynolds asked. "Jerry Shaw."

"Well, I'm not one-hundred per cent certain," Fox said. "But why would some guy call me out of the blue and tell me he's Jerry Shaw and wants to turn himself in to face possible criminal charges if it's not really him?"

"So, why'd he call?" Barrett interrupted. "Why not just turn himself in?"

Chief Reynolds answered for Fox. "Obviously, he wants to negotiate a deal," he said.

"Yes," agreed Fox. "He wants a deal."

"Like what kind of deal?" Barrett asked.

"Well, for one thing," Fox replied, "he was wondering if Global would simply take back the money and keep the matter of his returning it in house. Just let him resume his life as if the whole thing never happened."

"That's a non-starter," Barrett snapped. "First, of all, it did happen. And I mean, if it ever got out that we did that, prosecutor's offices, not only in Buffalo, but everywhere else, would go ballistic. They'd blackball us for sure. Plus, is that justice, considering what the guy did?"

"It might also turn us into accessories-after-the-fact," Reynolds suggested.

"Yeah, I didn't think of that," Barrett agreed.

Having expected that answer, Fox said, "Well, in the alternative, he'd like Global's cooperation in not demanding jail time, or at least, approving minimal jail time, considering his voluntary cooperation in turning himself in and giving back their money."

"I don't like that either," Barrett said. "I mean, for deterrent's sake if nothing else."

"Well, you have to give him something," Fox said. "I mean, the guy's turning himself in and giving back Global's money."

"Yeah, money's he's had for almost five years," Barrett sniffed.

"Well, you make it too harsh for him, you play hardball," replied Fox, "he just might decide not to turn himself in after all and continue leading the life he's leading. And keep Global's money."

"You mean, be perpetually on the lam," Barrett said. "Maybe it's finally starting to eat at him, constantly looking over his shoulder, not being able to live a normal life in the light of day."

That was exactly it, thought Fox, what was eating at poor Jerry. But, he replied, "Well, he's gotten away with it this long."

"It's not our call to make anyway, Jack," Reynolds said. "You know that. We'd have to get approval from corporate after review by the counsel's office."

"But your recommendation goes a long way with

the brass," Fox reminded him. "If you don't want to play hardball, they're likely to go along with that. Especially with full restitution."

"You sound like his defense counsel," Barrett snapped.

"No, just being reasonable," Fox shot back.

"Well, let us think it over," Reynolds said.

"How are you keeping in touch with him?" Barrett asked.

"He's calling me tomorrow," Fox said.

Actually, Fox planned on calling Jerry right after this call, and then after that, Dean Alessi.

"We probably won't have an answer by then," Reynolds said. "Depends what the corporate boys are into these days. I mean, this is hardly a priority. It's only a million bucks."

"Well, whenever you reach a decision, let me know," Fox said. "Jerry Shaw'll have to live with that." After a moment, Fox added, "Oh, I almost forgot. One other thing. He doesn't want to turn himself in until at least next May."

"Next May?" Reynolds said. There was a pinch of incredulity in his voice. "Why next May?"

"He didn't say," Fox lied. He couldn't reveal that Jerry wanted his resurrection to take place in conjunction with the release of The Anonymous Man movie.

"That's nine months from now," Barrett said.

128

"I know it is," Fox said. "But those were his terms."

"Well, I don't think Global'll want to wait nine months for its money," Reynolds said. "If we're gonna hafta wait to have him turn himself in, he should at least return our money. I don't know where he's stashed it, but I would think it's in an offshore account, or over in Switzerland. He could wire it in a way that'll keep its location a secret."

"Yeah," Barrett added, "that could be worked out. At very least, that."

"Well, I'll run it by him," Fox said.

"Alright," Reynolds said. "It is what it is, I guess. Is that about it, Jack? Anything else?"

"Nope, that's all I have."

"We'll get back to you," Reynolds said. "Though, like I said, it may take a few days." He laughed, then added, "But I gotta tell you, this is a friggin shocker. Friggin guy is still alive."

"As you said, it is what it is," Fox said.

***

After Fox hung up the call, he immediately called Jerry and reported his conversation with Reynolds.

"The bad thing is," Fox said. "Reynolds is retiring, and

this Barrett fellow who's taking over for him seems like a major asshole who loves to play hardball."

Jerry gave a long sigh on the other end of the call. Finally, he said, "It is what it is, Mister Fox."

"You gonna have a problem with at least giving up the money up front, should we reach a deal? No way Global's gonna want to wait nine months for their money, if not longer. I think Barrett's at least right about that."

"Sure," Jerry said. "I can do that. But that'll hafta to wait until the movie deal is greenlighted and I'm paid an initial advance. My agent seems to think that'll definitely happen, but until it does, you know…"

"Yeah sure," Fox said. "I get it. And like I told you yesterday, you have to decide what works best for you in terms of prison time," Fox said. "How much is too much. The problem is, now the cat's out of the bag. They know you're alive. And if you decide to remain an anonymous man instead of spending a few too many years in prison, they might decide it's worth it to come looking for you."

"Just what I need," Jerry said. He was beginning to regret his idea of turning himself in.

"When's Jade getting back?"

"This afternoon, around four. She's flying into Ft. Myers."

"That's good," Fox said.

"Yeah, being a single dad is exhausting."

"When's the last time you changed trac phones?" Fox asked out of the blue.

"It's been awhile."

"Jerry!"

"Yeah, I know. I know. I'll do it. Once Jade gets in, I'll cancel this one and then run out to Walmart and get a new one."

"Yeah, do it." Fox then added, "Look, I'm gonna call your lawyer, Dean Alessi, tell him about my call with Global, just to keep him in the loop."

"Alright, but don't make it a long call," Jerry said with a laugh. "I don't want his bill to end up being more than what I owe Global."

Chapter Nineteen

Hardball

"I say we play hardball," Barrett told Reynolds after he hung up the phone with Jack Fox.

He was pacing the Chief's office – soon to be his.

"It's your call," Reynolds said. "But corporate may simply want to get back the money and say the hell with deterrence and justice and all that crap."

"Well, I think we should fight for it," Barrett said. "Convince them it'll cost them more in the long run if we let this guy off the hook."

"You really seem to have a hard-on for this one, Neal," Reynolds said.

"Well, think of what the guy did," Barrett replied. "Made us look like fools."

"I don't feel like a fool," Reynolds said. "In fact, I kind of admire the guy. I mean, he became a dead man and nobody was the wiser, and then, he was essentially set for life doing what he wanted to do using our money."

"Yeah, but what kind of life is that?" Barrett asked. "Being dead doesn't sound like a valid life choice to me. He must have had help. And whomever helped him is guilty of a crime, too. You know, that could be our bargaining chip."

"Bargaining chip?"

Barrett stopped, turned to Reynolds and with a nod, explained, "Yeah, our bargaining chip. An accessory-after-the-fact. His lover, probably, man or woman. I'm sure he doesn't want to see that person get hurt when he turns himself in."

"Or, if we threaten that, it'll convince him not to turn himself in at all."

Barrett shrugged and relented, "Yeah, maybe." He began pacing again with his right hand to his chin, thinking things over. Then, he turned to Reynolds and said, "What about Jack Fox?"

"What about Jack Fox?" Reynolds asked.

"You think he's on the level? I mean his story sounded a

bit strained – you know, that this guy Jerry Shaw called him out of the blue."

"What else could it be?"

"I'm not sure," Barrett said. "I just have a funny feeling about it. Like Jack Fox knew a whole lot more than what he was telling us."

"Look, he worked for me for five years," Reynolds said. "I always found him to be a straight shooter. And for years before that in law enforcement, not a single blemish."

Barrett returned to the chair facing Reynolds' desk and sat down.

"Well, I'm just spit-balling here," he told Reynolds. He laughed and added, "In two weeks, it won't matter to you. You'll be retired sleeping until ten or eleven every morning. Going golfing whenever you want. Getting excited about that?"

"Can't wait," Reynolds said dismally.

***

After returning to his makeshift office across the hall from the larger one still occupied by Chief Reynolds but soon to be his, Barrett sat down behind his desk and called Victor Lenkov.

Now fifty-two, Victor was born in the United States

after his parents escaped from the former Soviet Union in the early 1960s. They'd settled in the Brighton Beach area of Brooklyn known as "Little Odesa." Home to numerous Russian restaurants, markets, Brighton Beach had become the preeminent melting pot for Russians, Ukrainians, Georgians and other Russian speakers.

While a teenager, Victor joined a gang with ties to the Russian mafia. At some point, this gang partnered up with an Italian mafia crew and together they stole expensive cars for shipment overseas. After his arrest at the age of twenty-two during a sting operation conducted by a task force of the New York State Police and FBI, he and a few of his fellow gang members were recruited to become freelance operatives for both the FBI and CIA in exchange for the dropping of the RICO and grand theft charges that had been lodged against him.

Over the next thirty years, Victor made a fortune conducting undercover operations, mostly black ops, on behalf of those agencies both here in the United States and overseas. He also worked freelance for private parties, including corporations and millionaires. It was during one of the FBI's undercover operations when Neal Barrett met Victor.

When Barrett got the job at Global, he reached out to Victor and asked if he's want to make a few extra bucks now and then working on Global cases. Victor agreed and without Dick Reynolds' knowledge, Barrett got approval from the senior vice-president in corporate who was in charge of Global's fraud unit to put Victor on Global's payroll as an independent contractor.

Victor was a good-looking man who fit the stereotype of the crude but brave eastern European, a brutish warrior from the steppes. He was tall, muscular and brusque, with thick, disheveled sandy-blonde hair, broad shoulders and a distinct Russian accent.

"Victor! It's Neal Barrett, from Global," Barrett said. "How's things?"

"They good," Victor replied. "You?"

"Good as well."

"How's new job?"

"It's okay. It'll be better in a couple weeks when I'm totally in charge. How's the gambling. Your teams winning?"

"No, not so good," Victor said. "Damn Yankees cost me plenty rubles Sunday."

Barrett laughed. Victor was a proud degenerate gambler who'd lost a significant part of his fortune on sports and racetrack betting.

"I got a job for you," Barrett said.

"Yeah, what?"

Barrett explained the broad strokes of the Jerry Shaw case.

"So you want I should find this Shaw. Be like a, what you say, bounty hunter."

"Yes, a bounty hunter," Barrett said. "We'd also like you to find Global's money that this Shaw fellow took."

"If I find this Shaw," Victor boasted, "I find money. So where I start, find this Shaw?"

"You start with a guy named Fox, Jack Fox," Barrett said.

Barrett spent the next couple of minutes explaining Fox's relationship to Global insurance as a former investigator, and that he'd worked on the Shaw death claim and helped prove it being a murder perpetrated by Jeff Flaherty and Shaw's wife, Holly.

"Only, Jeff and Holly told the cops that they hadn't murdered Jerry Shaw," Barrett went on. "That they'd helped him fake his death in that garage fire. That he was now setting them up for his murder."

"Double-cross," Victor interrupted.

"Well, yeah, a double-cross," Barrett said. "But after all, they double-crossed him."

"True," Victor agreed.

"But that doesn't matter," Barrett went on. "What happened is, the cops didn't buy their story and they ended pleading guilty to killing this Shaw guy. Only they weren't lying. Jerry Shaw was still alive."

"Crazy story," Victor said.

"Yes, crazy," Barrett said. "And I'm only half done with it."

"But, what about this Jack Fox?" Victor asked. "What is he to do with?"

"Well, Fox called us today, actually looking for the current fraud chief, Reynolds," Barrett replied. "He claimed that Shaw had called him out of the blue wanting to turn himself in and return Global's insurance money."

"Why do this?" Victor asked. "Turn self in. Give back money."

"He's tired of being a dead man," Barrett said. "Wouldn't you?"

"Maybe yes, maybe no," Victor said.

"Doesn't matter," Barrett said. "What matters is that Fox's call confirms that Jeff Flaherty and Holly Shaw were telling the truth – Jerry Shaw, Global's insured, didn't die in that garage fire. The three of them had faked his death and he's been hiding out ever since. With Global's money. Over a million bucks."

"So, what we know is this Jerry's calling Fox," Victor said.

"At least that. Maybe more, we find out later."

"Yes, exactly."

"So, through Fox, we find Shaw's cell number," Victor went on. "And once we got his number, we got him. It's simple."

"Shaw's probably using a trac phone," Barrett said.

"Don't matter," Victor said. "Number is number."

"So we should just ask Fox for that – Jerry's cell number?" Barrett asked.

"Nyet," Victor said. "My idea – Fox more involved than he say. So, I think Fox not give up his cell phone number so easy to you, just be ask. At least, not of free will." After a sigh, Victor added, "But, there are other ways."

"I'll leave that up to you, Victor. You never disappoint me."

Chapter Twenty

A Real Solid

~~~

About eleven the previous night, after Holly's parents had gone to bed, Wes Chandler snuck into Holly's room and made love to her for the third time that day. While they were laying in the darkness afterwards, he told her, "Can you take me someplace tomorrow morning?"

"Where?"

"Indian reservation," Wes said.

"Indian reservation? Why? You need smokes?"

"Nope," he said. "I need to find Billy Ray."

"Who the hell's that?" Holly asked.

"Old friend," Wes replied. "We did some work together, long time ago. I owe him something."

"What something?"

"This," Wes said. "A chance to earn a share of what we're gonna get from your Jerry Shaw."

"What are you talking about? How much of a share?"

"Hundred grand. Like I said, I owe him."

"Why?"

"Well, first of all because I think he can get us a gun," Wes said. "In fact, I know he can. He already told me that. And second of all because he did me a real solid twenty-five years ago, when we were kids. You know, when we were just getting started dealing drugs, robbing gas stations."

"What?"

"Just listen," Wes said. "See, there was this 7-Eleven in Silver Creek, just off the reservation. Me, Billy and this other kid, Dan Menke, decided to rob it late one night. More for grins than anything else. Anyway, I was driving this old beat up Chevy. Rust everywhere, carbon monoxide filling the cabin.

"We got there late, just before midnight. Nobody in the place, no customers, just us, and this clerk, some older guy, not some kid. He's getting ready to close the place. Gives us dirty looks for stopping in at the last minute. Last thing he needs. A minute after we go in, Billy takes out his pistol, some piece of shit stolen gun we'd picked up for like fifty bucks from some ex-con a few months earlier.

"Anyway, the clerk starts giving Billy Ray grief. You know, a wannabe Clint Eastwood. They're fucking shouting at each other. Billy Ray's yelling, 'just give me the fucking money,' and the clerk with this sour look, was being slow about opening the register. Finally, Billy fucking shoots the guy. Just shoots him. Not a kill shot. Shoots him in the upper left arm. This got the guy's attention, told him we were serious, not some teenage amateurs. Fuck, it got my attention. Holy fuck, I'm thinking. Crazy Indian just shot the asshole clerk.

"After the clerk picks himself off the floor, his arms oozing blood, him starting to go into shock, he finally manages to get the register open with his right hand and Billy goes around and scarfs up the money. 'Let's get the fuck out of here,' he's shouting at us and we go scrambling for the door. Doing so, we had our backs to the clerk and didn't see him somehow lift out a sawed off shotgun from somewhere under the counter. We didn't see him bring it up, aim and shoot at us. Two shots. I was in the lead, first one out the door. Behind me, one shot hit Billy Ray in the leg. The other hit Menke in the back of the skull, dead instantly. Billy fell and was writhing on the floor when a third shot rang out smashing out the glass on the door.

"I ran man, like a fucking jack rabbit running from a fox. I got into the car and it surprised the hell out of me by starting right away. I sped off leaving Menke dead and Billy wounded. The fucking superhero clerk called 9-1-1 and the police were passing me going the other way in like a minute.

"Anyway, the DA ended up charging Billy with felony-murder, because Menke was killed during the botched robbery. Thing was, he wouldn't cop a plea that involved him naming me as the third robber identified by the store clerk. He went to trial and got twenty years to life instead. He played the good Indian in state prison upstate at Great Meadow. He finally got paroled a couple years ago and moved in with his mother in some trailer on the reservation.

"It took me another five years after the 7-Eleven fiasco before I got pinched by that state police, DEA sting. When I was paroled, I called Billy Ray and promised to pay him back for keeping his mouth shut about me. Then, I came to see you about Jerry Shaw's money."

"So I have to pay for your stupidity?" Holly asked. "Or should I say, cowardice?"

Wes turned to Holly and crooked a grin. "No, darling," he said. "It'll come out of my end." His grin widened. "But when you marry me, it won't matter, will it?"

"Marry you?" She asked. "What makes you think I wanna marry you?"

"Once you suck this," he said and took her hand and moved it down to his crotch, "you never want to taste another."

"Yeah, right." She sighed. Pulling her hand out of his grasp, she asked, "So, you really want to bring this Injun Joe into this?"

"Yeah, I do," Wes replied. "Like I said, I owe Billy Ray a solid. Plus, it wouldn't hurt to have a bit more muscle. Billy Ray's fearless. And like I said, he's got a gun."

"Fearless? Sounds like he's more stupid than fearless. Even stupider than you. But you do have a point about the gun."

Wes smiled, bent down and kissed her. She didn't resist.

Chapter Twenty-One

Billy Ray Blacksnake

~~~~~~~~

Around ten the next morning, Holly let Wes drive her seven year old Ford Fiesta to the Seneca Indian Reservation. Wes was careful to drive the speed limit for the twenty-five minutes along westbound Interstate 90, called the Thruway in New York, until they reached the Irving/Silver Creek exit onto US Route 20. After a short time on Route 20, Wes turned right onto State Route 438 that became 4 Mile Level Road as it crossed onto the reservation past the familiar large blue sign stating, "Entering Seneca Nation Territory." Below that statement was the Seneca Indian language translation:

"*O Notowa Ke:Ono' Oh Lyo:No.*"

After driving a couple miles on 4 Mile Level Road, Wes

made a left turn onto a dirt road called Lane Drive.

"Where the hell you taking me?" Holly asked.

"To Billy Ray's house," Wes said. "It's a trailer. He lives there with his mother and aunt. But I think maybe his aunt died. Just so you know, Billy Ray's Seneca name is Billy Ray Blacksnake."

"Great name," Holly commented sarcastically. "What happened to his father?"

"He drunk himself to death when Billy Ray was a kid, even before I met him."

"How'd you meet him?"

"We were inmates at Lakeview Shock," Wes replied. "Here, this is it."

Wes made another left turned down a narrow, bumpy dirt and gravel road that after almost a tenth of a mile led to a tattered, rusting mobile home that looked like it had been planted there a century ago. Weeds grew out from under it and it's backyard was a stretch of straggly brush and woods.

"Is he gonna be home?" Holly asked.

"Well, if he ain't, his mother should know where he is," Wes replied. "I doubt he left the reservation." Wes laughed. "Not too many places to go when you ain't got a car or a cent to your name and you're a fucking Indian felon."

"How long's he been out of prison?"

"Couple years," said Wes.

"How'd you know he's still living here?"

"Like I told you, when I got paroled, I called him," Wes said. "Told him I wanted to look him up when I got out, maybe do business together. He said, sure, look me up. He gave me this address – same one he had before the 7-Eleven robbery when we was kids."

As it turned out, Billy was home. His mother, a bent, heavy-set woman with withered skin the color of leather opened the side door a snatch and greeted Wes and Holly with a scowl. There was a cigarette hanging from the left corner of her mouth.

"Yeah?"

"Billy home?"

"Who wants to know?"

"You don't remember me, Mrs. Blacksnake?"

The old woman's scowl deepened as she squinted up at Wes' face for a time. Finally, she said, "Wes?"

"Yeah, Wes."

"Who's the lady?"

"A friend."

"Girlfriend?"

Wes looked at Holly and cracked a grin. "Maybe," he said, after which Holly frowned disagreeably.

"Let me get Billy," his mother said.

She left them standing at the door as she hobbled back into the interior of the trailer.

A minute later, Billy Ray Blacksnake pushed through the side door wearing a scowl equal to his mother's. After stepping outside, he wrapped himself into what looked like the same old, worn leather jacket Wes remembered he used to wear from their days before they went to prison.

Billy Ray had long, jet black hair that flowed down to his solid, square shoulders. He'd was tall, around six foot two. He'd gained some weight over the years but he still presented an imposing figure. He'd always been a hard-ass, another dangerous, crazy Indian, especially when drunk, but now with that perpetual scowl, he seemed to Wes doubly tough and dangerous.

Billy walked forward, limping slightly from the gunshot wound to his leg he'd gotten during the botched 7-Eleven robbery from long ago. It was a chilly for late in the morning in early July, and he huddled into his jacket as he limped ahead of Wes and Holly. After stopping at a stand of trees behind his mother's trailer, he turned to them.

"Got any smokes?" he asked Wes.

"No, man, I quit," Wes sad. "Too fucking expensive. Plus, they'll kill ya."

"A lot of things'll kill ya," Billy said. "So what the fuck you want, man?"

"I don't want nothing," Wes said. "I came here to pay you back."

"Pay me back?" Billy laughed. "How the fuck you gonna pay me back?" He looked at Holly. "With her?"

Wes glanced at Holly, then laughed and turned back to Billy. "With this skank? No, I can get you better than that."

Glaring, Holly pushed Wes's shoulder and said, "Fuck you, asshole."

"So what you talking about, man?" Billy Ray asked.

"Making some money, that's what I'm talking about."

"Yeah, like how?" Billy Ray laughed. "Rob another 7-Eleven, like your last great idea?"

"No, nothing lame like that. Kidnapping a geek is what I'm talking about."

"Huh?"

Wes laid it out for him, his and Holly's plan for getting what was left of the Global life insurance money, totaling around a million dollars, still in Jerry's possession.

"You help us with that," Wes said, "and we get the money, I'll give you a hundred grand out of it." He cracked a grin. "That payback enough for you?"

Billy rubbed his chin and gave a short nod. "Maybe," he said. "But how you gonna find out where this Jerry geek is? You said he's hiding down in Florida, but you don't know where down there. It's a big fucking state." Billy shrugged. "So?"

"We track him down through her," Wes said, nodding at Holly. "She's got his cell phone number. They talk every now and then. Right, Hol?"

"Yeah, right," she said.

"He still got a thing for you, then," Billy said. "His ex-wife." He looked her over. "Well, can't blame him." He glared momentarily at Wes, then back at Holly, and said, "Contrary to this asshole, you ain't no skank."

"Thank you," Holly said. She glared at Wes and he shrugged back at her.

Billy turned to Wes and said, "So, she calls him, he calls her. What's that got to do with anything?"

"Because you can find a person's whereabouts simply by knowing their cell phone number," Wes explained with a laugh. "That's all you need. Can you believe that? A number.

I studied up on it in the can, on the internet after her old man, Jeff, told me about Jerry hiding down somewhere in Florida, with the insurance money. You load a person's number into a program you can buy online and it'll take you to the exact location of the person you're looking for. I mean, the address where he's using his cell phone from."

"Jerry uses a Tracfone," Holly chimed in. "You know, one of those pre-paid cell phones you can buy at Walmart or wherever. He changes the number ever couple of months."

"Don't matter," Wes said. "Like any cell phone, a Tracfone can be traced and located. All we need is the number of the latest Tracfone Jerry is using. Then we pay a cell phone tracking site, like Phone Trace, to locate the phone as long as it's on and working. It's cheap to do that, no more than twenty bucks. And like I said, Holly babe over here has Jerry boy's latest Tracfone number."

Wes turned to her and said, "Why don't you call him. Isn't his girl coming back today?"

"Yeah, this afternoon."

"So go ahead."

Holly shrugged, stuck her hand in the pocket of her jean jacket and took out her cell phone. She went to her contacts and clicked on Jerry's number. After several rings, someone picked up. Only it wasn't Jerry. It was a girl's voice with a Hispanic accent.

"Jerry?"

"Jerry? No. This Melinda. Who this?"

Holly clicked off the call. She turned to Wes and Billy Ray and shouted, "Fuck!"

Chapter Twenty-Two

The Call

~~~

Billy Ray was laughing. "Great fucking plan, Wes. Some things never change."

"Fuck you, Injun Joe," Wes snapped.

"So what's next?" Billy Ray asked.

"Nothing's next if Jerry doesn't call her with his new number," Wes said. He turned to Holly and asked, "You think he'll do that?"

She made a dismal shrug. "He's always called in the past after he changed phones," she said. "But this time, I have no idea. The last time we talked, I got the sense that he was getting antsy about our calls, that I'd become an aggravation he doesn't need any more with all his other bullshit going on. Maybe with this change of phones, he won't call back and cut me out of his life for good."

"Fuck that," said Wes. "If the guy kept the connection going all this time, I don't think he's about to stop. He's addicted to your pussy."

"Look, man," Billy Ray said, "let's go inside. My mother spends all day in her bedroom smoking Lucky Strikes and watching TV. We can talk this out over some coffee."

"Fuck the coffee," Wes said. "You got any beer?"

"Yeah, man, I got beer. Let's go."

Wes and Holly followed Billy Ray back to the trailer. Entering through the side door, both of them had to hold their breath a minute getting used to the stale smell of cigarettes and sweat and years of greasy food cooked on a cheap propane stove. Even after taking a breath, Wes gagged before taking another.

"I know, it fucking stinks in here," Billy Ray said with a laugh. "My mom ain't much of a housekeeper, or cook."

Billy Ray cleared a small table that was propped up on metal bars across from the stove. Wes and Holly then sat at it while Billy Ray put some grounds and water into a worn out coffee maker. He opened a small fridge and fetched out a can of Natural Ice beer that he handed to Wes. Wes pulled the tab with a whoosh and took a gulp.

"Nothing like a cold one in the morning," he said.

"You want something, honey?" Billy Ray asked Holly, seeming to be flirting.

"Cup of coffee'll fine," she said and flashed a smile at the Indian.

"You got it, darlin," he said.

"Joanie and Chachi wanna get a room," remarked Wes, glaring at Billy Ray.

The Indian laughed. "Back off, honcho," he said. "I know – she's all yours."

"Hey, I'm nobody's," Holly said.

"Except Jerry Shaw," countered Wes.

The coffee percolated and Billy Ray poured himself and Holly cups of the brewed cava while Wes drank half the can of Natural Ice. Sitting down between them, Billy Ray took a long sip of coffee, turned to Wes and asked, "So what was the plan?"

"Well, we were gonna locate the creep and kidnap him, his main squeeze and their baby, and demand the insurance money as ransom. You still got the pistol?"

"Yeah, I got it," Billy Ray said. With a menacing smile, he added, "And bullets, too. And after we kidnap this guy and his broad and baby, then what?"

Wes cracked his customary shit-eating grin and said, "Then we get him to give us that insurance money and we live happily ever after." He glanced at Holly still grinning. "And me and Holly get married."

"Yeah, right," Holly said.

"And what happens after we take Jerry's money?" Billy Ray asked. "He gonna keep quiet about that?"

Wes shrugged. "What else can he do?" he asked. "Call the cops and complain that someone stole the money he stole?"

"Or maybe he does just that," the Indian said. "Call the cops. Just to get on the good side of them. See, he's still gonna wanna turn himself in, right? To get a good deal and make the movie honchos happy."

"So what are you saying, Billy?" Holly asked.

"What I'm saying is, once they give us the money, we hafta off them."

That statement was followed by cold stone silence.

Wes said, "Man, that's radical." He laughed. "I ain't never killed no one."

Billy Ray stared at him. "But, instead, you'd want to go back to the can?"

"No," Wes said flatly.

"And to avoid that?"

"Yeah, I see your point."

"Wait, wait, wait," Holly said. "You're talking about killing Jerry and Jade, and, and the baby?"

"Maybe," Billy Ray said. "Once we got the money. Well, maybe not the kid. He's too young to make a good witness. Right?"

Holly looked at Wes. "This is more than I bargained for, Wes," she said.

"Kinda late to be worrying over that, lover," he replied with a wink.

"No, it's not," she said. "What if I don't give you Jerry's number." She sighed. "If he even calls. This whole thing may be moot anyway."

"Moot?" Wes asked. "What the fuck's moot."

"Moot," Billy Ray said. "Doesn't matter. If she don't get Jerry's number, there's nothing to talk about."

"No, he'll call." Wes nodded at Holly. "Like I said, he's still in love with you, and your pussy."

"Well, I ain't gonna participate in his murder." She swallowed. "Maybe, maybe I still have feelings for him, too. And maybe when he calls me, I'll warn him about you two fuckers, tell him to get another phone and never call me back again."

"Alright, alright," Wes said. "Killing them ain't a done deal. It's just talk. Right, Billy Ray?"

"Yeah," he said. "Just talk." He laughed and said, "Theoretical, anyway. I mean, we don't even have his phone number." He looked at Holly. "And like you said, he may never call you again."

Just then Holly's cell phone rang. She looked down at the screen. It said, "Unknown caller." She clicked on the answer icon and put it to her ear.

"Hello?"

"Holly?"

It was Jerry Shaw.

Chapter Twenty-Three

Jack Brewster

~~~

At about quarter past one that same Thursday afternoon, Dean Alessi entered the reception room of the Erie County District Attorney's Office on the fourth floor of an old musty building at 25 Delaware Avenue in downtown Buffalo. He gave his name to a tall, thin girl behind the long faded green Formica counter in the reception foyer and told her he was late for an appointment at one to see Assistant District Attorney, Jack Brewster, the head of the office's Special Investigations & Prosecutions Unit – or SIP for short.

At five-thirty that morning, Dean had arrived at the small airport in Punta Gorda, Florida to take an Allegiant

Airlines flight scheduled to depart at seven-ten for the nearly three-hour trip north to the even smaller airport in Niagara Falls. The flight was delayed and didn't leave until almost nine moving his arrival time in Niagara Falls to Noon. By the time he got his rental car and made the forty minute drive from the Airport to downtown Buffalo, it was one-fifteen.

Jack Brewster didn't make him wait. About Dean's age, forty-five, he was a tall, slightly overweight though solidly built man with bright red hair and an Irish brogue. Indeed, he thought himself more Irish than American and had been a long-time supporter of the Irish Republican Army. He always drank dark Guinness beer.

"Dean, nice to see you, laddie?" he said as he stuck out his right hand and gave Dean a long, hard handshake. "How's Florida treating you?" He stepped back and smiling, regarded Dean a moment. "You don't look like you spend much time out in the sun. I was expecting you'd have a solid tan."

"It's hard to practice law on the beach," Dean said with a laugh. "And I suck at golf."

Three years earlier, while Acting Director of the state's Lawyer Discipline Office, with headquarters up in Buffalo, Dean had interviewed and then offered Brewster a job as an assistant disciplinary counsel for the office only to have the state Supreme Court's Chief Justice, Alexander "Chip"

Krane, call Dean and nix the hiring. The Chief Justice instead insistedd that Dean hire a much younger and inexperienced lawyer, Pete O'Brien, for the job based on Pete's political connections.

"C'mon back," he said. "My office is a mess, files everywhere, but the SIP conference room is tied up."

Brewster led Dean through a door to a maze of inner offices of the bureau he led. After walking down a dusty hallway, they came to Brewster's office at the far end, a cramped space with a small desk piled with files, court papers, indictments, correspondence, and three law books stacked precariously on top of each other. A government issue laptop computer was set in a small, clear space among everything.

"I told you it was a mess." Brewster laughed as he moved an armless plastic chair from a side wall to the front of his desk. "Here, take a seat."

As Dean sat, Brewster went around and sat in a swivel chair that noticeably leaned to the right.

"Goddamn budget gets tighter every year," he said. "The last things these Demo-rats running Erie County want to do is fund anything to do with law enforcement." He sighed, crossed his arms and leaned back precariously in his chair. "Well, that's my political rant for the day." He sighed and asked, "So what can I do for you?"

"Well, before that, I'd like to tell you sorry again about

the LDO job," he said.

"Water over the bridge," Brewster said. "Wasn't your fault. And anyway, my staying here got me into this glamorous office. Though the best thing about staying on was seeing up close and personal that asshole, Sam Marcum, and his whore, Susie Hines-Laurence, get the heave-ho and have to spend the next half-century in prison. Heard you had a major role in that."

"Yea, but where'd it get me," Dean said.

"I heard it got you a pretty wife and trip down to Florida practicing law in a state with a real governor and no income tax. Another ten years, I'll be joining you there for sure"

Dean laughed. "Yeah, I guess that's the way I should look at it."

"So, what brings you to see me this hot and muggy afternoon?" Brewster asked.

"A client," Dean said. "He did something up here five years ago, a pretty serious fraud involving the theft of a whole lot of money."

Brewster laughed and said, "What else is fraud good for?"

"Anyway, this client of mine wants to pay back the money he stole and turn himself in," Dean said. "But he'd like some assurances before going forward, as you might expect."

"So, he's been lamming it and wants to come out of the shadows and rejoin the living," Brewster guessed.

"Exactly," Dean said.

"How much did he steal?"

"One point three mil," Dean replied.

Brewster let out a whistle. "That's Larceny in the first degree. A class B felony. He could be sentenced to eight-and-a-half to twenty-five years."

"Yeah, if you guys caught him in the act," Dean said. "But he's turning himself in and giving back the money. Sounds like pretty solid mitigation to me."

"I don't disagree with you, Dean," Brewster said. "But it'll depend on how the victim feels. We always try to make our victims happy in fashioning any plea deal. You know that."

"Yeah, I realize that," Dean said.

"So who's your boy's victim?"

"I'd rather not reveal that right now," Dean said. "Let's just say, it's a big company and a theft of even a million dollars didn't make a dent in its bottom line."

"Well, I'll have to run it by the DA at some point at any rate," Brewster said.

"But can you at least give me a guestimate what you'd

offer?" Dean asked. "So I can give my client a ballpark figure what he's looking at."

Brewster sighed and looked up at the grungy ceiling with several dented and bent foam tiles lingering up there. Finally, after shaking his head back and forth a few moments, as if calculating something, he looked across at Dean and said, "Well, I think a reasonable disposition would be a plea to attempted grand larceny second. Max sentence would be two-and-a-third to seven. We'd likely recommend a sentence somewhere in between, depending on the probation report. But jail isn't mandatory so there's a chance for your boy to get off with probation. As I said, depends on the victim's position, and which judge he ends up pleading before. Basically, thought, it all comes down to what kind of story your boy has to tell."

"Oh, it's a good tale, Jack. A real good one."

"Well, there it is then," Brewster said. "But that's not an offer. Just a guestimate."

"I can't believe Sal Parlato's the new DA," Dean said.

"Well, he certainly deserved it after what Marcum and Susie Hines-Laurence put the poor guy through."

"Yeah," Dean said. "Sometimes there really is justice in the world."

Chapter Twenty-Four

Doppelgänger

After leaving the DA's office, Dean drove twenty minutes to the modest Cape Cod house of Jack Fox in the Village of Depew. After he'd pulled into the driveway and parked the rental, Fox came scrambling out the front door to greet him. When Dean saw him, he laughed to himself. Fox looked a lot like his old friend and mentor and ultimate sidekick, Stu Foley, his Chief Investigator when he was still working for the Lawyer Discipline Office.

After Dean exited the car, Fox said, "Nice to meet you, Mister Alessi."

"Please, call me Dean."

They briefly shook hands and stood back looking each other over for a time.

Squinting at Fox, Dean said, "You don't happen to know an ex-cop and investigator by the name of Stu Foley, do you?"

Fox frowned as he thought a moment. "No, can't say as I do," he said. "Why? Should I?"

"No, guess not," Dean said. "He was my Chief Investigator at the Lawyer Discipline Office. Retired down to Florida - the Villages." Dean let out a short laugh. "You remind me of him."

"Maybe it's because all investigators look alike?" Fox suggested with a smile, then nodded to the front door. "C'mon inside," he said. "I've got some turkey and ham and salami from the deli. Some Kaiser roles. You must be starving."

Dean was starving. He followed Fox up three steps onto a narrow porch, then through the front door into a foyer.

"This way," Fox said as he led Dean through a living room into a cramped kitchen.

On the center of a granite counter, there were lunch meats set on a platter with some rolls on another with mustard and mayonnaise in bowls and a jar of pickles.

"Come eat," Fox said. "What'dya want to drink. I got beer in the fridge."

"Water works for me," Dean said. "If I have a beer, I'm likely to fall asleep on you. Been a long day already."

"I bet," Fox said. "Go ahead, make your sandwich, sit at the table. I'll get you a water. We'll have some privacy. My wife's out of town visiting the grandkids in Philly, our hometown."

Dean laid some ham on a roll with a slather of yellow mustard and brought it on a paper plate over to the kitchen table. Fox came over with his sandwich and two bottles of water and sat across from Dean.

As Dean bit into his sandwich, Fox asked, "So, how'd it go at the DA's office?"

After swallowing his bite of sandwich, he said, "Pretty much as expected." Dean shrugged and added, "No promises. What they can offer depends on what the victim wants. The ADA I spoke with, Jack Brewster, who runs the Special Investigations and Prosecutions Bureau, mentioned an attempted grand larceny second. Our client might have to serve some minimal time, but maybe not. Jail time isn't mandatory on such a plea."

"I'm a little worried that the victim's gonna play hardball," Fox said. "The former chief, my boss, Dick Reynolds, was hard-nose as they come, but reasonable. I don't think the new guy - name's Neal Barrett - who's about to take over for him in a couple weeks, has the same temperament."

"Then they might end up losing a million dollars," Dean said.

Fox shrugged. "Small potatoes to them," he said. Then, he sighed and added, "Jerry really wants this. He wants to stop being a dead man. I don't think a short prison sentence will deter him."

"Depends what you mean by short," Dean said. "A week in jail can seem like a century to some. Plus, you're not mingling with the best examples of humanity in the can."

"I realize that," Fox said. "But part of this Jerry brought on himself."

"So why didn't you turn him in? Why'd you keep his existence a secret all these years?" Dean took another bite and added, "I been kinda wondering about that."

"I don't know," Fox said wistfully as he chewed his sandwich. "I think I admired him, doing what he did – escaping a life he wasn't happy leading. That took balls. I think a lot of us fantasize about doing that sometimes. Plus, I admired his smarts." He laughed. "I mean, the guy watched his own funeral and attended the trial of his own murder – a trial he set up. He figured out a way to get his vengeance over his deceitful and murderous wife and best friend."

"He told me you guessed it," Dean said. "That he was still alive."

"Yeah, it came to me a few weeks after he was almost killed down in Florida," Fox said. "None of it made any sense - I mean, Holly and Jeff Flaherty's capture down in Kissimmee on a drug deal gone bad. So, I took a chance and staked out Jerry's gravestone on his birthday less than a year after he'd faked his death. I wasn't surprised that he showed up. I expected it. That's Jerry Shaw."

They finished their sandwiches in silence. Dean washed it down with a long gulp of water, then told Fox, "Well, we'll see what we can do about getting Jerry a good deal. At least, we have time on our hands. There's no rush."

"You read his comic books, Mister Alessi?"

"Dean. Call me Dean."

"Dean. You read his comics?"

"No," Dean said. "I mean, I skimmed the first issue on the plane. I really liked it. Clever. I plan to read more of it. Can't wait to see the movie version."

Fox laughed and said, "Yeah, it's really a good story. And for Jerry, his life imitates his art. His superpower is his fictional Anonymous Man's superpower – helping people escaping their troubled lives." Fox sighed and asked, "So what's next?"

"Next?" Dean thought a moment. "Next, I find out from Jack Brewster what his boss thinks of the case. If the

DA has no problem with an attempted grand larceny second then, with Jerry's permission, I reveal that Jerry is the thief turning himself in and Global is the victim. Of course, I keep secret Jerry's whereabouts until Global goes along with a firm commitment on a plea deal. Then, Jerry comes to town and turns himself in. We beg for mercy at sentencing with a ton of mitigation and hope for the best – a sentence of probation or a short prison term."

"Alright, sounds like a plan," Fox said. "Let me work on Global. I know a couple people in corporate who may be sympathetic."

"I'll call Jerry this afternoon and give him an update," Dean said.

"Sounds good. When are you going back down to Florida?"

"I could leave tonight on Allegiant, but I'm gonna stay until Friday, Allegiant's next flight after that. My better half is on trial all week – a personal injury case - and like me, when she's on trial, she's hard to live with. She does most of the heavy-lifting for the firm. I hate private practice. Maybe it was true that some lawyers had thought about me when I was disciplinary counsel."

"What's that?"

"That I only became a disciplinary lawyer because I couldn't hack being a real one." He laughed. "A lawyer gone bad told me that once." He sighed and continued, "Anyway, I'm thinking of giving up private practice and getting a job in the Florida attorney discipline system." He winked. "I already put an application in, but don't go telling my wife."

Fox laughed and said, "I promise."

"Plus, I have a kid up here living with his mom, a son, three years old," Dean went on. "This'll give me some extra time with the boy."

"At your age, you had a child? How old was your wife?"

"Same as me, forty-six," Dean said. "And yeah, it was a miracle."

"Must be hard being away from him," Fox said. "With you down in Florida, and him up here."

"Yes, it is. But under the divorce decree, I have him almost the entire summer, and for a few weeks here and there during the year. Yeah, it's hard, but I couldn't stay up here in Buffalo a moment longer once I left the Lawyer Discipline Office."

"Why? The weather?"

"That," Dean said, "and the politics."

"Yeah, the politics," Fox agreed. "Wrong people getting the important jobs. That sort of thing?"

"Yeah, that sort of thing."

"Proving of course," Fox added, "that there's no justice in the world."

Dean burst out laughing.

"What's so funny?" Fox asked.

"Not only do you kinda look like my former investigator, but you sound exactly like him," Dean explained. "He used to say that all the time. You really are his doppelganger."

Chapter Twenty-Five

1215 Manasota Beach Road

~~~~~~

"That was quick," Wes said. "What'd he say?"

"Nothing," Holly said. "He got a new phone. He called to give me the number."

"Man, he's definitely all over you," Billy Ray suggested with a smirk.

Holly shrugged and a small curl of smile formed on her lips. Somehow, the Indian's assessment made her feel good, gratified somehow.

"Once you taste a pussy you like," Wes said to Billy Ray,

"you never forget it. Right, man."

"You got that right," Billy Ray laughed.

"You're fucking gross," Holly told Wes.

"So, what's the new number?" Wes asked.

"It's on my phone," Holly said. She held up her i-Phone-13 and clicked to the recent call link. "Right here. I'll put it in my contacts." She tapped on the phone a few moments, then said, "There, done."

"So now what?" Billy Ray asked.

"Now, we locate Jerry boy," Wes said. He turned to Holly and said, "Give me your phone. Mine's a piece of shit."

"Why?"

"I'll go to the phone locator site and type in Jerry's new number," Wes explained. "Cost us ten bucks. Within a minute, we'll have Jerry boy's address." Wes' eyes narrowed. "Where the fucker actually lives."

Holly handed Wes the phone and in the browser, he typed in, "Phone Trace." A moment later, he was on the site. There was a bar at the top asking him to type in the number of the cell phone he was trying to locate. After typing in Jerry's new number, a box came up asking him to remit a nine dollars and ninety-nine cents and another box asking for a credit card number.

Wes turned to Holly. "I need your credit card," he told her.

"Really? It might be tapped out."

"Well, I don't have one," Wes said. He looked at Billy Ray. "You got one?"

"Shit no," he said. "A paroled felon's credit rating ain't so good."

"Alright, alright," Holly said. She dug into her purse, found her wallet and handed Wes her plastic credit card.

Card in hand, Wes squinted at the numbers and typed them into the field requested by the phone tracking site. A minute later, they had Jerry's address: 1215 Manasota Beach Road, Englewood, Florida. Wes laughed and asked Billy Ray, "You got a piece of paper, pen?"

Frowning, Billy looked around the kitchen, plucked a napkin off the counter across from the table. Holly gave him a pen from her purse and watched him jot down Jerry's residence address on the napkin.

"Now, we got the fucker," Wes said. He turned to Billy Ray and asked, "So you in or what?"

"For a hundred kay, you said, right?"

"Yeah, a hundred kay," Wes said. "All you gotta do is let us use your pistol to kidnap Jerry and his whore and baby and make him ransom himself and them free."

After thinking about it for a time, Billy Ray nodded and said, "Yeah, I'm in. All in."

Wes looked over at Holly. "But no killing them. We just take their money." He turned back to Billy Ray. "Right?"

"Got it," Billy Ray said. "No problem."

"Next, we need to rent an house down there," Wes said. "One of those Air-Nibs."

"Air-nibs?" Billy Ray asked and laughed. "You mean, Airbnb?"

"Yeah, whatever the fuck. I just got out of the can, asshole. But yeah, we rent an Airbnb and then we take a vacation. Once we're down there, we rent a cargo van to do the job."

"With what money are we gonna afford all that?" Holly asked. "I told you, my card's maxed out or just about maxed out."

"What about your mother?" Wes asked. "Doesn't she have a credit card?"

Holly shook her head. "No way," she said. "You know how much she and my dad've given me the last two years. She ain't gonna stand for it so I can take a trip down to Florida."

"You know where she keeps it?" Wes asked.

"Keeps what?"

"Her card."

"Yeah, in a wallet in her purse."

"Well, sounds easy enough for you to lift it," Wes said.

"Lift it? Steal from my own mother?"

"It's been done," Wes said. "And when you get your share of the money, you can pay her back - triple."

"Jesus Christ," Holly said, shaking her head. "Yeah, okay. I'll lift it."

Wes turned to Billy Ray and said, "Pack some shit for the drive, kiss your mother goodbye, and come with us. As soon as Holly lifts her mother's card back at her house, we're off and running. The sooner we get down there, the sooner we'll be a million dollars richer." He swigged down what was left of the beer and added, "And don't forget the gun."

Chapter Twenty-Six

The Credit Card

~~~

When Holly, Wes and Billy Ray came tramping through the front door of her parents' house an hour later, her mother was vacuuming the living room.

"Hi, Mom," Holly called out. They stopped and waited a moment for her mother to turn off the vacuum cleaner before Holly said, "Say hello to Billy Ray, Ma."

Holly's mother frowned at Billy Ray and then, with a short nod, said. "Hello, Billy."

"Hi," he replied.

"We're going upstairs to my bedroom," Holly announced. "Okay?"

Holly's mother gave the three of them a baleful look. "Yeah, sure," she said. "It's your bedroom."

Upstairs in her bedroom, Wes said, "Man, your mother looked pissed."

"Well, what'd you expect? I come home with you and a tough looking Indian. She's gotta be wondering if I'm up to no good again. I better go down and talk to her."

"Hey, man," Wes said, "we need that credit card of hers if we're gonna do this caper. Remember?"

"Yeah, I remember," Holly said. "I know where it's at. There's an old wallet in her purse where she keeps it. She doesn't use it much. They pay cash for just about everything. Only time she uses it is in an emergency, like when I needed to pay my lawyer for my murder trial."

"Well, this is another emergency," Wes said.

"Lemme go down there and talk to her first," she said. "Last thing I need is for her to call up my brother Raymond and have him come over and read me the riot act again."

"Whatever, darling," Wes said. "You just get that card."

"And you just look up a decent place for us to rent close by to Jerry's house," Holly said. "Here, use my laptop."

After powering up her laptop, Holly left Wes and Billy Ray while she went downstairs, first to talk to her mother and second to try and sneak her mother's credit card out of the wallet in her purse.

When Holy entered the living room, her mother turned off the vacuum cleaner and turned to her with a scowl.

"What are you up to?" she asked. "And who's that other guy? He staying, too."

"That's another kid from school that both Wes and I know," Holly said. "What, I can't have friends over to the house."

"He Indian?"

"Yeah, a Seneca," Holly said. "Name's Billy Ray. He's straight off the reservation. Why? You don't think Binghamton let's American Indians attend their college? Only the Asian variety? And no, he's not staying, just visiting."

"He doesn't have a car either?"

"Yeah, he's got a car," Holly replied. "We're going out in a bit and figured why take two cars. Jesus, it's always the third degree with you."

"You have to wonder why?"

"Look, I got in trouble, bad trouble," Holly said. "I admit it, but that's behind me now, okay. You and dad have nothing to worry about."

Holly's mother smirked.

"Where is dad anyway?" Holly asked.

"Golfing. You gonna be home for dinner?"

"Probably not," Holly said. "We'll probably get something out."

Holly's mother sat down on the couch. She put her hands on her lap and after wriggling her fingers around a moment, she looked up at her daughter with sad eyes.

"Holly, look," she said. "I just worry who you're getting yourself involved with. Lately, you seem to be gravitating toward the wrong kind of men. Ever since you...well, ever since Jerry."

"Ever since what Jerry? Ever since I killed him with Jeff – is that what you're saying?"

"No, I..."

"I told you, Jerry's not dead," Holly said. "Jeff and I didn't kill him. I was guilty of insurance fraud, not murder. But so was Jerry. I know you think he's this perfect guy, but he's not."

"But, but the police, they..."

"The police are idiots," Holly snapped. "And you can believe whatever you want, but Jerry's still alive, hiding out somewhere. Anonymous. And someday, he's gonna be found out and sent to prison where he belongs. As for Wes and Billy, they're college friends who, like me, haven't found themselves yet. So, so that's why, why we're thinking of driving down to Florida. There's plenty of decent jobs down there in construction and what-not."

Standing in the middle of the living room, after telling that story, Holly made a snap decision. Rather than steal her mother's credit card, she'd ask her for it. This would kill two birds with one stone. First, if her mother had noticed her card had gone missing, she'd call it in and cancel it. Second, if Holly went missing with Wes and Billy, she might call the police and they might catch them and find out what scumbags they were. Even her.

"So I was wondering," Holly blurted. "I was wondering if you'd let me use your credit card to rent a place down there – you know, an Airbnb, until we found jobs and an apartment. You know, for a little while."

"My credit card," her mother said. "Geez, Holly."

"Look, mom, mine's maxed out and I really do want to do this. Change the direction of my life. Get the friggin hell out of here, living with you and dad. I'm a big girl. I'm smothering here."

"What about them? They got no money, no credit cards?"

"Maxed out, too. Wes just got laid off – from some software firm," Holly lied. "And Billy's job is as bottom barrel as mine."

Her mother stared down at her hands in her lap for a time.

"Mom? What'dya say? Can I, can I have it?" Her mother finally looked up at Holly. "Your card. It'll only be a few hundred dollars. I'll pay you back. I promise."

After sucking in a breath, her mother gave a decisive nod. "Yes, okay. But don't tell your father." She stood and went over to her purse on a table across the room. She fished her wallet from it and slipped out a credit card. Holly walked over and took it from her mother. The feel of the plastic, obtained with a gross lie, thrilled Holly.

"I promise, I'll pay you back," Holly said.

Her mother had heard that before. Holly's murder trial had nearly bankrupted them.

After Holly hugged her and she'd stepped back, her mother said, "There's a six-thousand dollar limit on the card. Try not to use all of it, okay?"

"I told you it's just for a temporary place until the three of us get jobs."

"You gonna live with those two?" her mother nodded upstairs.

"At first, that's the plan," Holly said. "But as soon as I'm working, I'll get my own place. Maybe I'll finally meet the right guy down there."

Her mother gave a short, doubtful nod.

"Okay, lemme go upstairs, pack," she said. "You don't know how happy this makes me."

Her mother's tight smile belied her concern. "Maybe you'll run into Jerry down there," she said. "That's where you told the police he went. Right?"

That statement gave Holly a brief shock. She let out an empty laugh and said, "Yeah, that would be quite the coincidence."

Holly stepped forward and hugged her mother again, then kissed her on the cheek.

"You won't regret this, Ma," Holly said. "I promise."

Chapter Twenty-Seven

Florida Bound

~~~

Upon returning to her bedroom, Holly held up her mother's credit card. Wes stood up from an old, rackety wooden chair at a small desk against the far wall. From Holly's bed where he was stretched, Billy Ray opened his left eye. The knapsack that he'd stuffed with clothes and, presumably, the stolen pistol, was being used as a pillow.

"You swiped it!" Wes said. "Good girl."

"Well, I didn't hafta swipe it," Holly said. "My mother gave it to me. I told her we were going down to Florida to look for jobs."

"Actually that was only half a lie," Wes said and winked at her. "We already got a job." He nodded to the card. "Well, hand it over."

"No way," Holly said. She pulled her arm back as he reached for it and put the credit card in the front pocket of her jeans.

"Okay, be like that," Wes snapped.

"Whatever," Holly said with a shrug, then asked, "So, did you find any decent Airbnb's?"

"Yeah, I think so," Wes replied. He walked over to Holly's desk and pointed to the screen of her laptop. "What about this one?"

She scrolled through the photographs of the place, an older, three-bedroom, sixteen-hundred square-foot ranch with low ceilings and furnished with worn furniture on Torrego Street in a sleepy residential neighborhood in North Port, Florida, near something called the Warm Mineral Springs.

"Looks comfortable enough, and clean, decent reviews," Holly remarked, and seeing that it cost only eight-one dollars a night, added, "and the price is right."

"And it's only twenty-minutes from our boy's place," Wes added.

"Book it, then," Holly said.

"A bunch of beaches are pretty close by, too," Wes said.

"All of them only about fifteen minutes." He clicked a sound and a wink at Holly. "So make sure you pack your skimpiest bikini."

"We're not going down there on vacation," Holly reminded him.

Wes laughed.

"What about reporting to our POs?" Billy Ray asked Wes.

"How often do you have to report?"

"Used to be weekly, now once a month," Billy Ray said.

"When's your next report?"

"Coupla weeks."

"Then, you're cool," Wes said. "We only need a couple days to do this job."

"Well, I'll be fucked if my asshole PO drops in unannounced on my mother's trailer looking for me while I'm away," Billy Ray said. "The prick does that every now and then." He nodded to Wes. "What about you?"

"I reported yesterday," Wes told Billy. "Just before I dropped in on Miss Holly over here. So I'm good. I don't need to report back for a couple weeks. In fact, I gave my PO Holly's address as the place where'd I be staying for a little while."

"My address?" Holly asked, incredulous. "What if he comes around looking for you? My mother'll tell him you're with me looking for work down in Florida."

"He won't come," Wes said. "Those guys are overloaded with cases and they're lazy bastards anyway. My guy has a ho-hum get me to retirement attitude. He ain't no dedicated soldier of justice. And like I said, we only need a couple of days down there to pull this off." He slapped his upper chest and smiled at Billy Ray. "To become filthy rich, man," he added. "Right, man?"

Billy Ray nodded sleepily with his eyes still closed while Holly said, "Yeah, right. So we ready to get going or what? We gotta long drive ahead of us. At least twenty hours."

"Yeah, first, give me the credit card and lemme book the house," Wes said. He turned to Holly. "Put it under your name, right?"

Holly shrugged. "I guess," as she handed over the credit card.

Wes sat at the desk and typed in tomorrow's date for them to check-in and three days after that for the rental to terminate. He clicked on the "reserve" button that took him to the next page where he typed in the credit card numbers and security code. After that, he clicked on the "confirm and pay" button and that was it. The house where they'd take Jerry, Jade and their baby after kidnapping them was booked.

Looking up at Holly, Wes said, "Now we need to rent a cargo van. That Fiesta ain't gonna work in the kidnapping."

"So, see what's available," Holly said.

Wes found an Enterprise-Rental place in North Port not too far from the Airbnb and rented a Chevrolet Express Cargo Van for a week and arranged for pick-up before 5 P.M. the following day.

"Okay, we're all set," he told them.

"Well, let's go then," Holly said. "I'll fix us some sandwiches and we're out of here. "

"Good idea," Wes said. "Don't wanna waste our money on McDonalds." Wes turned to Billy Ray and asked, "You bring the gun, man?"

Billy opened his eyes, lifted his head and gave Wes an annoyed look.

"Yeah, I brought the gun," he said. He slapped the knapsack. "It's in here. What'dya think I am - a stupid Injun?"

"Well, aren't you?" Wes said, then pointed at Billy Ray and made a clicking noise out the side of his mouth. "Just like the rest of your tribe. That's why you live on a fucking reservation."

"Fuck you," Billy Ray hissed.

Chapter Twenty-Eight

A Real Person

~~~

Jerry was waiting in the cell phone lot of the Ft. Myers International Airport when Jade finally texted him that she'd claimed her bags and would be waiting in front of Section 5 at the arrival level of the terminal. It was just after four and Seius was snoozing in the car-seat in the back passenger row of seats in their Nissan Rogue when Jerry drove up there.

Jerry couldn't wait to see Jade, to hold her in his arms and, of course, to make love to her that night – provided she was up to it which, he sadly admitted to himself, was probably unlikely. She'd be experiencing serious jet lag for sure tonight and be beat even without it after flying out west for three long days of meetings and celebrations and all the stress that came with attending Comic-Con two evenings ago. Despite that, Jerry smiled, having had some additional Facetime sex last night and knowing that he'd shortly not only be holding Jade in his arms but he'd be grasping his newly won Wil Eisner Award as well. And soon after that, his anonymous world would dramatically change forever.

There was the usual quick hug after Jerry had pulled up and parked where Jade stood with her bags. She was so pretty despite her tired eyes and he could hardly restrain himself. Seius interfered, of course. He had awakened and was begging for his mommy. Jade sat in the backseat with her son as Jerry pulled out and headed to the entrance to I-75 northbound.

"So, what's been going on around here?" Jade asked.

"Nothing," Jerry said. "Absolutely nothing."

During the hour-and-a-half drive to Englewood, both Jade and Seius snoozed. Tired, himself from a week of caring for a rambunctious two and a half year old, and all the stress that had been brought by the award ceremonies and the many changes in his life to come, Jerry yawned and fought off sleep as they sped along with the moderately heavy traffic to the exit off I-75 onto Jacaranda Boulevard that would take them at long last to their Englewood home at 1215 Manasota Beach Road.

Once settled in and unpacked, Jade said, "I thought we'd do dinner at Briandi's."

"You're up for going out? I could get us a pizza."

"No, definitely Briandi's," Jade said. "We should celebrate. But first, you need to call Vince Benson. He wants to talk to the real anonymous man – and set up a schedule to review your script and some other details. As he told me, he wants to hit the floor running. And anyway, I want to get reacquainted with my baby boy."

"Vince Benson? Really? He's one of the best Marvel guys."

"Yep. The studio is going full board," Jade said. She smiled and kissed Jerry on the cheek.

"You can do better than that," Jerry said as he pulled Jade to him and kissed her fully on the mouth.

"Later, honey," she said, "you'll get all the kissing you want." She laughed and said, "If I'm able to stay awake." After a deep yawn, she added, "But really, Jer, you need to call this guy."

Jade handed him Vince Benson's business card. On the back was a printed cell phone number. "That's his personal cell," Jade explained. "Put it in your phone."

"What about the other stuff?" Jerry asked. "The contracts and all that."

"Gabe's working on all that," Jade said. "You're getting three-hundred thousand for an option on the story and script, plus residuals. If they don't use the script, or have to make substantial changes, you'll still get story credit, be credited as an executive producer and likely be brought on as creative director. I learned a lot on the business of moviemaking the last couple of days. More than I ever wanted to know. Bottom line, depending on how well the movie does, and the sequels, we're going to be set financially. The Marvel execs and Vince think it's a slam dunk." She winked at him and added, "And you're right, we won't need Global Insurance's money anymore."

An odd thought occurred to Jerry right then – that might work against him in his quest to become a notorious man. His becoming wealthy, independent of the money he'd stolen from Global, might dampen the mitigating factor that entailed his giving the money back. He'd have to talk to Dean Alessi about that and get his opinion as to how badly it might hurt him.

"Jerry? Penny for your thoughts?" Jade asked with a curious frown.

"Oh, nothing. Just tired."

"Maybe we should get pizza after all," Jade said. "Eat it with champagne. Save Briandi's for tomorrow."

"As usual, you're reading my thoughts actually," Jerry

said with a smile. "As always, we're on the same page." In the next moment, Jerry had the dark thought, *except when it came to keeping Holly out of his life.*

Jade suddenly wrapped her arms around his waist. From the couch, Seius looked up at them with wide, blue eyes. Seeing his mommy and daddy embrace and kiss seemed to satisfy his every need. But, as the kiss lingered, the boy, as they will, began to fuss.

"Well," Jade sighed, "I'm off to being a mommy again."

"Thank god," Jerry said with a laugh.

"Go call Vince Benson," Jade said. "He said something about arranging a Zoom reading of your script in the next couple of weeks."

"They really want to use my script?"

"Maybe," Jade said. "At least some of it. Benson said it's pretty good, though maybe not cinematic enough."

"What the hell does that mean?" Jerry said with a laugh.

For her part, Jade shrugged.

"Alright," Jerry said. "Lemme go call him. Get this show on the road."

After Jade left the room cuddling Seius in her arms, Jerry took Vince Benson's business card and retired to his den. He sat at his desk and after a sigh, tapped out the Hollywood number on it.

After four rings, someone answered.

"Hello, Vince Benson here."

"Ah, Mr. Benson, this is ... well, this is the anonymous man who wrote The Anonymous Man comics, and the movie script based on it."

"Ah, yes," Benson said. "So you really are a real person."

Chapter Twenty-Nine

Rest Stop

~~~•~~~

Holly, Wes and Billy Ray didn't crowd into Holly's Fiesta until just after four in the afternoon for the twenty-hour drive down to the Airbnb rental in North Port, Florida. If the Fiesta held up and they didn't get bogged down in traffic from an accident or construction zones, they figured to arrive there no later than one the following afternoon.

Holly started out the drive and just after entering I-79 from the I-90 in Erie, Pennsylvania, about two hours into the trip, complaining that she had to pee, she pulled the Fiesta into a rest area near Edinboro.

"Already?" said Wes from the front passenger seat. "Jesus."

"Too much coffee," Holly replied. "I told you stopping

at Tim Horton's was a mistake."

"I gotta take a shit anyway," Billy Ray said from the backseat.

After Holly parked the Fiesta, each of them climbed out of the cramped car and ambled and stretched up a sidewalk to the grimy looking restrooms. It was still hot and humid that July afternoon, still in the mid-80s with the sun still high above them in a hazy blue sky.

Holly was glad that there were only a couple other lady travelers in the women's room as she entered. Grimacing after sniffing the stale smell of sweat and pee and washed out Clorox, Holly pushed open the door to an empty stall, undid her shorts, and sat down. After relieving herself, she checked her phone. No one had texted or called.

Sitting there on the toilet, Holly made a snap decision to call Jerry on his new trac phone number even though she knew that at that hour, just after six, Jade was likely home from San Diego. With a sigh, she clicked on the contact link to Jerry's cellphone number, not expecting him to answer. But after the third ring, he did.

"What's up, Holly?" Jerry asked, just above a whisper. From the glum tone of his voice, Holly could tell he wasn't happy about the call. "You're supposed to text first, remember?"

"Yeah, I remember," Holly said, keeping her voice low as the next stall had become occupied. "Jade back?"

"Yes," he said. "She flew in at four. She's with the baby. I'm in my studio."

"She must be tired."

"Where are you? What's wrong with your voice?"

"I'm, I'm in the living room. My mother's in the kitchen. Don't want her to hear me."

After a moment registering that, Jerry asked, "So, what'dya want?"

"I wasn't too happy about the way our last call ended," she said. After a sigh, she added, "I'm sorry, Jerry, sorry for everything."

"Look, Holly, you know, these calls really do have to stop," Jerry blurted. "I've been lucky, real lucky, that Jade hasn't found out about them." Holly let out a bitter laugh and said, "Yeah, if she did, she'd come up here and kill me. She promised to do that, you know."

"Yeah, you've said," Jerry replied. "But, she'd probably kill me first."

After another sigh, Holly said, "I just wish…"

"Wish what?"

"I just wish I hadn't lost faith in us," she said. "I just wish you still loved me."

Jerry kept silent.

"Jerry?"

"Look, Holly, we just have to end these calls, okay," he said. "I should never have let it happen. They're counterproductive to us moving forward with our lives."

You let it happen because you're still in love with me, she wanted to tell him.

"I love you, Jerry," she whispered. That was the second time in two days she'd admitted that to him.

Jerry didn't respond.

"I'm sorry," Holly told him for the second time. "I'm sorry for everything."

Whether or not she loved him and was sorry for everything was an open question. Sometime along the way of their eight years together, she'd let go of her feelings for him. He'd lost his appeal and while Jeff was not a meaningful replacement, his energy and dark spirit had cast a spell over her eclipsing her love for Jerry. She realized now how wrong her attraction to Jeff had been, what a bad man he was. Then she wondered what the hell she was doing falling under a similar dark masculine spell cast this time by the likes of Wes Chandler.

"Look, I just can't do this anymore, alright," Jerry said. "Please consider this our last call."

The realization of that suddenly hit Holly and she began to cry. "I, I can never speak with you again?" she whimpered. "Is, is that what you're telling me?"

Jerry drew in a breath and said, "Yes, that's what I'm telling you." Then, he clicked off the call.

Holly drew in a breath, looked at her phone. She waited a full minute for him to call her back. When he didn't, she hissed, "You motherfucker."

Chapter Thirty

North Port

When Holly returned to the car, Wes and Billy Ray were leaning against the front hood.

"What the hell took you so long?" Wes asked. "You got the runs?"

"Shut up," she told him.

Billy Ray laughed. He opened the door and rolled into the back seat.

As she strolled past Wes to get in the driver's seat, Wes grabbed her left arm and wrenched her around to face him. "Who the fuck you think you're talking to?" he asked, glaring at her.

"C'mon man," Billy Ray called out. "Keep it civil. You're attracting attention."

Wes looked to the back seat and snapped, "Go fuck yourself, Billy Ray. This's between me and this cunt."

Holly yanked her arm out of Wes's grasp. "Get your fucking hands off me," she said. "I'm not your whore."

"No, you're not. You do it for free. You suck my dick and fuck me and I don't have to pay a dime."

Shaking her head with disgust, Holly strode off to the driver's side. She opened the door, got it and slammed it shut.

Wes turned around to face her inside the car, lifted his shoulders up as to say, what the fuck's the matter. Then, he walked around, opened the door to the passenger side and slid into his seat.

"Enough of this bullshit," Billy Ray said. "We got a long ride ahead of us. We don't need this animosity bullshit. You two are like an old married couple."

Wes lifted his arm over the backrest and glaring at Billy Ray, said, "I meant what I said a minute ago. Stay out of it. This is between me and her."

"So, she's your squeeze now?" Billy Ray asked. "Don't seem it to me. Seems as if she's open game."

"You keep your dirty red mind and smelly red dick off her," Wes warned. \

By now, Holly had started the Fiesta and was backing out of the space.

"Or what, hombre?"

"Or we're gonna have a serious problem."

Billy Ray laughed.

"The both of you, shut the fuck up," Holly said. "Like Billy Ray said, we got a long ride ahead of us."

***

The rest of the trip was relatively amicable. There were moments of distress and anger, but for the most part, Holly, Wes and Billy Ray got along.

In a parking lot after downing some burgers and fries at a McDonald's near an exit off

I-77 near Wytheville, Virginia, Wes strode up to Holly, took her arm, turned her to him and kissed her. She resisted at first, but within moments, she was kissing him back. Behind them, Billy Ray shook his head and silently mouthed, "Shit. Hey, Joannie loves Chachi, get a fucking room." They ignored him and kept kissing for a few seconds more.

Wes drove the twelve remaining hours from Wytheville

to North Port, Florida. Around three in the morning, while Billy Ray was fast asleep sprawled out along the backseat, Wes reached over, grabbed Holly by the back of her neck and pulled her to his lap.

"What're you doing?" she gasped, as she pushed back and looked up at him.

"I need you to blow me," he whispered. "Keep me awake."

"What?"

"Just do it," he told her.

She lifted up a moment, and looked into his sad blue eyes. Ahead of them, the headlights of the Fiesta showed a stark white path along the interstate. She sighed and reached a momentous decision. Then, shaking her head a moment, she helped him lower his shorts, bent her head onto his lap and got into it as the Fiesta cruised down the southbound I-77 in northern North Carolina at seventy-five miles per hour. He came into her mouth ten minutes later just north of Statesville.

Holly rose up and wiped her mouth clean with a napkin from the glove compartment.

"See, was that so bad?" Wes asked her.

As she crumbled up the napkin, she glared at him and said, "You're a mean, sick bastard, you know that?"

"So I been told," Wes said. "But whoever did that to me before, always told me they wanted more."

Holly shook her head as she turned and stared out at the blackness of the night rushing past her.

***

At around one in the afternoon that same day, Wes took the exit from I-75 onto West River Road. Fifteen minutes later, following the directions being called out by a lady's voice from Holly's cellphone, he pulled the Fiesta into the driveway of the Airbnb rental on Torrego Street in North Port just south of Venice.

Using the code to open the front door, Wes, Holly and Billy Ray entered the house carrying their knapsacks. They were pleased to find that the house was a spic-and-span clean, airy place with plenty of room for them and later, their captives, Jerry, Jade and their baby boy.

"Let's go get the van rental," Wes said to Holly. He turned to Billy Ray and added, "You can stay here and crash."

Forty-five minutes later, Wes was pulling the rented cargo van into the Airbnb house driveway.

"Well, we're all set," he told Holly. "Let's get some shut-eye, eat something, then stake-out your Jerry boy's house."

Holly gave an unenthusiastic shrug. She was beat and felt

soiled by her association with Wes. He was a black knight even worse than Jeff Flaherty had been.

The Airbnb rental was a three-bedroom twenty-one square foot fairly typical Florida ranch house built with cinderblocks covered by stucco. Out back, there was a small screened-in pool. The AC worked well and Wes put the temperature down to a cool seventy-four degrees. Outside it was a humid, hazy ninety-four.

After exiting the cargo van and entering the house, Wes and Holly found Billy Ray asleep on a chaise lounge on the pool deck.

"Let's take the master," Wes told Holly. With a laugh, he added, "Hope you won't snore again like you did last night."

"I don't snore," Holly shot back.

"That's right," smiled Wes. "You purr."

Though Wes quickly fell asleep moments after climbing under a sheet on the king-sized bed in the master bedroom, Holly couldn't. She tossed and turned, her thoughts racing about what they were about to do. She had betrayed Jerry so many times before she couldn't figure what number this one would be. She hoped this would be the last time.

A part of her agreed that betraying Jerry was just fine. He'd treated her badly the last two years, stringing her along with those stupid, useless phone calls, and just yesterday afternoon, had dumped her unceremoniously. But she worried that her participation in Jerry's kidnapping could end up with his murder. She vowed not to let that happen.

Wes started snoring, guttural inhalings and exhalings that Holly could not ignore. She sat up, wracked with guilt and worry, and gave up trying to nap. Sliding out of the bed, she tramped to the spacious open area with a kitchen overlooking what in Florida was called a gathering room. She plopped down on the couch, laid down and closed her eyes. After a couple minutes, she felt the soothing, soft embrace of sleep coming on when another body squeezed in next to her. Opening her eyes, she saw that it was Billy Ray.

"Thought you'd like some company," he said.

Without hesitation, he was kissing her and for some reason Holly couldn't fathom, she was kissing him back. His hands were soon down to her hips and ass and he was pulling off her shorts and moving his finger to her crotch. Soon enough, he had his shorts off and rolled on top of her.

Chapter Thirty-One

Lawyers Gone Bad

Later that same afternoon, following his phone call with Vince Benson, Jerry called Dean Alessi, still up in Buffalo.

"So where do we stand?" Jerry asked. "Any news?"

"It's still up in the air," Dean said. "I told you about the possibility of a grand larceny second plea. So far, haven't heard back from Jack Brewster, the ADA I met with who heads the Special Investigations Bureau - where a case like yours would most likely land – about the DA's position. At some point, we're gonna hafta contact Global, run it by them. The DA ultimately decides what he thinks is a fair disposition, but he won't piss off a victim, especially a corporate victim."

"Jack Fox is helping with that, right?"

"Well, he told me they might play hardball," Dean said. "The guy taking over for his old fraud unit chief seems to have a more aggressive attitude."

"Just my luck," Jerry said. He sighed and added, "Well, it is what it is. But should they go along with the grand larceny second plea, you said I'd likely get minimal jail time - if any."

"Yeah, that's possible," Dean said. "But no guarantees. Plus, remember, they have some bargaining chips. As we also discussed, your – what'dya call her – oh, yeah, your front, Jade, she's at risk in all this. By harboring you the past five years, she became an accessory-after-the-fact. Plus, she benefitted from at least some of the money. In exchange for no exposure to her, they might want more of a pound of flesh from you. Get it?"

"Yeah, I get it." Jerry was again having second thoughts about giving up his anonymity to become the notorious man. But his inability to interact with the real world as an anonymous man still seemed to eclipse these risks.

"One other worry that came to me only yesterday," Jerry added, "as if I didn't have enough already, is that my turning the money in might be questioned as a real mitigating factor."

"How so?" Dean asked.

"Because of the movie deal and all that," Jerry explained, "I really don't need Global's money anymore. They're think that's the only reason I'm giving it back."

Dean thought about that for a time, then said, "Yeah, I see what you mean." After a sigh, he added, "Well, let's hope no one picks up on that and makes the argument."

"Yeah, let's hope," Jerry said, then asked, "So, what did you think of Jack Fox? Interesting guy."

Dean laughed and said, "He reminds me of my former chief investigator, a great guy by the name of Stu Foley. Same age, same attitude. He lives down in the Villages now. Had these sayings like, 'There's no justice in the world,' and 'What goes around never comes around.'"

"A true cynic, then," Jerry commented.

"Yep, that he was, and still is. So, how's your movie deal with Marvel going?"

"It's proceeding right along," Jerry replied. "They've set up a Zoom reading of my script for next Sunday. They'll be some top actors involved." He laughed. "I'm nervous as hell. If they use my script, my value to the movie increases significantly. Could be worth a quarter million dollars, maybe more. At least, that's what my agent's telling me. So that's what got me to thinking about the effect of making all that money on the mitigation question."

"Yeah, you said. No use worrying about it. And Jade, she got home alright yesterday?"

"Yes, thank God," Jerry said. "She's worn out, with the

baby now. I'm worn out, too. Being a single parent was no fun. Plus, there's too much shit on my mind."

"Yeah, I get it," Dean said. "Got a lot of shit on my mind, too."

"Yeah, like what?"

"Oh, several things," Dean said. "My legal career going forward for one thing. I'm not a huge fan of private practice. Hell, sometimes I regret having become a lawyer in the first place."

"What else would you want to do?" Jerry asked.

"Write," Dean said. "I've been dabbling in writing stuff for years, mostly crime short stories, some science fiction. I've got journals full of ideas, drafts of whole stories even. Some of its been published." He laughed and added, "And my father gave me a great idea for a TV series a few years back."

"He alive, your father?"

"No, he died a few years ago," Dean said.

"Sorry to hear that."

"Yeah, he was a great guy," Dean said. "And you? Your father still alive?"

"Yes, he is," Jerry said. "Thing is, I don't think he ever really grieved over my passing. I had this older brother, Pete

– Petey, we called him. He was a stellar athlete, a football star in high school. My parents adored him. And why not, everybody adored him.

"Before Petey's senior year, he got a scholarship to play at Michigan and he and my parents had dreams of him making it to the NFL. Then, after a game late in the season his senior year, he was a passenger in a car driven by a friend. The friend was drunk and they were driving in the country hills on their way to some party house. Anyway, it'd been slick that night, a rain, snow mix and the idiot friend was going too fast and they went off the road and crashed into a tree. Petey was killed. The asshole driver survived. For Petey, it was instantaneous, the coroner said, as if that was a blessing." Jerry sighed. "And that was it. My parents never recovered. Left a dark hole in my soul as well."

"I'm sorry, Jerry," Dean said.

After a long moment of silence, Jerry asked, "So, what was the idea your father gave you? You know, for the TV series."

Dean laughed. "Oh, yeah... It was based on what I was doing back then, when I ran the Lawyer Discipline Officer up here in Buffalo. A series about a guy like me who ran the office and had to chase down bad lawyers – you know, lawyers who committed all kinds of serious ethical and even criminal misdeeds.

"And my father's idea stuck with me," Dean went on. "It took me awhile, but I've drafted a pilot script. I think it's pretty good actually. And you know, I was wondering if you could run it by your agent. Maybe show her a copy, see if she could pitch it for me."

"Sure," Jerry said. "I could do that. What's it called, the series?"

"Lawyers Gone Bad," Dean said.

Chapter Thirty-Two

The Stake-Out

~~~

Before driving out that evening to stake-out Jerry's house at 1215 Manasota Beach Road in Englewood, Holly used the satellite and ground features views on Google maps to get a look at the place from above and at street level,. From those views, she, Wes and Billy Ray were able to select where Wes could park the Fiesta so they could conduct a meaningful surveillance.

"This road over here looks good," said Billy Ray, pointing to what looked like a dirt and crushed shell road intersecting Manasota Beach Road almost directly across from Jerry's house. "Gives us a good view of the place. You know, help us figure out how best to approach the house tomorrow morning."

"Yeah, I agree," Holly said.

"Give the redskin a fucking gold star," Wes snapped.

It seemed to Holly that Wes had become annoyed with Billy Ray ever since they'd entered their North Port Airbnb rental. This gave Holly the idea that somehow Wes had become aware of her indiscretion with Billy Ray earlier that afternoon.

"What the fuck's your problem," Billy Ray countered.

"You," Wes snapped back.

"Fellas," Holly interrupted. "Look. Check this out."

She had called up the Zillow dot com site and typed in 1215 Manasota Beach Road. Within seconds, the house popped up.

"It's a typical Florida ranch house," she told Wes and Billy Ray, "pretty much the same design as our Airbnb only bigger - twenty-five hundred square feet with four bedrooms and big pool out back covered by a cage. From my talks with Jerry, the front guest bedroom has been converted into his work studio.

"According to the Sarasota County Tax Assessor's site," Holly went on, "Jade is listed as the owner. Guess what Zillow estimates its market value is?"

"Not a fucking clue," Wes replied.

"Eight-hundred fifty grand," Holly said.

Billy Ray whistled and said, "Man, nice."

"Who gives a shit," Wes hissed. "Over-priced, you ask me." He pointed to Holly's laptop screen and said, "From this, looks like the best way to approach the place is by sneaking through the bushes along the side of the house off this side road - Dennison Road."

"We'll know better when we stake it out," Billy Ray suggested.

"No shit, Chief Sherlock," Wes said.

"I asked you before – what's your fucking problem," Billy Ray shot back.

"You," Wes replied. "You fucked her, didn't you, while I was napping."

"Jesus Christ," Holly said.

"You ain't married to her," Billy Ray said.

Wes grabbed him by the shoulders and yanked him up. As Billy Ray lurched forward, he swung his arms up and flung Wes's arms off him. Stepping back, he pulled out his stolen pistol that he'd tucked inside the waistline of his jeans, unlatched the safety and pointed it square at Wes's chest.

"Keep your fucking hands off me, asshole," Billy Ray barked. "I'll shoot you like I shot that clerk. Actually, it was fun doing that. Shoulda aimed at the fucker's head."

Wes raised his arms and after a long moment, smiled. "Whoa, buddy," he said. "Just venting some steam. Next time you wanna fuck my girl, just ask me first."

"I'm not your girl," Holly said.

Wes glared at her and said, "Yeah, cause you're a useless, cheating skank."

"Fuck you," she said.

"Look, we gonna argue about this shit or work out a plan here," Billy Ray said as he clicked back the safety on the pistol and tucked the weapon back along the waistline of his jeans. "There's a million dollars at stake. And my one hundred grand."

That seemed to calm everyone down. Wes even patted Billy Ray on the back. Stepping back, he asked, "So how was she?"

"Jesus, man, give it up," Billy Ray said. "I told you, I'm sorry. I shouldn't have done it. But you're not the only horney sucker out here."

"This's bullshit," Holly said. "I'm going home."

As Holly tried to stalk off, Wes grabbed her by the right arm and pulled her to him. Looking down into her eyes, he said, "You ain't going nowhere, sweetie. You're part of this caper now, whether you like it or not. And they next time you go to fuck someone, it better be me."

"Don't worry," Billy Ray said from behind them. "I had my taste. Now she's all yours."

Wes bent down and planted a kiss on Holly's lips. She kept them tight for a time before relenting and giving him some tongue.

"Alright, now that you two have patched things up, we gonna get out there?" Billy Ray asked. "See what's what."

"Yeah," Wes said as he grabbed Holly by the arm again and started pulling her with him toward the hall leading to the master bedroom. "As soon as I drop a load in her."

"Jesus fucking Christ," Billy Ray whispered as he watched Wes drag off a mostly compliant Holly.

***

Half an hour later, before taking the twenty-minute drive from the Airbnb rental to 1215 Manasota Road, they stopped at an Ace Hardware along the way and purchased some rope and nylon ties for use in tying up Jerry and Jade once they'd invaded the house and kidnapped them the following morning.

By five-thirty, Wes was parking Holly's Ford Fiesta along the dirt and crushed shell road that Billy Ray had pointed out as a good stake-out site.

"Nice house," Billy Ray commented.

"Still not worth eight hundred grand," replied Wes.

After five minutes, Billy Ray said, "Not much going on."

"What'd you expect?" Wes asked. "They're probably back in the pool. It's still what, ninety degrees. I'm fucking dying in here."

"Turn the car on," Billy Ray said. "Get the AC cranking,"

"And risk blowing out the engine of this piece of shit?" Wes asked.

"Yeah, you better not," Holly said. "Anyway, we've seen enough, right? Like you said, that area along Dennison next to the property should be how we approach the house. It's secluded enough, no neighbors to see us. From there, we head to the pool, rip out the side screens of the cage to get onto the pool deck and the patio, lanai, or whatever it's called. Then we smash in the sliding glass doors if they're not open. They won't know what hit them. It's a surprise attack."

"Just hope Jerry boy doesn't have a gun," Wes said.

"But we got the element of surprise," Holly said. "Still, we hafta be quick." She sighed and added, "Wish we had another gun."

"Well, we don't," Wes said. "And no way to get another.

So, we'll just hafta be fast." He turned and looked back at Billy Ray. "Right, Billy Ray?"

"Right," he replied.

"Let's get the fuck out of here," Wes said. "We've seen enough. And I'm fucking starving."

Chapter Thirty-Three

Outfoxed

Late the same afternoon as Wes, Billy Ray and Holly were staking out Jerry's house in on Manasota Beach Road, Victor Lenkov met with Gregor Vasiliev and Boris Lebedev, two thick, brutish men who'd once been members of the Russian paramilitary organization, The Wagner Group. They sat in Victor's room in the same Holiday Inn where two years earlier Jerry had screwed Holly – but not the same room. Victor had arranged for Gregor and Boris to fly to Buffalo from their Brooklyn apartment and they'd arrived late that morning. Victor had also booked a separate room for them at the same Holiday Inn.

"So, here's deal," Victor began the meeting. "We go to house of this guy, Fox."

"Fox?" Gregor asked. "like animal"

"Yeah, like animal. His name, Fox," Victor replied, then continued, Using this index finger, he traced what he was telling them on the top of the bed on which he sat. Boris and Gregor occupied chairs along the side of it. "We go from here, we park on street, then we bust into house, surprise Fox, then find number of this guy, Jerry Shaw, on his cell phone. Is easy."

"Jerry Shaw," Boris said. "They guy who stole money."

"Yes, yes," Victor said. "Guy who stole money, from insurance company."

"When we go do this?" Gregor asked.

"Right now," Victor said with an annoyed shrug. "When you want go?"

Gregor answered with a sheepish shrug.

"See, he, this Fox, is alone," Victor went on. "Wife's gone some place. No alarm system. Plus, he's old, like seventy. Armed, maybe, so we be careful." He shrugged and went on, "Ah, you know, little bit. Like I say, all we want, his cell phone, find number of Shaw. Supposed be down in Florida. We get cell of this guy, Fox, find number, find Jerry. That's it."

"What we do with Fox after find phone and use phone to find Jerry?" Boris asked.

"We tie up," Victor said. "Keep in basement. One of us – you, Boris – you stay with him. Me and Gregor fly to Florida tomorrow morning, first thing, rent car down there then find this Shaw. Once find, we drive back up with him, one day. Turn him in to cops. Then, Boris, you leave house, leave Fox tied up in basement. You both, go back Brooklyn. I make a call, someone goes, unties Fox."

Gregor and Boris exchanged glances.

"What?" Victor asked.

After they turned to Victor, Gregor said, "You say ten each for job."

"Yeah, ten each."

"Twenty," Boris blurted.

Victor laughed and replied, "Fuck no. Ten. That's it. You don't like, I call other guys."

Boris and Gregor looked at each other. After a moment, Gregor turned to Victor and said, "Okay, ten."

"Good," Victor said. "You ready, do this?"

"Yeah, sure," Gregor said.

"Yeah, sure," Boris said.

***

Ten minutes later, Boris and Gregor herded into Victor's

rental car for the fifteen minute drive out to Fox's modest three-bedroom, fifteen-hundred square foot Cape Cod house in Depew, about twelve miles east of Buffalo. Victor drove while Gregor took the front seat and Boris occupied the back.

"Pew?" Gregor said as Victor pulled out of the driveway of the Airbnb. "What kind name that?"

From the back seat, Boris laughed and said, "*Vonyuchiy*," the Russian word for smelly.

"Keep quiet," Victor said. "Think job, you *p'yanyye idioty*." He'd just called them drunken idiots.

Gregor and Boris grumbled curse words in response to Victor's insult.

The July sun was still high up at the hour as Victor parked the van a few doors down from Fox's house. Gregor and Boris hopped out of the van with him and without hesitation, they strode to the side entrance. After pulling open the storm door, Gregor used a Halligan bar to pry open the inner wooden door.

Hearing his side entrance door having been snapped open, Fox stood up from the couch where he'd been watching Fox News and strode into the kitchen. When he saw Victor with his two burly Russian henchmen, he stopped in this tracks, his eyes wide with surprise and fear.

"What the fuck is this?" he shouted.

In the next moment, Boris and Gregor were on him. They lifted Fox under his armpits and carried him, as planned, into the master bedroom and tossed him onto the queen bed. Fox's attempt to wriggle free was easily thwarted by the full weight of Boris' six foot two inch, two hundred forty pound frame on top of him.

"Tie him up," Victor ordered Gregor.

"Keep still," Boris said, as Fox tossed and turned under him in a hopeless attempt to escape.

"Motherfuckers!" Fox shouted.

"*Zamolchi*, shut up," Gregor grunted as he deftly applied the nylon ties around Fox's ankles and, using a thin rope, secured his hands behind his back. Boris rose up and he and Gregor laughed as Fox continued wiggling about looking like a giant, helpless old worm on the bed.

"Stay still, idiot," Boris rasped.

"Okay, good," Victor said. "Now, Gregor, go find cell. Look living room."

"What is this?" shouted Fox.

"You quiet," Victor said with a vicious glare, "or we gag you, tape mouth shut."

Fox sighed and toned down his hysteria. "Just take what you want and leave."

Now, Victor smiled. "Yes, we will."

Gregor went out to the living room and quickly returned with Fox's cell phone. Handing an Apple i-Phone 13 model to Victor, he said, "Here is cell."

"Good," Victor said. He smiled seeing that it used face recognition to unlock the device. He sat on the bed and held the phone within a foot of Fox's face.

"What're you doing?" Fox asked.

Victor smiled when he saw that the phone had unlocked. Then, he looked down at Fox and said, "You behave now. Okay."

Scowling, Fox nodded and said, "Okay. But what do you need on my phone?"

Victor clicked the contacts icon on Fox's cellphone and searched for Jerry Shaw's number. When he found no such listing, her decided to scroll through Fox's contact list, starting with the letter "A." He smiled when he came upon, "Anonymous Man," remembering what Neal Barrett had told him about this Shaw guy faking his death and becoming, well, anonymous.

He looked at Fox and said, "This gotta be it, right? Anonymous Man. In your contacts."

Fox tried to hold a poker face, but a slight twinge at the right corner of his mouth and three rapid blinks of his eyelids told Victor that he'd found Jerry Shaw's number.

Turning to Gregor and Boris, Victor said, "Take him down basement. Tie him to a pole or something down there."

"Bastards," Fox snapped. "How'm gonna piss, shit?"

Victor shrugged and said, "Better hold it."

"Fuck you," Fox said.

"Just do my job, Mister Fox," Victor said. "You got bathroom down there?"

"Yeah."

Looking at Boris, Victor said, "He got shit, piss, you take him. Okay?"

Boris shrugged.

"Now, take him," Victor said to Gregor and Boris. "No more time to waste."

While they escorted Fox to the basement, Victor called Neal Barrett.

"We done here," he told Barrett.

"You found Shaw's number?"

"Yes, number. Now we find address, fly down there."

"When?"

"In morning," Victor said. "We fly Jet Blue. Leave

Buffalo, like by six, fly to New York. Arrive Sarasota like eleven."

"Alright," Barrett said. "Once you grab him, call me. In the meantime, I'll contact the DA's office up in Buffalo and file a criminal complaint."

"Good," Victor said. "We drive up with the guy, hand over to cops next day."

"Good work," Barrett said. "You'll make a good payday when you complete this job."

"Of course," Victor said. "Always."

Chapter Thirty-Four

Jerry-Rigged

~~~

At eight the following morning, Jerry sat at the desk in his studio reviewing his screenplay for The Anonymous Man. He'd gone over it twice and made minor changes since waking up at six. He intended to keep tinkering with it until he believed it was the best work he could possibly submit to Marvel Entertainment's executive producer and showrunner, Lee Stanford. Like most good writers, Jerry had long ago accepted that the real work of writing came during the revision process.

As he leaned forward and re-read for the fourth time the clunky dialogue spoken by a minor character in a scene, he was startled by the explosion of smashed glass. Must be the sliding glass door, was Jerry's first thought.

After jumping up out his chair, Jerry trotted from the studio to see what had happened. Entering the gathering room, he stopped when he saw standing a few feet within the smashed out sliding glass door two rough-looking men – one, light-skinned and blonde and the other, dark-skinned with long jet black hair – and, of all people, with them, was his very own Holly.

"What the hell?" he shouted.

A moment later, Jade had bolted from the master bedroom and ran to Jerry's side, her eyes wide with fright as she saw what he was seeing. As Jerry placed his left arm around her shoulders and brought her close, it became frightfully apparent that the dark-skinned man was pointing a black pistol at them.

"Seius," Jade whispered up to Jerry.

"He'll be alright," Jerry whispered in reply, though not really sure of anything right then.

"You," the light-skinned man shouted. "Shut the fuck up."

Jade finally focused on the woman among the three intruders. She did a double-take and said, "Holly?"

"Yeah, it's me, Holly," Holly snapped. "Remember your promise that you'd kill me if I ever bothered Jerry again?"

She laughed. "Well, you may get your chance. Why don't you ask Jerry how I found him?"

As Jerry frowned, Jade shot him a disturbed look.

"Cut the chit-chat," the light-skinned, blonde haired guy said. "This ain't no reunion party. Name's Wes by the way. And this over here with the gun is Billy Ray. And you already know my girlfriend, Holly."

"I'm not your girlfriend," Holly shot back.

"Ain't she neat," Wes said. "Well, folks, in case you're wondering, this is what's called a kidnapping. The ransom's gonna be all that Global insurance money you got hold up in some secret bank account somewhere."

Jerry turned to Holly and said, "Damn-it, Holly."

"You gave me no choice, Jerry."

Now it was Jade turning to Jerry. "What the hell's going on?" she asked him.

"We got no time for this fucking bickering," Wes said. "What we want is for Jerry to transfer the Global money in whatever secret bank account it's in to a secret account we've set up to receive it. You comprehendo, Jerry?"

Jerry nodded. "Yeah, I comprehendo. But it's not as easy as you think. It's actually in four accounts in four different foreign banks. It may take a couple days for the transactions to clear."

"All we got is time, Jerry boy," Wes said. "But you start playing games, you'll regret it. Understood?"

"Yeah, I get it."

"Alright, the first thing we gotta do is tie you and the missus here up," Wes said. "And because Billy Ray is holding a gun on you, and has an itchy finger, you're gonna let me do it without complaint. Right?"

Jerry and Jade nodded.

"Right?" Wes was now demanding an answer.

"Yeah, right," they both mumbled.

Then, Jade said, "But I got a baby asleep in his crib back in his bedroom. He can't be part of this."

"Oh, yes, he can," Wes said. "Consider him kidnapped, too." He turned to Holly. "While I'm tying up Jerry and Jade, here, why don't you go back and grab their little bugger and bring him out here."

"No, please," begged Jade. "Look, you can tie up my legs, but let me keep my arms free so I can hold my child. I need to feed him, change his diaper and all that."

"You mean, he ain't potty trained yet?" Billy Ray asked. "Jesus."

Jade shot him a look and snapped, "Are you?" As Billy Ray smiled at her in recognition of the quick comeback, she added, "No, he's not potty trained. He's not there yet. He's only two and a half." She turned back to Wes. "So, you see, I really do need my hands free."

"I don't see no harm in that," Wes said as he looked to Billy Ray and Holly. "Do you?"

"Whatever works, man," Billy Ray said. "We can't exactly take the kid to daycare."

After hesitating a moment, Holly said, "Yeah, I'm okay with that. Let her take care of her kid. I sure don't want to." She looked at Jerry. "I have no experience in that, right Jerry?"

Jerry looked away, having no response to her old accusation that it was somehow his fault for not getting her pregnant.

"Alright, then," Wes said. "Holly, you go get the baby and give it to Jade while I tie Jerry up. Then, I'll tie her."

While Holly went down a short hallway off the gathering room to Seius' bedroom to fetch the child, Wes brought over two armless dining room chairs and ordered Jerry and Jade to sit down on them. After digging through the plastic bag Holly had carried into the house and dropped on a coffee table, he pulled out two lengths of rope both cut to seventy-two inches, some nylon ties, and duct-tape that they'd purchased the evening before at an Ace Hardware store. There were also two pieces of cloth for use in gagging Jerry and Jade.

"Man, you don't need to do this," Jerry pleaded as he watched Wes prepare to tie them up. "There's no need to kidnap us. There's no need to tie us up. I'll get you the money. Then, you can leave us alone."

"Sorry, pal," Wes said, "But we need some time to get away."

"Get away? From what?" Jerry asked. "It's stolen money I'll be handing over to you. If I report it to the cops, I'm slitting my own throat." He nodded to Jade. "And hers, too. We'd both go to jail for sure. So, it doesn't make sense for me to turn you in. You caught us red-handed. Good for you and bad for us. But, there's no need to do anything after the money's in your hands and out of mine."

Holly had returned to the gathering room holding the baby just in time to hear Jerry's spiel. Seius was fussing, whining and stretching, seeming intent on getting out of Holly's arms.

Battling to hold the kid still, she hissed, "That's bullshit, Jerry."

Jerry and Jade simultaneously turned to her.

"You're turning yourself in anyway," Holly said. "You're tired of being the anonymous man. At least that's what you told me yesterday on the phone. Remember?"

Jade glanced at Jerry, her eyes hot. "On the phone?" she asked.

Jerry gave a sheepish, sad nod and hung his head.

"Yeah, on the phone," Holly replied for him. "Jerry's been talking to me behind your back for the last two years. Ever since you dropped me off that time right after I killed that federal marshal guy and saved both your asses." She directed her gaze to Jerry. "Right, Jerry?"

Jerry nodded, seeming helpless.

"You bastard," Jade said to him.

"And that's how we found him," Holly added. "Through his cell phone."

"Jesus Christ," Jade whispered to herself.

"Look, don't matter to me who told what to who," Wes broke in. "We're taking you and Jade and the baby with us. We got an Airbnb nearby, in North Port. Once the money's transferred, then we'll boogie out of there with you still tied up. Once we're safe and sound in a galaxy far, far away, we'll make an anonymous call to the cops and let them know where you are."

Jerry doubted that. He felt in his bones that the only way for this character, Wes, and his buddy, Billy Ray, to feel safe and sound was for he and Jade to be dead. And Seius, too. As for Holly, he had no idea where she was coming from. That convinced Jerry that he had only one choice right now - to go along with whatever they were planning and hope that some opportunity would arise somewhere along the way to save himself and Jade and Seius from ultimate harm. Of course, after that, he'd have to deal with Jade's fury.

"You wanna hand her the baby," Wes said to Holly.

Holly looked dumbstruck a moment.

"Holly?" Wes repeated. "Ah, the baby?"

Seeming reluctant to give up the child, Holly drew him close to her bosom while Seius started fussing and struggling against her.

"Holly, Jesus, what's your fucking problem?"

Wes's shout finally broke the spell. Holly gave a meek smile, then strolled over and handed Seius over to Jade.

"Thank you," Jade said.

There were tears in Holly's eyes. "My one regret, never giving Jerry a child," she whispered, woman to woman. Jade had nothing to say to that. She looked down at the baby in her arms and smiled. Mollified and comforted, Seius seemed to relax and stopped fussing.

"Let me finish tying them up," Wes said.

He came over and used the nylon ties to secure Jerry's hands together on his lap. As promised, he kept Jade's arms free so she could hold the baby. Then he took the rope and tied it tightly around Jerry's and Jade's ankles with a fifteen inch width between them so that they could perp walk but not run off. After that, Wes told Holly to go get the cargo van and pull it into the driveway. It was time to get this show on the road, as he put. Billy Ray was on the couch, his eyes drooping as he aimed the pistol at the carpet.

"C'mon, Sleeping Bull," Wes said to him. "Help me move them to the van."

"Fuck you," was Billy Ray's response.

Chapter Thirty-Five

Kidnapped

~~~~~~

Wes had Billy Ray sit in the back compartment of the cargo van with Jerry and Jade holding the baby while Holly sat in the front passenger seat for the ride to their Airbnb rental in North Port.

A minute into the drive, Holly turned to Wes and said, "What did you mean back there when you mentioned after this going to a galaxy far, far away? You're not going back up to Buffalo from here after we get the money?"

"No," he said. "Why would I? There's nothing for me up there except bad memories."

"And where am I supposed to go?"

"I was hoping with me," Wes said. He winked at her and his mouth made a clicking sound.

"I hardly know you," she said.

He reached down and grabbed his crotch. "You know me well enough," he said. "And anyway, what the hell you got up there? Your mommy and daddy?"

She shrugged, turned and stared out the window.

"So, why not hide out with me?" Wes asked. "Become anonymous, in a galaxy far, far away."

"What - are you into that Star Wars shit? Next you'll be saying, the force be with you."

He laughed and told her, "And with you, too."

Holly turned to him again and asked, "What about your parole officer?"

"Fuck him," Wes said. "They'll never find me."

"Famous last words," Holly said. "Jerry's a lot smarter than you and he got found."

Holly turned and looked back at Billy Ray. "What about you, Billy Ray? Where you going after this?"

"He'll go back to the reservation and blow his hundred grand on booze and drugs," Wes chimed in, then glanced back at Billy Ray. "Right Crazy Horse?"

"Right, man," Billy Ray said. "Because that's what the red man do. Stay on the reservation, get drunk, get high, and screw fat Indian squaws, then beat them up."

Wes said, "That's about right. Just like your father."

After a silence, Billy Ray added, "I don't know what I'm doing, man."

After another couple minute lull in the conversation, Holly leaned toward Wes and whispered, "And you're not gonna kill them, right?" She nodded to the rear compartment.

Wes frowned, then shook his head. "No," he said, keeping his voice down. "No way."

Whispering, Holly asked, "You speaking for him, too?"

Holly glanced over her shoulder at Billy Ray who scowled back at her. She had no idea what he was thinking, but whatever it was, it worried her.

Then the baby was howling.

"He's hungry," Jade said.

Before leaving Jerry's house, Wes had let Jade pack a carton of milk, baby food, cereal, and apple juice containers in a large plastic baby storage container. Then, he let her fill up a diaper bag.

"Where we gonna go?" Holly asked Wes.

"What?"

"When we get the money," Holly said. "What state?"

"Montana," Wes said.

"Montana? Why there?"

"I don't have a fucking clue. Sounds like a wide-open space to hide out in." Then, Wes sang a line from a Frank Zappa song, "Going to Montana soon, gonna be a dental floss tycoon."

***

Fifteen minutes later, Wes backed the van into the Airbnb rental's driveway. Then, using a remote to lift the garage door, he pulled the van into the garage. After closing the door, he helped Billy Ray perp walk Jerry and Jade, still holding the baby, from the van's rear compartment, through the garage and into the house. As they did so, Wes backed off and broke out laughing.

"What's so fucking funny?" Billy Ray asked.

"They look like fucking penguins," Wes said.

Once inside, Jerry and Jade, holding the baby, were made to stand sheepishly in the middle of the gathering room waiting for orders.

Wes told Holly and Billy Ray, "We need to separate them. Put her and the baby in the extra guest room across from Billy Ray's, and Jerry in the walk-in closet of the master bedroom." He looked at Holly and laughed. "That way, he can watch us fuck." Turning to Jerry, he added, "I heard that from Jeff, may he rest in peace, that Jerry boy likes to watch people fuck."

"Shut up, Wes," Holly snapped.

The baby was wailing again and Jade said, "Look, I need to feed my son."

Wes shrugged. "Go ahead, feed him," he told her. "Does he still tit suck you? Now that, I'd like to see."

"Would you please shut the hell up, Wes," Holly said.

Wes frowned and said, "What? No, you shut up. Or I'll shut you the fuck up." He nodded to Jade holding the baby and added, "Help her and the kid to the table so she can quiet his screaming."

Holly went over, picked up the food storage container, and led Jade and the baby to the table.

"When we gonna make him transfer the money?" Billy Ray asked. "Get this over with."

"Now," Wes said.

He looked at Jerry and asked, "You can do it online, right? On our laptop?"

"Yes," Jerry replied. "But the money's scattered in foreign accounts, all under either Jade's name or an LLC we opened in New Mexico when we first hatched the plan to fake my death. Jeff Flaherty spearheaded that."

"Why fucking New Mexico?" Wes asked.

"Cause New Mexico's the only state that allows you to open an LLC without revealing the identity of the members," Jerry explained.

"So where these banks at?" Billy Ray asked. "What countries?"

"Cayman Islands, Switzerland, Singapore," Jerry answered. He looked across at Jade.

"Jade, what's the other one?"

"Belize," Jade replied, glaring at Jerry, still looking pissed as hell having learned only minutes ago that he'd been cavorting with Holly on the telephone the last two years.

"Alright," Wes said, "Have a seat at the dining room table over there, Jerry boy, across from your wife, while I go fetch the laptop. I'll do the typing but you gotta give me the bank information and passwords."

"I can't remember all that," Jerry said.

"What?"

"The accounts, the passwords," Jerry said. "All that's on my laptop back at the house. It's automatic when I call up the accounts, just to check the balances, make sure nothing's happened. I do that about twice a week or so."

Wes walked over to Jerry and gripped his right arm. With a sneer, he said, "Now you tell us? Why didn't you fucking mention that when we were at your fucking house?"

Jerry was about to say, well, you didn't ask, thought better of it, and merely shrugged deferentially and said, "Sorry, I didn't' think of it. Too much other shit on my mind, if you know what I mean."

"Fuck," Wes spat. He let go of Jerry's arm and gave him a mild shove, then turned to Billy Ray and Holly. "I gotta go back there, get his fucking laptop, bring it here."

Holly shook her head and whispered, "Idiot." Wes wasn't quite sure if she was talking about him or Jerry.

Wes turned to Jerry and asked, "Where is it, your fucking laptop?"

"In my studio, near the front of the house just off the foyer." Jerry said. "I think it's still on. Remember to bring the battery pack with it."

"Gimme the keys to the Fiesta," Wes told Holly. Shaking his head in disgust, he grabbed the Fiesta keys from Holly's outstretched hand and strode out the front door of house.

Sprawled out on the couch holding the pistol lazily on his lap, Billy Ray laughed and said, "What a cluster-fuck."

Chapter Thirty-Six

Swingers

Not five minutes after Wes left to retrieve Jerry's laptop, Billy Ray got up from the couch, crossed the room with the pistol dangling from his right hand and approached Jade at the dining room table as she was feeding Seius some dry Fruit Loops. From the other side of the table, Jerry tensed as the Seneca Indian with long, sticky wet, stark jet black hair leaned in close to her and, cheek to cheek, sniffed.

"You sure smell good," he whispered.

As he was doing that, Holly had gone and sat on a recliner.

"What're you doing?" Holly asked. "Leave her alone. Better watch it with her. She'll take you down."

Billy Ray stood up and laughed. "I needed a whiff of her beauty." He leaned down again within a couple feet of Jade's face. He jerked his head toward Holly and said, "Man, anyone ever tell you that you and her could pass for sisters?" He stood and glared at Holly. "She's your better looking younger sister."

"I'm younger," Holly said. She turned to Jade. "A year younger, right?"

"I have no idea," Jade said. "Nor do I care."

"Ah, c'mon," Holly said. "That's the only reason Jerry picked you. Isn't it, Jerry?" When Jerry didn't answer, she repeated, "I said, isn't it Jerry?"

Jerry seemed preoccupied staring at Billy Ray hovering over Jade.

"What?"

"The only reason you picked Jade is because she looks like me," Holly said.

The baby was shifting in Jade's arms as he reached for more cereal.

Jerry shook his head, signifying it was a silly question not worthy of an answer.

Billy Ray stood up and said, "What I wanna know is does she fuck like you, Holly?"

"I wouldn't know," Holly said.

Jade scowled in disgust.

He turned to Jerry and asked, "Well, does she?"

"Fuck you," Jerry said and glared up at Billy Ray.

"I'd really, really, really love to find out," Billy Ray said. He brushed the pistol through Jade's thick platinum blonde hair. "In fact, I'm getting hard thinking about it. See, I already fucked Holly."

Jerry put his elbows on the table and tried to stand, but the rope tied to his ankles caused him to buckle forward against the edge of the table.

"Sit down, hero," Billy Ray said. "I'll save my hard-on for later when me and Wes fuck your woman in front of you. Is it true what Wes said – you like watching that sort of thing?"

Holly got up and came over to Billy Ray. Standing next to him, she reached down and massaged his crotch.

"Forget about her," Holly told him. "You got me."

Jade swung Seius up against her shoulder and said, "Look, he doesn't need to hear this kind of talk. Lemme take him to the guest room. It's his nap time anyway. Okay?"

Billy Ray nodded and turned to Holly. "Yeah, go ahead take her," he told Holly.

Holly made a face, pushed herself out of the recliner and went over to the table. She helped Jade out the chair, lifted the storage container and diaper bag and led Jade to the short hallway leading to the guestroom.

While she was gone, Billy Ray strolled back to the couch and plopped down on it. He placed the pistol on the cushion next to him.

"You still married to Holly?" When Jerry didn't reply, Billy Ray grabbed the pistol and pointed it at him. "I asked you a question."

"Yeah," Jerry said. "Technically, we're still married. Legally, since I'm considered dead, I don't think so."

"Man, my head's fucking spinning with all this shit," Billy Ray said with a short laugh. "Well, as you like watching Holly fuck other men. So, when she gets back, I'll give you a treat. Alright?"

Jerry pursed his lips, shook his head. This situation was getting sicker by the moment. He was worried about what their ultimate plan was, if there was one, after the Global money was transferred over to whatever account that had been opened to receive it. He knew that once that happened, the double and triple and quadruple crosses would commence, and he had the definite feeling none of them was good for him and Jade and the baby, and likely for Holly as well.

"Man, dude, I asked you another question," Billy Ray

said. "You want the treat of watching me fuck Holly?"

"Fuck you," Jerry hissed.

From the couch, Billy Ray chuckled. After a moment, he said, "You know what? When she gets back, I'd rather be the...what's it called." He frowned. "The voyeur." Billy Ray laughed and added, "I'll have her suck your dick."

Holly walked into the living room just then and, frowning, asked, "Who's sucking who's dick?"

"Go over and suck his," Billy Ray told her.

"Screw off," Holly replied.

Now, he pointed the pistol at her.

"I said, go, do it," Billy Ray. When Holly gave him a double-take, he snapped, "Yeah, right now. In fact, go get that Jade broad first so she can watch you suck her man's cock."

"You're sick," Holly said and made a face.

"I'm not kidding around," Billy Ray said, "I'm telling you to go fetch that Jade bitch, bring her out here so she can watch you go down on her boyfriend."

When nothing happened, Billy Ray stood. In the next moment, he aimed the pistol at the wall to the right of Holly and fired. The sound was loud, hurting everyone's ears. A gash of blown up drywall marred the wall and splinters and dust from it settled onto the carpet below.

Jade scampered out from the bedroom, barely able to keep herself from falling down with her ankles tied together. Her wide eyes begged for an answer to her frantic question, "What was that?" From the guest bedroom, Seius cried.

Holly and Jerry were like statues, transfixed by the sudden violence of Billy Ray's actions. He stood across the room with the pistol in his hand, his mouth slack.

Then, he smiled and said, "Ah, perfect. You're here. You can watch Holly give your man a blow job."

Billy Ray pointed the pistol at Holly and said, "So, go ahead. Do it."

Holly swallowed and feeling light-headed, ambled over to where Jerry sat.

Billy Ray came over from the couch and sneering, pointed the pistol at Jerry and said, "Move your chair around so she can kneel in between your legs." After Jerry wiggled around and moved the chair on an angle away from the table, Billy Ray said, "Perfect," then, to Holly, he said, "Now get down in there, between his legs."

With a tired sigh, Holly did as he said.

"Lower his shorts," was Billy Ray's next order.

Holly put her fingers over the belt-line of Jerry's shorts

and pulled them and his boxers so that Jerry's limp penis was visible.

"That's a dick?" Billy Ray laughed. He looked at Holly and said, "No wonder why you went after fresh meat. Now, go ahead, get him hard."

Holly leaned forward to his Jerry's limp penis and started licking it. It was something she'd done countless times before and oddly enough, despite the situation, she enjoyed doing it now, and enjoyed it even more knowing that Jade was watching her. After a minute, she got a bigger thrill when Jerry started getting hard.

"Yeah, that's it," Billy Ray whispered. "Suck it."

Jerry had closed his eyes and whispered, "No, no." He opened them and squinted at Jade who stood there, her arms limp at her side, watching the spectacle of Holly sucking Jerry's cock. Then, she closed her eyes, bit her lower lip, close to tears.

"Come on," ranted Billy Ray. "Get fucking hard. I want you to come in her mouth. Then, I'll make her go over and kiss Jade."

Holly raised up and looked at Billy Ray. "I'm not doing this anymore," she said. "He can't get hard."

"No," Billy Ray snapped. He jutted out the pistol and said, "Keep trying. If you don't, this time I'll put a hole in you instead of the wall."

After a sigh, she lowered her head again to Jerry's crotch.

Then, in the next moment, Wes came walking through the front door of the house carrying Jerry's laptop. He stopped in this tracks and jerked back a moment when he saw Holly kneeling between Jerry's legs.

"What the fuck's that?" He laughed and said, "You guys having a swinger's party?"

"Jerry got horney," Billy Ray said. "Holly got horney. I got horney. Not sure about Jade."

Wes went over and set Jerry's laptop down along the side of the dining room table. Still on her knees, Holly had straightened and looked up at him.

"Billy Ray made me," Holly said.

Ignoring her, Wes said, "Well, since Jerry's doing my girl, I'm gonna hafta do his." He looked across at Jade and gave her a crooked smile. Then he looked at Billy Ray and said, "And since you've got the gun, I guess you're gonna hafta help me."

"Sounds like a plan, amigo," Billy Ray said. "Let's get this swinger party going."

Chapter Thirty-Seven

Gone

Victor and Gregor's Jet Blue flight into Sarasota-Bradenton International Airport was thirty minutes late. After taxiing to the gate, they didn't deplane until ten-thirty. Tired and crabby from having to get up so early, Victor was grumbling and cursing under his breath as he and Gregor strode from the gate to the main terminal and took an escalator down to the baggage claim area.

Victor had checked his TSA regulation gun case containing his two Glocks, one for him, one for Gregor, at ticketing back in Buffalo. Now, they had to wait another ten minutes for it to finally show up on the baggage claim carousel. While he was doing that, Gregor stood in the

Budget rental car line.

Grumbling again as they drove out of the airport in a rented Toyota Siena van at nearly eleven, Victor said, "Jesus, comrade, it's fucking hot down here."

"Yeah, hot," Gregor agreed.

Making a left turn out of the airport terminal exit road onto University Parkway, they had a forty-minute ride ahead of them when Victor called Neal Barrett.

"We here," he told him.

"Good," Barrett said. "You guys ready."

"Yeah, all set," Victor said.

"You're leaving right after capturing him, right?"

"Yes, we capture this Jerry," Victor said, "drive Buffalo."

"It's like a twenty hour drive from there, right?"

"Twenty, twenty-two," Victor said. "Depend how much we stop."

"So you'll arrive around ten, eleven tomorrow morning?" Barrett asked.

"Yeah, morning, ten, eleven, we make good time," Victor agreed. "If not, maybe later. one, two."

"I'm flying up to Buffalo this afternoon," Barrett said. "I'm meeting with a state cop named Dan Miller. Reynolds put me in touch with him. So, when you're a couple hours away, let us know. I'll have Miller and some cops waiting for you in a parking lot to take custody of Jerry. I'll tell you exactly where later. Okay?"

"Yeah, okay. As long as get paid," Victor said. Then, he asked, "He knows, this Reynolds, what we do?"

"No, I told him I was meeting with Miller to coordinate a plan for Jerry Shaw's voluntary surrender. He doesn't know I'm coordinating his actual capture."

"What about the million dollars this Jerry owe?" Victor asked.

"Well, if he wants a decent plea, he'll hand it over," Barrett said. "The point is, we'll have the leverage. He plays hardball, he goes to jail longer. You understand? *Ponyat*."

"Yeah," Victor laughed. "*Ponyat*." Then, he added, "We see."

***

At eleven-thirty that morning, Victor pulled the Siena along the side of Dennison Road about thirty yards from its intersection with Manasota Beach Road. A little more than three hours earlier, Wes Chandler had parked the rented cargo van along the exact same spot.

To the right of the van was some high brush and trees

that hid Jerry's house.

"It's beyond this shit," Victor said nodding to it as he turned off the van. He looked at Gregor and said, "You ready."

Gregor nodded and said, "Yes, ready."

"Get guns," Victor said. Gregor had the gun case on his lap holding their two pistols. He opened it and handed Victor one of them and took out the other one for himself.

With the pistol secure in his hand, locked and loaded, Victor nodded and said, "We go."

After exiting the Siena, they slipped through the bushes onto Jerry's property. It was quiet, too quiet, thought Victor. Holding the pistol in his right hand, he led Gregor to the back of the house. Turning a corner, they saw it – the smashed out sliding glass doors – and stopped in their tracks.

"*Kakugo khrena*," Victor growled, meaning "what the fuck," in English.

"Somebody here already, boss," Gregor said.

Victor looked at him and said, "No shit!"

They walked cautiously forward and entered the back of the house through the shattered sliding glass door. After searching every room and finding the house deserted, Gregor commented, "Somebody grab them already."

"Yes," Victor agreed. "I know."

"Who?"

"*Chto, yesli ya znayu*," said Victor. Fuck if I know, it meant.

For some reason, Gregor laughed.

"I call boss," Victor said.

After Barrett answered, Victor told him the news – Jerry's house had been broken into sometime earlier and Jerry, Jade and the baby were gone.

"Gone? Gone where?"

"Don't know."

"Fuck," Barrett said.

"Yeah, fuck."

"So, now?" Victor asked. "We fly back?"

Barrett didn't answer for time, then said, "No, stay put. Book a hotel room. We'll get Jack Fox to help us figure this out."

Victor laughed. "Yeah, good luck," he said

Chapter Thirty-Eight

Go F--- Yourself

~~~~~

Barrett told Victor to call Boris and have him untie Jack Fox. After that, he was to direct Fox to call him. Fox placed that call while still in the basement of his house with the thick-bodied henchman, Boris, standing sheepishly beside him.

"What the fuck is going on?" Fox demanded.

"I dunno," Barrett said. "You tell me."

"What's that supposed to mean?"

"Just wondering if you've been keeping a little secret about our mutual pal, Jerry Shaw," Barrett said. "Kinda curious that you had his number under Anonymous Man in your phone contacts. I'm sure if we checked, we'd find out it's been there a while."

While kidnapped, Fox had time to think about his response to an accusation like that. He hadn't come up with a good answer. "You think what you want," was the best he could come up with.

"Alright, maybe we'll get to the bottom of it, maybe we won't," Barrett replied. "But now your friend, Jerry, may have a bigger problem on his hands."

"Yeah, like what kind of bigger problem?"

"Someone got to him before we could," Barrett said.

"What'dya mean?"

Barrett told him about Victor's planned raid on Jerry's house with his "colleague," Gregor, that had come up empty and worse, gave them good cause to believe that someone had already kidnapped Jerry and whomever else had been living with him.

"Jade and their baby," Fox said.

"Who?"

It was at that moment when, having been summoned by Barrett a few minutes earlier, Chief Reynolds strolled into his makeshift office. As he sat down on a chair facing Barrett's desk, he shrugged as if asking why he'd been summoned.

"I've got your old investigator, Jack Fox, on the phone," Barrett said. "Let me put him on speaker."

Reynolds shrugged, still unclear what this was about.

"Okay, Jack, you're on speaker," Barrett said.

"Hey, Jack," Reynolds said.

"Hey, Chief."

"Let me fill the Chief in on what's going on," Barrett said.

Barrett spent the next couple minutes bringing Chief Reynolds up to speed.

"So, you hired some Russian free agent goons to kidnap Jerry Shaw?" Reynolds asked Barrett.

"It's not kidnapping," Barrett replied. "It's bounty hunting."

"How'd that work out for you?"

"As I just told you, it hasn't, at least not yet."

Reynolds called into the phone, "And, Jack, what's your role in this?"

"My role? I've been kidnapped by Mr. Barrett's Russian idiots and had my phone stolen."

"What about what Mister Barrett here says," Reynolds said. "That your in cahoots with our Mister Shaw?"

"He and his Russian stooges can go fuck themselves. And you too for that matter."

Despite feeling in his bones that Barrett was probably right, and that for some reason Jack Fox had developed some kind of bizarre connection with Jerry Shaw - a.k.a., The Anonymous Man – Chief Reynolds couldn't help but laugh at his old pal's brazen effrontery.

"Well, besides the history between you and Jerry Shaw, the point now, Jack," Reynolds said, "is there any way you can think of that'll help us help Jerry Shaw assuming he's been kidnapped by someone ahead of us?"

There was dead silence for a time.

Finally, Fox said, "Yeah, maybe." After another few moments, he said, "Through Holly. Holly Shaw."

"His wife?" Barrett asked. "How?"

"She knows Jerry's alive," Fox said, revealing more than he intended to by divulging that. "And she's kept in contact with him. So, she's the only one, other than me, who might be able to lead us to him – if, she hasn't already done that with someone else."

"Like who?" Barrett asked. "Who somebody else?"

"I have no idea," Fox said. "But my point is, she's the best and only lead we have. So, I suggest we check her out."

"We?" Reynolds asked.

"Yeah, we," Fox said. "I'd like to help this Jerry fella get out of whatever bind he's gotten himself into."

Reynolds looked at Barrett and said, "I suggest we take him up on it."

Barrett shrugged, not disagreeing. "Sure, what do you have in mind, Jack?"

"First thing we gotta do," he said, "is find Holly Shaw."

Chapter Thirty-Nine

Holly's Mom

The search for Holly Shaw led to her parents' three-bedroom, Cape Cod house on a side street in the small, in the rather dreary looking village called Blasdell just south of Buffalo. After shewing Boris out of the house, with Barrett's approval, Fox quickly showered and dressed. Right around two-thirty, he stepped onto the same porch where Holly had first met Wes Chandler.

Holly's maiden name was Blanchard. Her mother's name was Grace.

Grace opened the front door a crack a few seconds after Fox had rang the doorbell.

"Help you?"

"Yes," Fox said. "Name's Jack Fox. I'm here to see your daughter, Holly."

"Holly? Why?"

"I don't know if you remember me, Mrs. Blanchard," Fox explained, "but I was the investigator for Global Life and Casualty Insurance who investigated the Jerry Shaw claim. I testified at Holly's murder trial."

Mrs. Blanchard opened the door wider and squinted at Fox. "Yes, I remember you," she said without animosity. "Does this have something to do with that?"

"Maybe," Fox said. "I think Holly can shed some light on a certain something. So, if I could please talk to her, that'd be great." Then, he added, " I mean, she's not in trouble or anything." Not yet, at least, he didn't add.

"Well, Holly's not here," Grace said.

"Do you expect her back sometime today?"

"No. See, she's down in Florida. She went there with a couple, ah, friends, looking for work. And better weather, I guess, though this time of year it has to be hot down there."

"Speaking of hot," Fox said and laughed as he rubbed his brow. "It's quite steamy out here."

"Oh, of course, c'mon in," Grace said.

"That'd be great," Fox said.

Grace stepped back and let him enter into the short foyer, then gestured into the living room. She went over and nodded to a couch and said, "Here, sit."

As Fox obeyed, Grace asked, "Want a glass of water?"

"No, I'm fine," Fox said. As Grace sat in an armchair next to the couch, Fox asked, "So, were the friends Holly went down to Florida with men or women?"

"Men," Grace said. "Two of them, like I said. She supposedly knew them from college, at Binghamton." She shook her head and added, "Though they didn't look like college graduates."

"Look, I'm gonna level with you, Mrs. Blanchard," Fox said. "I think Holly's gotten herself into some trouble with those two lads traveling down with her to Florida."

Grace looked down at her lap and regretfully whispered, "I knew it."

"Is there any way you can help me get in touch with her down there?"

Grace looked up. She thought a moment, then told Fox, "Maybe. They used my credit card to rent a house down there."

"Yeah, that should work," he said. "You have the card number somewhere, and the security code?"

"Yes, I keep all that written down."

"Perfect," Fox said. "You have online access?"

"What's that?"

Fox smiled. "You can get access to the card online, on the computer. I can help you set it up at the bank's online site. I might need your social security number. Okay?"

"Yes, sure," Grace said. "Anything to keep Holly out of trouble." She laughed. "She's named after my Aunt Holly." She giggled, then said, "They're both troublemakers." Then, she frowned and asked, "Do you really think Holly killed her husband, Jerry? He was a such a nice boy. She claims she didn't, but I don't know." She drew in a breath and added, "She's been such a disappointment to Frank and me. Not like her brother, Raymond. He turned out fine. Has a good job, great wife, and gave us two wonderful granddaughters."

Grace sighed and continued, "We all felt that Holly would amount to something special, maybe even become a movie star. From the time she was a little girl, she wanted to be an actress. She went to lessons. She was good, too. A lot of people told her she had great potential. Frank and I used to love going to her plays, especially during college. But once she graduated, she seemed to give up on her dream of going to Hollywood. She got a job at a law office, and that was okay. And she and Jerry seemed to be happy, even though they couldn't give us grandkids." After another long sigh, she added, "Then she met that Jeff Flaherty, and it's been nothing but trouble ever since."

"A lot of people give up on their dreams, Mrs. Blanchard," Fox said. "Maybe that's what's wrong with the world."

"Yeah," Grace said. "Anyways, I just don't want her to get mixed up in any more trouble."

"Well, with your help, maybe we can prevent that from happening," Fox said. "Okay?"

Chapter Forty

Break In The Case

~~~

Around three that same afternoon, Dean Alessi took a call from Assistant District Attorney, Jack Brewster.

"We received a strange referral late this morning," Brewster told Dean. "Global insurance filed a criminal complaint against one Jerry Shaw. They claim he defrauded them by faking his death, collected four million dollars on their life insurance policy, and that he's been essentially living as a ghost down your way in Florida ever since."

"Yeah?"

"Yeah," Brewster went on, "See, it's related to a murder case our office handled not long after the insurance claim was filed with Global. The defendants were this Jerry fellow's widow, Holly, and her then boyfriend, Jeff Flaherty. The victim was – you guessed it – Jerry Shaw. Holly and Jeff claimed at the time that they hadn't murdered Jerry, but that they'd faked his death, that he was in on it, and that he was still alive. The police and our office didn't buy it, so we put them on trial for Jerry's murder. They ended up pleading to lesser charges after the trial started, but were released from their prison sentences six months later on a speedy trial technicality."

"Yeah, so?" Dean asked. "What are you...?"

"See, we just found out, they were being honest," Brewster said. "Jerry, with them, really did fake his death. And he's alive and well living down your way the last five years.

"Anyway," Brewster went on, "Global's criminal complaint against this Jerry Shaw was assigned to Special Investigations – it's the kind of case we handle – and, when I reviewed the paperwork, you know what, I thought of you. You know, that conversation we had a couple days back about some guy who's been in hiding for the same amount of years that this Jerry fellow went missing and now wants to turn himself it. A light-bulb clicked off in my head – maybe the guy down in Florida who'd hired you and wanted to turn himself in and give back certain money he'd stolen, happened to be this Jerry Shaw fellow. I became even more suspicious about that when I later learned that Jerry had been living in your neck of the woods in a house in a place called Englewood down there."

"Yeah, Englewood's the next town over from Venice," Dean said. "But where's this leading, Jack? My client, whomever that is, whether it's Jerry Shaw, or eight billion other people in the world, is still protected by attorney-client privilege."

"I realize that, Dean," Brewster said. "But I thought you might like to know that the game has changed since we spoke. See, charges have been filed on the strength of Global's criminal complaint and some other evidence, and a warrant for Jerry Shaw's arrest has been issued. It's been sent down to the Sarasota County Sheriff. They're in the process of serving it. Only, you see, there's a little complication that I thought you should know about, if, as it turns out, you really are Jerry Shaw's counsel."

"What kind of complication?"

"It appears that Jerry's been kidnapped by his wife, or former wife, or whatever she is - this Holly Shaw gal, and two male associates she's hanging out with these days," Brewster said. "We suspect they came for Jerry to, you know, convince him to hand over the million bucks Global says is still missing out of the four they originally paid out.

"Anyway, the local cops down there are arranging a SWAT team rescue operation at the location where they think Jerry's being held – an Airbnb rental in North Port, Florida. That near you, too?"

"Yes, North Port," Dean said. "It's just south of Venice." After a sigh, Dean asked, "So, when are they moving on that, the SWAT operation?"

"They're planning it as we speak," Brewster said. "Hey, if you admit you're this Jerry's counsel, I could notify the cops down there and have you brought into their confidence. Because, you know, I wouldn't want those same cops to inadvertently violate any of this Jerry fellas constitutional rights."

Dean laughed and said, "You're one sly prosecutor. And friend, even though I did stiff you out of a job." He sighed and added, "Yeah, Jerry Shaw's mine. Unfortunately, looks like all the bargaining chips have been taken out of his hands."

"Well, it might end up being worse than that for him," Brewster said.

"How so?"

"He might end up dead."

***

Victor and Gregor were parked on Torrego Street a few houses down from the Airbnb rental where Barrett had told them within the hour that Jerry Shaw was being held by his ex-wife and her two male friends. According to Barrett, it appeared that this group of miscreants were the ones who'd broken the sliding glass door in the back of Jerry's Englewood house in the process of kidnapping him.

These facts made little sense to Victor. Now Barrett was ordering him to rescue Jerry out of the North Port Airbnb and drive him up north back to Buffalo. Barrett had also warned him to exercise extreme caution in doing so as the ex-wife, Holly Shaw, and her associates were likely armed and dangerous.

"Dangerous?" Victor had scoffed with a laugh.

But then, five minutes later, Barrett called Victor back and told him to stand-down.

"Stand-down? What mean?"

Barrett told him that it had been decided by his superiors, Chief Reynolds prominently among them, to file criminal charges with the local prosecutor up in Buffalo and turn this into an official police matter.

"*Der'mo*!" Victor shouted after he clicked off the call with Barrett and slammed his palms on the steering wheel of the rented Siena van. "Shit!"

"What?" Gregor asked.

"Bastards take case from us," he said. "I not fulfill contract, I not get paid. Except my expenses, a few bucks."

"Shit is right," Gregor agreed. "Why? What happened?"

"They found this Jerry guy, and other guys who kidnapped him before we could," Victor explained. "The cops, they in it now, will come, attack house, capture Jerry. Global has made formal charge with police. So, after they grab him, Florida cops will send him north to face judge.

"So goddamn Barrett wants us should fly back tonight and he settles with me in morning," Victor added. "But no way he's gonna pay my contract – I lose fifty fucking grand." He looked over at Gregor. "But you and Boris, I still pay."

Gregor nodded.

Victor took out his cell phone and started checking for flights back up to Philadelphia. Barrett said they could meet at two the next afternoon in his office to settle things. After a minute, he lowered the phone.

"You know what?" he said, then looked at Gregor. "Fuck them. Let's do job anyway."

"Do job? What job?"

"Capture this Jerry," Victor said. He nodded to the house a few hundred feet down the road where Jerry was being held. "Cops not come for a while. We got time. We can take him."

"Then what?"

"Then, we got leverage," Victor said. "I bargain. Give Jerry to cops, I get money under contract. Everyone happy."

"You think?"

Victor laughed and said, "What else they gonna do? Arrest us?"

Chapter Forty-One

Rescue

～●～

"We go in back to sliding glass door," Victor told Gregor. "We sneak up, check inside. See what's what." He nodded to the back row behind them. "Take crowbar." He gestured to the outside and said to Gregor, "*Poydem*," meaning, "Let's go," in Russian.

Victor and Gregor simultaneously exited the Siena with Gregor clutching a crowbar. They seemed calm, though their insides were churning. They were going into battle and there was no telling how it would turn out. Having the element of surprise on their side was a positive, but it didn't negate the ever-present danger of death toward which they might be heading. They had no idea about the capabilities of Holly

Shaw's two guy friends. Likely, they were idiots, amateurs, no match for Russian mercenaries. But there was always the possibility that they were professional killers and Victor and Gregor would be no match for them or that luck would not be on their side.

As they approached the front of the Airbnb rental, Victor pointed to his right and as he turned that way, he crouched down with Gregor duck-walking behind him. The house looked unoccupied, as if everyone inside was asleep, and Victor hoped momentarily that they'd caught them literally napping. The Ford Fiesta had turned in the driveway ten minutes ago, and the driver, a tall man with long sandy blonde hair, had exited the car and carrying a laptop, walked up the narrow cement path to the porch and then entered the house seeming without concern.

As they hugged the side of the house in the blaring, hot sun, with the air temperature registering in the mid-nineties and the real-feel above one-hundred, Victor turned to Gregor and said, "Ready?"

Gregor's eyes widened. His face was flushed. He nodded, smiled and said, "*Da.*"

They hustled along the side wall to the back of the house and found themselves standing at the rear corner looking into a screened in lanai with a sliding glass door that allowed entrance into the kitchen. Victor took box cutters from the rear pocket of his shorts, easily sliced through the black screen, and then loped through the opening with Gregor right behind him. Standing there a moment, Victor looked at Gregor, nodded and said, "Let's go. *Russkiy forvard.*"

***

Wes had led Jerry from the dining room table to a chair Billy Ray had placed in the master bedroom a few feet away from the large king-sized bed. While he was doing that, Billy Ray had pointed the pistol at Jade and gestured for her to follow Wes.

"C'mon, guys," Holly had said as she crowded into the bedroom behind Wes, Billy Ray, Jade and Jerry. "Don't do this."

"Just go check on the baby," Billy Ray snapped at her.

"Thought you'd like to watch," Wes said to Holly with a laugh after he grabbed Jade by the shoulders. Jade gave him a defiant snarl as he forced her to sit down on the bed.

With the pistol limp in his right hand, Billy Ray watched Wes as he pushed Jade backwards onto the bed and then swing her legs up and around so that she ended up in a prone position. As Wes tugged Jade's shorts, then panties, down to her tied up ankles, she whimpered helplessly.

"You motherfuckers," Jerry hissed.

Wes turned and grinned at Jerry. "Yes, we are both about to be motherfuckers," he said, trying to be funny. He turned to Billy Ray and asked, "Mind if I go first?"

From the guestroom on the other side of the house, Seius could be heard crying.

Billy Ray shrugged. "Yeah, go ahead," he said. "Break her in for me. But you're gonna hafta untie her legs to get your face and dick in there."

Wes looked down at Jade. Billy Ray was right. With her ankles tied together, there was no way to open her up.

"Yeah," he said. After a shrug, he looked at Billy Ray holding the pistol. "She ain't going anywhere."

As Wes snapped apart the nylon ties, Holly said, "You guys gotta stop this."

"Don't worry, hon," Wes said as he pulled down his shorts to his boxers. "You'll be next."

Holly edged over toward Billy Ray as Wes pulled down his boxers, then took off his tee shirt. Standing naked before everyone now, he raised his arms and grinned as he made a full circle turn to show off his manhood.

"You call that a dick," Billy Ray said with a laugh.

The gun was still hanging loose in his right hand and he didn't seem to notice that Holly had edged within a couple feet of him.

"Fuck you," Wes replied as he lifted his privates in a show of bravado for Billy Ray's benefit. "You wish you had a tool this ginormous."

As Wes stepped toward the edge of the bed, he started massaging his penis. Glancing back at Billy Ray, he said with a laugh, "Should I eat her out first?" His grin turned into a frown when he saw Holly suddenly make a grab for Billy Ray's right hand. "Look out!"

She was clutching the pistol and almost had pulled it from Billy Ray's hand when Wes strode over and threw an overhand right with all his force along the side of her head. Holly let go of Billy Ray's wrist and fell with a thud to the carpeted floor.

"What the fuck you trying to do, you stupid cunt?" Wes shouted.

***

Staring into the living room, Victor and Gregor saw nothing, no people, no activity. The only sound was the occasion cry of a baby.

"Where they?" Gregor asked.

Victor shrugged. He gestured to the locked sliding glass door and ordered Gregor, "Use crowbar, open. Try not break glass. Okay."

Gregor nodded and deftly inserted the pry end of the crowbar to snap open the door.

"Good," Victor said. "Now we go, do rescue."

After sliding open the door, Victor and Gregor crept into the living room and stopped a moment to listen to muffled conversation and laughter coming from the master bedroom.

Lifting his Glock to eye level, Victor nodded for Gregor to follow him. They edged forward cautiously into a small hallway past a door to the A/C unit only three steps to the open door that led into the master bedroom. All at once, there was yelling and a smack of a fist and someone shouting.

As Victor and Gregor slowly entered the room, a naked Wes, and his long-haired Indian accomplice, Billy Ray, were glaring down at Holly writhing on the carpeted floor. She'd clearly been struck by one of them. On the bed lay another woman, her shorts and panties pulled down to her ankles. On a chair sat a man with a deep scowl. Victor immediately decided that this guy must be Jerry Shaw.

Without comment, Victor pulled up his Glock and shot the naked man – Wes - through the back of the head. Before Billy Ray could bring up his pistol, Gregor had put a bullet through his forehead. It was over in less than ten seconds.

What remained were the screams and groans of Holly, Jade and Jerry. From a room somewhere at the front of the house, Seius shrieked.

Chapter Forty-Two

Another Kidnapping

Gregor went over to the bed and helped a shocked and sullen Jade to sit up. After she pulled up her panties and shorts, he gently moved her off the bed. On their way out of the master bedroom, she glanced back at the bodies of Wes Chandler and Billy Ray Blacksnake that still lay sprawled on the carpet stained with their blood and brains.

Once outside the master bedroom Gregor took Jade by the arm and escorted her to the guest bedroom where the baby was still crying.

"Your kid?" he asked along the way.

"Yes," she whispered, still shell-shocked and afraid despite Gregor's kindly demeanor.

Upon entering the guest bedroom, Seius looked up and saw Jade, and immediately stopped crying and reached for her. Jade hurried over and lifted him off the bed. Clutching his mother around her shoulders, Seius took several gulps of air as he settled down.

"You stay here," Gregor said. "Okay? We mean no harm - you, others. Okay?"

Jade nodded and said, "Okay."

While Gregor led Jade out of the master bedroom, Victor attended to Holly. She had a welt across her forward and she'd been sprayed with Billy Ray's blood.

Victor leaned down and asked her, "You okay? Can stand, walk?"

Seeming numb to some degree, Holly managed a short nod.

"Okay," Victor said. He reached his hand down. When she clutched it, he pulled her up. Standing now, Victor noticed that she was trembling.

"Look, I take you out of here," he told her. "Sit on couch. Okay?"

"Yeah," Holly said. "I'll be alright. Just wipe this blood off me."

With a nod, Victor led Holly into the en suite. "Here, you wash," he told her. He waited while she took some soap and splashed water on her face and used a towel to wash off the blood.

"Now, come."

Victor escorted Holly out of the master bathroom and out of the bedroom to the gathering room and sat her on the couch. She had a glazed look and a bump developing on the side of her head where Wes had smacked her. Taking a plastic supermarket bag from inside a drawer at the kitchen counter, Victor went to the fridge and filled it with ice. He returned to Holly and, after putting the bag of ice on the bump, causing her to wince, he told her to hold it there.

After that, Victor returned to the master bedroom for Jerry.

"Who are you guys?" Jerry asked.

"We?" Victor laughed. "Superheroes. Come for rescue."

"Yeah, right. Really, who are you?"

"We work Global. You know them?"

"Yeah, I know them." Jerry sighed and said, "So now what?"

"Now, we take you and girl from here," Victor said. "To safe place."

"Like where?"

"You see when get there," Victor said.

Gregor had walked into the master bedroom.

"What do here?" Victor scolded him. "Go watch girl on couch."

"She okay," Gregor said, scowling. "Sleeping."

Victor said something in Russian. Orders, Jerry figured.

After Gregor left the room, Victor looked at Jerry and said, "Now, we go."

"All of us?"

"No, just you and girl on couch," Victor said. "The other one, she stay here with baby. Okay with that?"

"Yeah. All I care about is that she and the baby are safe."

"She safe, baby's safe," Victor said. "Police coming, any minute. Okay?"

"Yeah, okay."

Victor came over and helped Jerry to his feet. He then led him out into the living room. Gregor was sitting next to Holly. Victor said something to Gregor in Russian. Gregor nodded, dug into his pants and pulled out a long nylon tie. Then, with the tie in his hand, he got up from the couch and strode across the living room to the short hallway leading to the guest bedroom. All the while, Holly appeared to be sleeping on the couch.

"Where's he going?" Jerry asked Victor.

"He tie woman's legs to bedpost," Victor said. "She be okay. Like I say, police coming."

"Can I say goodbye to her?" Jerry asked.

"No, no time for goodbyes," Victor replied. "We go." He nodded to the dining room table and said, "Laptop, that yours?"

Jerry nodded. This was no time to get cute.

When Gregor returned in the next minute after tying up Jade, Victor told Gregor to fetch the laptop on the table and hand it over to him. After Gregor did so, Victor nodded to Holly and said, "Bring her."

Holly groaned as Gregor put his hands under her armpits and lifted her off the couch.

"No," she whined. "Sleep. My head."

When Gregor looked at Victor, he shrugged and said, "She be okay. Has concussion. Help her. We go out back, same way we came in." Then, he nodded to Jerry and said, "Let's go."

Chapter Forty-Three

Ransom

Victor drove the Siena to a Hampton Inn in North Port only five minutes from the Airbnb rental where he and Gregor had killed Wes Chandler and Billy Ray Blacksnake. The rooms were surprisingly expensive, over two hundred dollars a night for what seemed like such an out of the way hotel across from a Lowe's hardware megastore and a Culver's restaurant.

Victor went into the lobby to book a room while Gregor held a pistol on Jerry and the still sleepy Holly in the back row of seats. The tinted windows of the van hid anyone outside from seeing him doing that.

Ten minutes later, Victor opened the driver's side door

and hopped up into the van.

"You get room?" Gregor asked.

"Yeah. First floor. Perfect. I park behind the hotel and we sneak them through back entrance, okay?"

"Yeah, okay, but let's go," Gregor said. "I need take shit."

Victor drew a breath and shook his head, tired of dealing with this Russian brute.

He drove the van around back and parked in a mostly empty row a few spaces down from a rear entrance. After waiting a minute to make sure no one was around, Victor exited the van with Gregor. Victor opened the sliding door to the rear compartment and grabbed Jerry while Gregor pulled Holly off the backseat and out the side door right after them. Jerry offered no resistance as Victor perp walked him to the back entrance door.

Within two minutes, they were in a cramped room stuffed with two queen beds, a small desk, a chair in the corner, and a three-drawer fake oak dresser with a cheap 50 inch, flat screen TV on top of it.

After Gregor laid Holly on one of the beds, he turned to Victor and said, "She bad off. Think need doctor?"

"No clue," Victor said. "But even so, cannot take her. She survive, she survive. If die, die."

"So what's your plan?" Jerry asked Victor, clearly the leader. "Where you taking me?"

"Taking you? Nowhere. We make deal with Global, tell them where find you, we go, they come, take you back to Buffalo."

Jerry nodded, getting it now. Victor was double-crossing Global. Jerry also knew that Victor's double-cross wasn't good for him. He'd cease being the anonymous man, but not on his terms. His bargaining power had been liquidated. But maybe that's what he deserved. He only hoped that Jade would avoid trouble for being his front all these years. That worried him more than his own well-being. He also couldn't be angry at this Victor fellow and his Russian henchman. After all, they'd likely saved his life and the lives of Jade and Seius. He looked over at Holly laying motionless on the bed and worried whether they'd saved her life as well.

Victor was on his cell phone now, calling whomever at Global, most likely Jack Fox's old boss, Chief Reynolds. But Victor surprised him when he asked to speak with someone named Neal Barrett.

***

"We gotta make new deal," Victor said.

"What?" Barrett asked. "What are you talking about? What new deal? Where are you?"

"I'm with that Jerry guy," Victor said.

"Shaw? Jerry Shaw?"

"Yeah. We stole him from you."

"What?"

Victor laughed and asked, "How much worth it to you knowing where he is? My contract was fifty. I say you send me that and another hundred."

"What for?"

"I told you. I got Jerry guy. And his laptop. Key to money. Million bucks." Victor laughed. "Fuck, maybe I take the million and fuck Global. Then let Jerry fellow go."

"I can't believe this shit, Victor," Barrett said. "You'll never work for Global again."

Victor laughed and replied, "Who wants work for idiots?"

After Barrett seethed behind the desk in his makeshift office across from the one Reynolds still occupied, he whispered, "So what's the deal."

"First, you send one hundred fifty to my account," Victor said. "Then, I leave Jerry. After couple hours, I call, tell you where Jerry is. He has his laptop, so he sends his million back to you. Okay?"

"Yeah, okay."

"Everybody wins," Victor said. "Right? Me, you." He laughed and added, "Only Jerry loses."

"Fuck you, Victor," Barrett said.

"Why? I make you look bad?" Victor laughed. "You still get money, be hero."

"Like I said, Victor, fuck you."

"As you wish. Now, I wait for one hundred fifty to my account. Better not wait long, okay?"

Victor didn't wait long. Immediately after hanging up with Neal Barrett, Victor opened Jerry's laptop and powered it up.

Chapter Forty-Four

A Triple-Cross

"What're doing?" Jerry asked.

"What password you?"

"Why?"

"I want get in."

Jerry frowned. "Why?"

Victor shook his head, as if Jerry had said something idiot. "Why, else?" he asked Jerry. "To get money – million dollars."

From the chair in the corner, Gregor laughed. "Yes, good idea."

Victor glared at him, then turned to Jerry. Jerry nodded, sighed, then said, "It's anonymous. The password."

"Of course. Why not?" Victor laughed. "Anonymous."

"So, you're triple-crossing Global?"

As Victor typed in "anonymous" and the laptop screened flashed with various icons, he shrugged and said, "Sure. Why not? I take money, use as leverage. I give most back. Some, I keep. Global, they no miss it. They billion dollar corporation." He turned to Gregor. "I give some you, Gregor, and Boris. Extra for job. Okay?"

"Yeah, sure."

"So where's the accounts, passwords, so we can make transfer?" Victor asked Jerry.

"But this'll fuck me up," Jerry said. "I'll have no bargaining chips left if you take the money."

"Listen – I won't take all money. Just a piece. Too much opportunity to pass up. Global know I'm the bad guy, not you. Plus, another thing."

"Yeah?"

"You have no fucking choice. I'm making offer you no refuse." Victor lifted his pistol and aimed it at Jerry's midsection. "I'm like Godfather. Capeesh?"

"Yeah, capeesh."

"So?"

Jerry told Victor where to look on his Word program for the overseas checking accounts and the login names and passwords for each of them. Within half an hour, Victor had put into motion the transfer of a little over one million US dollars from Jerry's secret accounts to a secret one in his name in a bank in Russia.

"Now, we tie up girl and you to bed and get fuck out of here," Victor said.

He stood and nodded to Gregor. "You have nylon rope?"

"In car," Gregor said.

"Get," Victor said.

While waiting for Gregor to return, Victor helped Jerry from his chair and walked him over to the bed and laid him on his back next to Holly. Holly moaned as he shifted her around onto her back.

"You okay?" Victor asked her just as Gregor had returned to the room.

Holly nodded, but didn't seem sure of anything. "My head," she said.

"Bad concussion, that's it," Victor diagnosed, hoping it wasn't a fractured skull. Turning to Gregor, he said, "Tie legs of him to legs of her. Okay? Then tie their hands together, so no way they can move, make escape."

Gregor thought a moment, then nodded. Over the next five minutes he tied the legs and wrists of Jerry and Holly together.

"Nice work," Victor told him. "Now, we go."

He said something to Gregor in Russian and they started for the door.

Before opening it, Victor looked back at Jerry and Holly tethered together on the bed and told them, "Not worry. Police come soon, get you. In meantime, you talk."

Then, he and Gregor were out the door. Before taking off for the back exit, Victor hung the "do not disturb" placard on the outer door handle.

***

"Should we scream for help?" Holly asked.

Jerry shook his head. "What's the use. Like they said, someone'll be here in short order." Jerry frowned. "How you doing, Holly? You okay? How's the head?"

On her back within a foot of Jerry, her hands and his hands and her ankles and his ankles strapped together, she stared up at the ceiling and said, "No, I'm not okay. My head hurts. My brain hurts." She turned to him and winced. "I fucked up everything again, didn't I, Jerry?" She was close to tears, full of regret.

Jerry shrugged as he looked at her. After a moment, he started laughing.

"What's so funny?" she whined.

"This," he said. "Us. Being tethered together like this. Waiting for the cops to come arrest us." He laughed some more. "It's so ridiculous, it's funny."

She sighed and started laughing with him. But that hurt and she soon stopped.

"At least, we ended up together," she said, and that set off another wave of laughter between them.

Then, Holly turned to him and said, "I love you Jerry. I really do. But, I also realize that too much shit's happened between us."

"That shit," Jerry said, "is called betrayal."

She fell silent, deep in regret again. Then, she whispered, "Tied up like this, we can't even fuck for old time sake."

Jerry had no answer to that. He knew that because of Holly, his relationship with Jade was badly screwed up, perhaps irreparably. Stuck here, he was desperate to speak with Jade, to somehow explain himself and make things right. But he knew deep down that talk would end up going nowhere. How could he explain what he didn't understand?

He had no sound reason for continuing his relationship with a woman who had betrayed him over and over again, who had on three occasions almost caused his death.

Holly turned to him. "But we can kiss," she said. She smiled, then winced.

Jerry looked at her with a scowl.

"C'mon, Holly. Really?"

"Why not? If nothing else, it'll kill the time. Make me forget how bad my head hurts and my heart aches."

Jerry looked up and stared at the ceiling for a time. Unable to stop himself, he sucked in a breath, and wiggled sideways the foot or so across to Holly. Her eyes were wide with desire. After hesitating a moment, knowing full well what he was doing was stupid and wrong, Jerry kissed her anyway.

Chapter Forty-Five

Chief Reynolds

Early in the morning exactly one week later, Dick Reynolds sat across from Jack Fox at Fox's dining room table in his house in Depew sipping a cup of coffee.

"So you're staying on as Chief for a while, eh," said Fox.

"Yeah, thanks to you."

"Me?" Fox shook his head and smiled.

"Yeah, you."

"How me? Neal Barrett was the one who screwed up."

"Never mind," the Chief said. "Yeah, Barrett screwed up. Big time. Enough for Global corporate to send him packing. He was a stupid fool, anyway. Can you believe he hired some

Russian operatives behind my back," He laughed. "And they go stealing half a million of Global's money of the million they'd gotten from Jerry Shaw."

Fox whistled, then laughed. "That much?"

"Yeah, half a mil," Reynolds said. "That's what the Russians asked for. Because Global didn't have any bargaining power in the negotiations, it was decided that half was better than none. And to make matters worse, the Russian behind it all, this Victor Lenkov character has some CIA immunity that makes him untouchable. He's like a Russian 007. Bastard's probably dealing arms to Putin." He seethed a moment, then went on, "Aside from that, Global's getting their pound of flesh. All the other culprits in this sad caper are either dead or they're stuck in prison or out on bail, awaiting trial on felonies that could earn them serious time."

"You're talking about Jerry and Holly Shaw, and Jade Martin," Fox said.

"Yes, them," the Chief said. His brow narrowed as he lifted up his cup, took a sip of coffee, the set the cup down. "You know, Jack, that Jerry Shaw fellow – he looks a lot like that nephew of yours I met a couple of years ago in your hospital room after you got waylaid doing freelance work in Binghamton. What was his name?"

"Who?"

"Your nephew."

Fox remained silent for a time, trying to remember the name Jerry had used when he'd stopped by for a last visit with him at the hospital before he and Jade took off on their drive back down to Florida. In fact, Jade had been with him as well.

Finally the name came to him, or he believed it did.

"Steven," he told Reynolds. "You must mean Steven. My, my brother's kid. Yeah, and he does resemble Jerry Shaw, now that you mention it."

"And he had a girl with him, this Steven, his fiancé, I believe," Reynolds said. After a short laugh, he added, "And from what I recall, she looked a helluva lot like that Jade woman – Jerry's front all these years. What was the girl's name?"

There was no way Fox could remember that or was even going to try.

"I don't remember," Fox said. "Those two never did get married. Steven goes through women like tee-shirts."

"Andrea," blurted out Reynolds. "Wasn't it? Her name."

Fox shook his head, shrugged and said, "I don't remember."

Reynolds took another long sip of coffee, then stood.

"Well, gotta run," he said. "I have a meeting with the ADA handling the prosecutions. They wanna know what pleas might be acceptable to Global."

"What's Global's position on that?" Fox asked.

"Probably not as harsh as Barrett would have been," Reynolds said. "But Global'll want its pound of flesh. Jail time for sure for Jerry and Holly Shaw. The other one, Jade, may get off with probation. She's got a child – Jerry's kid – to take care of. As for Holly, she's also in trouble for her involvement in the kidnapping of Jerry, Jade and the baby down in Florida." He laughed and added, "Although the State's Attorney down there seems confused as hell as to how it got to that. She may face a felony-murder charge, though from what I understand, because of Jerry and Jade's testimony, they may not pursue that. I guess she was trying to stop the two dead guys from raping Jade when the Russians intervened."

"What about the Russians?" Fox asked. "Is the Florida state's attorney pursuing anything on their involvement?"

"Doesn't look like it," Reynolds said. "Based upon what Jerry, Holly and Jade told them, they're saying that the shootings were justified – they stopped Jade's rape and Holly's getting further beaten up. Plus both victims – if you could call them that – were scumbag jailbirds who'd violated their terms of parole."

"Sounds like it's a better world without them defense," Fox said.

"Yep, that's it exactly," Reynolds said. "Plus, the whole thing is so goddamn confusing." After a sigh, he said, "Well, gotta run. Tomorrow I fly back to Philly to start looking for my replacement. This time corporate's gonna let me do the hiring." As he stood, the Chief let out a ironic laugh and said, "So after five long years, we finally solved the Jerry Shaw case. Except for Global not quite getting all its money back, justice has been served."

"We'll see," Fox said. "You know how I feel about justice."

Fox got up and followed Reynolds to the front door. As Reynolds opened it, he turned to Fox and said, "And you're a lying sack of shit, Foxy. Don't think I don't know that."

He winked at Fox and added, "But in your shoes, I'd have probably done the same thing. That Shaw guy is quite a compelling character. Has real balls. From what I hear, he attended his own funeral and murder trial. And now, after all that, he's a hot-shot comic book writer with a movie coming out."

"You'll have to attend the premiere up here in Buffalo," Fox said. "Supposed to come out next May. You can come as my guest. Get a front row seat."

"And maybe I'll actually be retired by then, God help me," Chief Reynolds said with a laugh. He gave Fox a friendly tap on the shoulder, turned and walked out the door.

Chapter Forty-Six

Jade's Visit

Around two that same afternoon, Jade entered the visitor's room of the Erie County Holding Center, where those under arrest for various crimes were held until they made bail or, if they couldn't – like Jerry, who'd been denied bail as a flight risk – had the unfortunate experience of waiting months until their case was resolved by plea or verdict after trial.

Jerry was escorted to the visitor's room and upon entering it through a thick metal door, he ambled his way to a booth with a glass window separating inmates from their visitors. After sitting down, he nodded sheepishly at Jade on the visitor's side of the glass window of the booth.

There were old-fashioned black telephones on each side of the booth counters and Jerry and Jade simultaneously picked up their respective receivers. It was the first time they'd seen each other in the two weeks following Jerry's rescue from the Hampton Inn hotel room by the SWAT team of the Sarasota County Sheriff's Office and was then extradited three days later up to Buffalo.

"How are you?" Jade asked. She looked at him with a mixture of sympathy and hostility. She missed him and yet having learned of his continued contacts with Holly over the past two years, she was angry and hurt.

Jerry shrugged and replied, "How am I? Lousy. Everything's screwed up and it's all my fault."

"How's it your fault?"

"If I hadn't decided to end my anonymity, none of this would have happened," he said. "I wouldn't have called Jack Fox, and so those Russian guys wouldn't have found my number in his phone, and then they wouldn't have found me."

"What about Holly?" Jade snapped. "Your continued contacts with her led her to us and put us – and our child – in grave danger."

Jerry bowed his head. "Yeah, that, too," he admitted. After a moment, he looked up at Jade, straight in her eyes, and asked, "Can you ever forgive me? Are we over?"

Jade drew in a breath. The small shake of her head didn't reveal to Jerry what she'd decided. Yes, they were over. No, they weren't. Perhaps the truth was she hadn't yet made up her mind.

"All I want to know," Jade asked, "is it finally over between you and Holly?"

"Yes," Jerry said. "It's over. It's been over. Oooo-ver."

She smiled and gave that same, small doubtful shake of her head.

"No, it's not," she said. "I can see it in your eagerness to stay connected to her." She paused, then added, "I can see it in your eyes."

Jerry bowed his head again. After a time, he looked up and said in a determined, forceful way, "I love you, Jade. You and only you."

Jade smirked and shook her head. It was clear that she wasn't totally convinced of that. Not so much of his feelings for her, but by the "you and only you" part of Jerry's claim.

"We'll see," was all she said. Then, after a moment, she added, "We're probably gonna have some time to dwell on all that – from inside our prison cells."

"No," he said. "For me, yes. Not for you. Dean thinks they'll offer a plea that'll keep you out of prison. Harboring a known criminal isn't good, but not as bad as being the criminal - me. Plus, I got you pregnant and you have our baby to take care of. He says your mitigating circumstances are solid. Plus, you spent very little of the money I took from Global, and worked in legitimate jobs on your own so we wouldn't have to take more."

"Yeah, I know all that, from my lawyer," Jade said. "That's why I made bail and you didn't. But still I gotta worry. Until the Judge orders probation, I'm preparing from the worst."

Jade lowered her head and stifling tears, she sucked in a breath and said, "My poor baby. If I'm sent...sent to prison," and then she looked up, "what will become of him?"

"Your mother?"

Jade drew in another breath and looked up at Jerry. "Yeah, her," she said. She let out a short laugh. "At least, because of this, she's back in my life."

"Anyway," Jade went on, "maybe this forced separation will do us good. We can sort things out in our minds. Decide what our true feelings are. Figure out where we go from here."

"I already know what my true feelings are," Jerry said. "I already figured out where I go from here – hopefully, back into your arms."

"Then why did you keep that lifeline to her?" Jade asked.

Jerry leaned back his head and sighed. He wondered if Jade could ever let go of that question. Finally, he whispered, "I don't know."

"That's the problem, isn't it?" Jade asked.

It was another question for which Jerry had no answer. Instead, he asked, "How's Seius handling all this mayhem? I miss him so, so much."

"He's fine," she said. "Like I said, my mother's been a real help." She laughed. "She just loves being a grandma, something she never thought she'd be with the life I was leading, until you came into it." She drew in another breath. "Anyway, I rented a house up here for the three of us. It's in a nice, clean neighborhood. I even got one of the small portable Intex pools. Seius loves it." She laughed. "I do, too."

"I'd love to see you in a bikini splashing around in it," Jerry said. "And hold and kiss you while you're wearing it. God, I miss that. Holding you. Kissing you."

Jade shook her head. "Best to not think of that."

"Yeah, well." After a silence between them, Jerry asked, "What's going on with the movie? Or did I screw that up, too?"

"So far, so good," Jade told him. "Gabe notified them as soon as you were arrested and as far as she knows, it hasn't soured them on the project. They still think that your arrest is a selling point for the movie."

"Man, I hope I haven't blown it," Jerry said.

"Only time will tell," Jade replied. "The script you sent is being gone over. Marvel still likes it and they've assigned some experienced screenwriters to look it over – you know, smooth out the rough edges and make it more cinematic. They're called showrunners, whatever that is."

"Alright, at least that's positive news," Jerry said.

"Gabe also told me they've already hired a casting director and she's making some contacts."

"Anyone yet for The Anonymous Man."

"Yes, she started there first," Jade replied. "Alan Tudyk's been contacted and he seems interested. But no decision yet."

Jerry thought for a moment but was unable to call up an image of the guy, he shrugged.

"He was the pirate in Dodgeball and some other stuff," Jade said. She laughed and added, "One of the Marvel execs is pushing for Tom Cruise. He's never been in a superhero movie."

"Why should he be," Jerry said. "He's a superhero all on his own. But yeah, he'd work. Only thing's his age. He's like sixty, right?"

"I have no idea. Anyway, the point is, your arrest hasn't put the kibosh on the movie."

Jerry let out a breath, relieved over that. Then, he told Jade, "You know, I have another idea for the ending. Is it too late to revise it again and send it over?"

"I'll run it by Gabe," Jade said. "You have your laptop in here?"

"No, but I can do it in the library," Jerry said. "Believe me, there's lots of dead time and not much in the way of company."

"Holly's in here, too, you know," Jade said. "In the woman's wing."

"Yeah, I figured," Jerry said.

"Well, just don't go contacting her behind my back," Jade said.

"Never again, my love. Never again. I promise."

Chapter Forty-Seven

Jack Fox's Visit

The next morning, Jack Fox signed in to see Jerry.

"You look good," Fox said after Jerry appeared in the booth and raised the receiver to his right ear.

"I look better than I feel, I can tell you that."

"Coulda worked out worse," Fox said. "You coulda ended up dead."

"I suppose," Jerry said.

"Thanks for keeping me out of it," Fox said.

Jerry laughed and said, "Hey, I was tempted to bring you in, get me a better plea deal. But I figured you saved my life

– and Jade and the baby's, so what the hell."

"So what's the scoop?" Fox asked. "They gonna give you something decent?"

Jerry shrugged. "Not sure. Dean Alessi's meeting with the prosecutor handling my case as we speak. I should know something by lunchtime."

"Well, you'll be glad to know that Neal Barrett's been canned over at Global," Fox said. He laughed and added, "That means my old boss, Dick Reynolds, has been forced to delay his retirement a few weeks. I don't think he'll be as hard on you as Barrett would've been. Deep down, I think Dick has a soft spot for you, just like me."

"Well, I can only hope," Jerry said. After a silence, he said, "Jade was here. Yesterday afternoon."

"Yeah? How'd that go?"

"She's hurt, angry," Jerry said. "I can't blame her, after what I did – I mean with Holly, letting her call me, keeping in touch. Anyway, there seems to be a glimmer of hope for us. Actually, I think it's up to me."

"Well, do the right thing then," Fox advised. "Stay away from Holly – permanently."

"I don't think that'll be too hard," Jerry said. "She's likely to spend a few more years in the can than I am. I mean, not only does she have the new charges up here, but she's got the kidnapping rap down in Florida."

"That might give her more of a reason to hold on," Fox said.

Jerry shrugged. "Maybe."

"Sometimes you gotta fight against your urges, Jerry," Fox advised. "Use your brain instead of your, well, heart." He laughed and said, "Or is it your dick that's guiding you in this, whatever you got going with that woman."

Jerry shrugged and said, "I don't know. Both maybe."

"Well, you got your wish anyway," Fox said.

"What's that?"

"To become a notorious man," Fox said and laughed "You've become quite notorious. The papers are having a heyday with this story."

"Shit, I was afraid of that."

"You even made the New York Post," Fox said.

"Double-shit." Jerry sighed and looked suddenly troubled. "I just hope it doesn't sour me with the Marvel Entertainment people."

"How's that going?"

"So far so good, according to Jade," Jerry said. "The movie's still greenlighted. They've even started casting."

"Nice," Fox said.

"Only thing is, looks like I may not be around for the premiere."

"When do expect that's gonna be?"

"They're still planning next May. You know, during blockbuster release season."

"Maybe you'll get lucky and the DA will take pity," Fox said. "Especially if Reynolds doesn't push so hard."

They fell silent for a time, then Jerry asked, "So what's next for Mister Fox?"

"Wife wants me to finally move down to Florida," Fox said. "Spend my days out on a pool deck getting sun-burned and taking up golf. She's really tired of the Buffalo snow and gloom. And the taxes. And I gotta say, I can't blame her."

"So, when're you moving?"

"She's busy looking for a place. Wants to move us down to the Villages. Has a sister down there. But the prices of houses. Whoosh! Through the roof. You gonna keep your place?"

"I don't know yet," Jerry said. "Depends on how much time I get. Jade's moved up here for the time being to stay close depending on whatever prison sentence I get sent to. That is, if she decides to stay with me."

"Well, that's a good sign, isn't it?"

"Yeah, I guess."

"Well, hope that happens," Fox said. "And on that note, let me leave you with some friendly advice, even if I'm repeating myself." His narrow eyes bore into Jerry. "Stay away from Holly. You get it?"

"Yeah, I think so," Jerry said. "I completely get it."

Chapter Forty-Eight

Dean Alessi's Visit

About two that afternoon, Jerry was escorted to one of two jail interview rooms in the Holding Center - cramped, square ten-by-ten foot cells with cinderblock walls in serious need of a paint job. There was an old, rackety wooden table in the center of the cell with two armless orange, plastic chairs on each side.

After the guard deposited him in the cell, Jerry sat down on the chair at the far end of the table facing the locked metal door and waited. At ten after two, Dean Alessi arrived.

"How're ya Jerry? They treating you okay in here?"

"Oh, it's just dandy," Jerry said. "Like a stay at the Waldorf Astoria."

"Well, hopefully it won't be for too much longer," Dean said. "Though getting your bail reduced from the one mil Judge Lattimore set at your arraignment is likely a non-starter. Your history of anonymity works against us on that issue, shows that you're a serious flight risk. Still, I've filed a bail reduction motion returnable this Friday. The argument is that you had contacted Jack Fox, and me, before you were kidnapped and all the rest showing an intent to fact justice."

"Think it's got a chance?"

Dean shrugged and said, "I doubt it, but who knows. What is looking more promising is getting this case pled ASAP. The ADA handling it is offering something I think we can live with – attempted grand larceny in the second degree, a class D felony, and attempted insurance fraud in the first degree, a class C felony. The C felony has a range of five to fifteen years in prison. But as we discussed before, a prison sentence is not mandatory. And although we don't have as much mitigation as we had if you'd turned yourself in, we still have an indication, as I said, through Jack Fox and myself, that you were certainly planning to do so.

"Plus," Dean added, "Global insurance is not playing hardball. They're essentially leaving it up to the DA and have even indicated that they'd vouch for the fact that they've received full restitution – from you, even though the Russian that Barrett hired to find you took half what you had left in your offshore bank accounts."

"So, how soon can I plead?"

"As soon as next week," Dean said. "You'll be saving the prosecution from having to present the case to a grand jury. All that works in our favor. Shows cooperation, repentance, and all that crap. The DA'll probably recommend prison, but I seriously doubt if they'll go for the full fifteen years. One thing though, the court will have to run a probation report, and get a recommendation. That'll delay things another month or so."

"What's your opinion? You best guest-estimate?" Jerry asked. "I won't hold you to it, but how much prison time do you think I'm looking at."

Dean shrugged and said, "Look, I'm no expert at this, but I have talked to a couple of my brethren up here that are. They think you'll look at no more than a sentence of two to four. And with time served and good time once you're inside, you could be out in a year or so."

"A year," Jerry said with a sigh of displeasure. "Well, I guess that'll give me plenty of time to write more comics, and maybe another screenplay or two."

"Or, you could get time served," Dean said. "Lattimore's even-keeled and fair. He's not known to slam guys just for the sake of slamming."

Jerry thought for a time, then came to an abrupt decision. "Alright, let's do it," he said. "Tell the DA I accept. Let's get this over with."

"One other thing, Jerry," Dean said.

"Yeah?"

"I'm going to need to withdraw from your case," Dean said. "But don't worry, I have someone good taking over. His name's Dan Walters. Good, honest guy. At least, his name never came across my desk when I was working for the Lawyer Discipline Office."

"Why're you withdrawing?"

"Well, two reasons," Dean said. "First, as you know, I live in Florida. Second, I'm quitting private practice."

"To do what?"

"I've been hired by Florida Bar Division of Lawyer Regulation," Dean replied. "I'm in the chasing bad lawyers business again."

"Well, congratulations," Jerry said. "Good luck with that."

"But I was wondering if you could help me with something," Dean said. "I have this pilot script for a TV series called 'Lawyers Gone Bad,' you know, about what lawyers who chase bad lawyers do and all the stuff in between." He laughed and added, "My dad gave me the idea just before he passed away – said what I was doing would make a good

TV series. Anyway, I was wondering, with whatever contacts you're making in Hollywood, if you could help me pitch it and sell it."

"Sure, Dean," Jerry said. "I'll see what I could do."

"Oh, thought you'd get a kick out of this one," Dean said as he opened his briefcase and pulled out the morning edition of the New York Post. He flipped a few pages before finding the story he was looking for. Turning the paper around, he pushed it across to Jerry and pointed to the headline, "From Anonymous To Notorious."

With a laugh, Dean said, "That's just what you wanted, isn't it?"

After reading the first couple sentences of the story, Jerry looked up at Dean and said, "Yeah, kinda." He laughed and added, "Except for the jail part."

Chapter Forty-Nine

Big Pete

A few days later, Jerry had another visitor – his sister, Joan.

"I can't believe you did this to Dad," Joan said the moment she lifted the receiver.

"Dad?" Jerry laughed. "Does he even care either way – whether I'm dead or alive?"

"What are you talking about?"

"We've had this conversation before over the years, Sis," Jerry said. "Many times. How Mom and Dad doted so much over Petey and how they ignored us, our achievements, especially after he died. They gave up on life even though they had two pretty good kids to live for."

Joan bowed her head. All of that was true. Having invested so much in Petey, their parents seemed to have little left for them. And Jerry was right – he and she often had discussed it. She remembered crying bitterly into Jerry's arms at their mother's funeral.

"Tell me, then," Jerry said, interrupting this sour memory. "Did he genuinely grieve over my passing? I mean, I saw him at Marzulak's, at the wake, then funeral, keeping that poker face, never shedding a tear. At least, when I watched anyway."

"You watched all that?"

"Yeah, the wake, even the funeral," Jerry said. "How could I resist? Seeing how I'd be mourned. I sat in my rental car and watched people come and go. You and Dad, Aunt Judy and Bernice and Uncle Lenny and our idiot cousin, Lenny Junior, my co-workers from Micro-Connections and Dan and Andy from Binghamton, and Joe Reed and my other friends from high school. I was so blown away watching that. During the evening viewings those two days, I got out of the car and snuck up to the window on the side of Marzulak's and peeked in. And you know what, it seemed more like a group getting together for a party than my family and friends gathering to mourn my passing. Anyway, the times I spotted Big Pete, he didn't seem all that broken up. At least, a couple times, you broke down."

"I can't believe you did that," Joan said, shaking her head.

"Well, I did." Jerry laughed and added, "I even attended my own funeral mass."

"What?"

"Yeah, I followed the procession of cars over from Marzulak's. Then, in the parking lot, I actually put on a cheap disguise that I'd gotten at some spy store on the west side of Buffalo, snuck in the back and took a seat in the last pew in the back of the church." He smiled and continued, "I watched as poor cousin Lenny Junior got stage fright giving the first reading and was snapped out of it when Uncle Lenny shouted up something to the poor guy forcing him to finally stutter out the words."

"Of course, I didn't go up for communion," Jerry went on. "But during it, I made the mistake of glancing up and when I did, Holly's cousin, the ever plump, Mary Grace McDonnell, happened to be looking down at me. As with all funerals in Holly's family for years, Mary Grace had been tasked with playing the church organ and belting out sorrowful funeral tunes with her hearty soprano voice from up in the balcony of the church.

"That morning, when our eyes met in that instant, I gave a start fearing that she'd recognized me. I suppose the silly disguise saved me because in the moment after that, she looked away without uttering a sound.

"After communion, I then listened to friggin Jeff Flaherty give my eulogy. As he gave it, he knew full well that I wasn't dead. And, he knew full well that he was screwing Holly."

"Yeah, I wondered about that," Joan said, "especially at their murder trial. Had he eulogized the man he'd murdered?"

"I was there, too, you know."

"At their murder trial?"

"Well, yes. I'd lost weight, grown a beard. It was daring, but it worked. Nobody recognized me, not even you."

"And then, you became this fantastic comic book writer," Joan said. "And what's this I hear there's a movie coming out based on your superhero – The Anonymous Man."

"Yep," Jerry said. "Hopefully, next May." He sighed and asked, "You think that'll be good enough to draw Big Pete's attention and praise?"

"It always comes down to that," Joan said. "You're still craving the old man's attention."

"Like you don't."

"I didn't say I don't," Joan replied.

"You know I saw you and dad at Mom and Petey's grave one time, a couple years back," Jerry said.

"You did?"

Jerry remembered following Joan and Big Pete out to Holy Cross Cemetery from Joan's quaint Cape Cod at 89 Arbor Lane where the old man was presently living. He'd followed a safe distance behind them in his rental car as they negotiated the narrow, curvy cemetery roads until they came to the "Angels of Heaven" section directly across from a long, community mausoleum where dozens of the dead were entombed above-ground.

He'd stopped aways back from where they finally parked and watched as they strolled up through the gravestones until they stood before the dull granite family headstone with the names of his mother, Mary Shaw, his brother, Peter Shaw, Jr., and his name, Jerry Shaw, with the dates of their birth and death etched in. To the immediate right of Mary's name was Big Pete's, Peter J. Shaw.

With them standing there with sullen expressions, their hands folded in front of them, staring silently at the headstone, Jerry had exited his car and crept forward and hid behind a stranger's gravestone where he had a clear view of Big Pete and Joan.

"Yeah, and what I saw was quite disturbing."

"Why?"

"Why? Lemme tell you. After you guys were standing there for a little while, Big Pete started sobbing. You tried to comfort him, but it did no good. And then, I heard him moaning, 'Petey, my Petey.' He broke into tears and sobbed as you held him. Know what bothered me – there was not a single peep of grief out of him for me. He was crying only for Petey, but had nothing in his heart for me. I stamped away, angry and hurt. Down at my car, I couldn't help myself. I slammed the car door and both of you looked my way."

After a few seconds, Joan said, "You know what - I remember that. So, that was you."

"Yes. Me. Pissed off because my own father couldn't shed a tear for me. Not one tear."

Joan stared at Jerry, unable to come up with a thing to say in defense of Big Pete.

"He's scheduled to visit you tomorrow," Joan said. "Do you, do you want to see him."

Jerry drew in a breath, thought a long moment, then said, "Of course, I do. He's my father."

Chapter Fifty

A New Ending

D ean Alessi had put the final touches on the plea he and Jerry had agreed upon, and then put Jerry in touch with Dan Walters. Walters was an affable guy around Dean's age to whom Jerry took an immediate liking. More importantly, he seemed competent enough to develop a compelling argument to keep Jerry's prison time to a minimum. The hope was that the Judge would sentence him to probation, though that outcome, according to the Walters, was highly unlikely. The plea was set for Tuesday afternoon the following week.

While waiting to enter his guilty plea to attempted Grand Larceny in the Second Degree and Insurance Fraud in the First Degree before Judge Lattimore, Jerry spent his free time working on a new ending for The Anonymous Man screenplay on a computer in the Holding Center library. It seemed only fitting that the scene would mirror what he was going through in real life. The audience would want to know, he decided, what punishment had been issued for The Anonymous Man's thefts and fraudulent actions both before and after his escape into anonymity on 9/11.

After several revisions, Jerry was finally satisfied with the scene. With permission from the corrections staff under the Holding Center regulations, he was permitted to print out the changes and provide them to Jade during her visit the following afternoon.

As she silently read the new scenes from her side of the visitor's stall, Jerry waited apprehensively.

```
From the empty prisoner's gallery, the
handcuffed THE ANONYMOUS MAN is escorted by
two overweight Sheriff's deputies to the
defense counsel table on the left side of
a courtroom. The courtroom's gallery is
packed with reporters, lawyers and various
civilian onlookers.


THE ANONYMOUS MAN sits next to his counsel,
FRANK BOLTON, who clasps his left forearm
in a show of support.


After a few moments, JUDGE MAXWELL KANE, a
stern looking man in his sixties, enters
the courtroom by a door behind the uplifted
bench. With his sudden entrance, a bailiff
```

shouts, "All Rise!" and THE ANONYMOUS MAN and FRANK BOLTON stand with tight expressions. The Judge sits and scowls down at them. After a moment, he nods, ready to pronounce judgement.

Standing at the back of the packed courtroom that afternoon, trying to look inconspicuous, is NICK HOLLISTER, aka KING MIDAS. He wears a fresh pair of tan slacks and a polo shirt, and looks about, desperate not to be recognized by those charged with monitoring the use of his powers to control the minds of others within reach of his brain energy.

                    JUDGE KANE

        Will the defendant and counsel for the

        defendant please rise.

THE ANONYMOUS MAN and FRANK BOLTON stand and grimly face the judge.

                    JUDGE KANE

        Upon consideration of the defendant's
        testimony, and letters and other
        correspondence from numerous individuals
        on his behalf; upon the testimony of
        those called by both the prosecution
        and defense; and, upon review of the
        probation report, I hereby sentence
        you, for the crimes for which you have
        entered pleas of guilty to, to –

The Judge stops and seems momentarily puzzled. He blinks several times, bows his head. Then, he rubs his brow and momentarily looks up at the packed courtroom, seeming thoroughly confused and at a loss for words. Everyone in the courtroom is wondering - is he sick, wasted or what?

One of two young ADAs turns to his trial partner.

>   ADA #1
>   (to ADA #2)
>   What's wrong with him?

>   JUDGE
>
>   I, I -

Judge Kane bows his head again and swallows several times before finally looking up. He swallows, takes a drink of water from a glass on the counter before him, draws in a breath and, with a nod, seems to have reached a momentous decision.

>   JUDGE (cont'd)
>
>   - I, I hereby ...sentence ...you ...
>
>   to ... to time served, and a term of probation not to exceed five years.

There is a murmur of surprise from the audience. The two young ADAs look at each other with shocked expressions. A few members of the considerable audience filling the courtroom gallery cheer the decision and the Judge suddenly pounds his gavel.

                    JUDGE
            Quiet in the courtroom!

THE ANONYMOUS MAN looks relieved. He is a
free man.

From behind and unseen by him, KING MIDAS
briefly smiles from the back of the courtroom,
then slips out through long, ornately
carved wide wooden doors. A moment later, a
middle-aged man in a suit, perhaps a lawyer,
perhaps not, quickly follows after him.

                    JUDGE (cont'd)
            This case is ... is closed.

Still looking off, Judge Kane turns to The
Anonymous Man's Sheriff Deputy escorts.

                    JUDGE (cont'd)
            You may unshackle the defendant.

            This court is now adjourned.

As the Judge stands, the Bailiff calls out,
"All Rise!"
THE ANONYMOUS MAN turns to FRANK BOLTON.

                    THE ANONYMOUS MAN
            What just happened?

```
                    BOLTON
          I have no idea.
```

Grinning, Frank Bolton slaps The Anonymous Man on the shoulders as one of the Sheriff Deputies comes over and wordlessly removes his handcuffs. The Anonymous Man raises his hands and with a wide grin, turns to the gallery behind him. He is then crowded by reporters who want to know how he feels.

```
                    THE ANONYMOUS MAN (cont'd)
          How do I feel?
          (pause)
          Free.
```

"Free?" Jade asked as she put down the script.

"Yes, free," Jerry said. He smiled and added, "Now, if only King Midas shows up for my sentencing."

Of course, King Midas didn't show up for Jerry's sentencing. He was a fictional character that was born out of Jerry's mind. Jerry already had in his mind the idea that in the sequel to the movie, The Anonymous Man would communicate his displeasure to King Midas for compelling the sentencing judge to issue such a light sentence.

***

A month later, like The Anonymous Man, a handcuffed Jerry Shaw stood before Judge Lattimore next to his counsel. Only the judge didn't sentence him to time-served and five years' probation.

After a rendition of the more aggravating circumstances of Jerry's criminal conduct, including the extensive planning, amount stolen from Global, and the length of time Jerry spent in hiding and in possession of over a million dollars of Global's money, and then the mitigating factors, including Jerry's intent to turn himself in and the return of most of the money taken from the victim, Judge Lattimore paused for a few moments, before announcing, "I hereby sentence you to time served plus an additional term of imprisonment in a state corrections facility of one year. Upon your release from prison, I sentence you to an additional term of five years' probation to be monitored by the New York State Parole Board."

Judge Lattimore then continued, "Let me now advise you of your appeal rights, Mr. Shaw. Both you and the prosecution essentially waived rights of appeal of this sentence in paragraph eleven of the plea agreement, but I advise you that should you wish to file an appeal, you should do so within fourteen days of the entry of this judgment and commitment order pursuant to Section 450.10 of the Criminal Procedure Law. If you could not afford an attorney to represent you on appeal, an attorney could be appointed once again to represent you. Do you understand this, Mr. Shaw?"

Jerry said, "Yes, your Honor."

"Very well," said the Judge. "This case is closed and this court stands adjourned."

Smiling, Dan Walters turned to Jerry and said, "That's good. That's very good. With good time, you just might be out just in time for the premiere of that movie of yours."

In the next moment, two heavy-set, brooding Erie County Sheriff's deputies came over, took Jerry by the elbows, and escorted him back to jail.

Chapter Fifty-One

Nuptials

Having earned four months of good time, Jerry was released from the Collins Correctional Facility, a medium security prison, in Collins, New York, about forty-minutes south of Buffalo, on a crisp, cold day in early April, eight months to the day after his sentencing by Judge Lattimore.

Jade had decided to remain in Florida after all during Jerry's incarceration rather than stay up in the Buffalo area so that Seius' life would not be disrupted unduly. Jerry agreed that his son should sleep in his own bed in his own bedroom in their house on Manasota Beach Road down in Englewood, Florida.

During her last visit before returning to Florida, Jade revealed to a relieved Jerry that she was determined to forgive his two-year phone relationship with Holly. Despite his protestations, she told him that she'd have to accept that Jerry's feelings for Holly were deep set and beyond his control. He had once loved the woman, as she had once loved him, and they had their history apart from their relationship. Bottom line, Jade told him, "I love you."

Jerry nearly cried hearing that and promised never to betray her again.

"Don't make promises you can't keep," Jade warned him. "Because never is a long, long time."

But Jerry was adamant and humbled by her forgiveness.

"You'll see."

***

While down in Florida over the weeks that followed, Jade devoted a good deal of her time ensuring that Jerry's comic book episodes for King Midas that he'd written and illustrated in prison were sent to the publisher, properly edited and then published. Through the work of Dan Walters, the state corrections department allowed Jerry use of his laptop with the special comic book creating programs so that he could continue earning a living.

Jade also spent considerable time monitoring the

progress of The Anonymous Man movie. Upon Gabe Tivoli's recommendation, using Jerry's power-of-attorney, she hired an entertainment lawyer from LA who wrote an ironclad production agreement that had the potential to make Jerry and Jade millionaires depending, of course, how well the film did at the box office and on a streaming network thereafter.

While still an inmate at the Erie County Holding Center awaiting his sentencing on his guilty pleas, Jerry hired a Buffalo matrimonial attorney, Pat O'Rourke, upon Dan Walters recommendation, to untangle and extinguish his marital relationship with Holly. When it was all said and done, he and Holly were legally divorced by December, thus freeing Jerry to marry Jade.

Immediately after filing the divorce judgment, O'Rourke made arrangements for Jerry and Jade's nuptials. In early January, pursuant to New York State Corrections Directive 4201, a marriage license for them was issued by a Collins Correctional Facility official who'd been designated under the state corrections regulations as a town clerk. A week later, on a gloomy, damp though snowless day on the thirty-first day of January, the facility chaplain solemnized the marriage between Jerry and Jade in a brief ceremony in the chapel with two grim-faced corrections officers acting as witnesses.

"I'm finally Missus Jade Shaw," Jade whispered into Jerry's ear as they strolled arm-in-arm down the center aisle toward the exit of the chapel. Their marital bliss was immediately dampened when Jerry and Jade saw the two burly, glum corrections officers who'd been their marital witnesses waiting for them in the gloomy corridor just outside the chapel door. One escorted Jade out of the prison and the other, equally morose, took Jerry back to his work detail.

Out in the corridor, Jerry whispered in Jade's ear, "In a few short months, I'll be out of here and we'll properly celebrate this day." He then stole a long, passionate kiss before being pulled apart by their grumpy correction officer escorts.

***

During his eight months in prison, Jerry had plenty of time to keep abreast, through his phone calls with Jade and her occasional visits, of the progress of "The Anonymous Man" movie. After it was greenlighted in August, it was cast rather quickly with Ryan Gosling playing his alter ego, The Anonymous Man, and Regé-Jean Page cast as King Midas. The role of The Anonymous Man's nemesis, private investigator, Oscar Plato, who chases after Jerry, always on his heels but never quite capturing him until near the end of the movie, was filled by Michael Weston. The Anonymous Man's love interest, Karla Hanson, was to be played by an attractive, though unknown starlet.

The filming of the feature took five months, much of it on location in New York City and Buffalo with additional, fill-in scenes done at a studio in Hollywood. It frustrated

Jerry to no end that he couldn't be present to watch how the making of the movie was accomplished and to mingle with the director and actors about his creation, and perhaps give a tip or two as to what he was thinking for a particular scene, what the motivation was of The Anonymous Man or King Midas, or some peripheral character.

Dan Walters tried four times with motions to the court to get Jerry released, even agreeing to pay the expenses of his travel to the filming for the day, especially for the Buffalo shots. He argued that the movie's success would go far toward insuring Jerry's rehabilitation. But his submission by motion papers to Judge Lattimore was opposed each time by the DA and a denial order was quickly issued.

Finally, in mid-April, after weeks of editing and reshooting certain scenes, the movie was deemed ready for release. Not long after that, Jerry was released from prison and was finally reunited with Jade and Seius. He had never been happier in his life the moment Jade greeted him at the Punta Gorda Airport with a warm hug and deep, passionate while somehow balancing Seius on her hip.

Chapter Fifty-Two

The Premiere

It's my premiere, Jerry thought as he exited a long, black stretch limousine at the end of the red carpet for the Buffalo premiere of "The Anonymous Man" at the North Park Theatre in Buffalo's artsy northside on a cool but thankfully dry evening in mid-May. As was customary for big-budget Marvel Entertainment superhero films, a more glitzy red carpet premiere was scheduled for the following Saturday night at the iconic Los Angeles Convention Center.

As Jerry emerged from the limo in his stark black tuxedo, he was momentarily blinded by the blare of television camera lights and flashing bulbs of the paparazzi's Nikons and Canons clicking in his face. Squeezed against the roped-off red carpet were local and national reporters together with a sizable crowd of ordinary civilian gawkers many of whom were recording the event with their cell phones.

Jerry's exit from the limo was followed by Jade in her thousand-dollar Jacqueline white one-shoulder crepe gown. As they started their stroll down the red carpet, the crowd cheered. By now, their faces and back stories were well-known from the many articles that had graced newspapers and magazines across the world together with the many TV segments that had aired on local and national news stations during Jerry's prison term and especially in the run-up to the premiere.

Jerry and Jade waved to the crowd and smiled like the stars they had become as they promenaded arm-in-arm up the red carpet toward the glass door entrance leading into the movie theatre's vast lobby. Before stepping inside, they turned and waved to the reporters and paparazzi and onlookers. As they finally turned to enter the theatre, another loud cheer rose up from the crowd that was even louder from when they first appeared.

Once inside the lobby, Jerry and Jade were greeted with firm handshakes and hugs and sometimes, kisses, from each of the family members and friends they'd invited as VIPs for the local premiere, including Jerry's father, Big Pete, looking uncomfortable in his black tux, and his sister, Joan, also wearing a formal gown, and those many other relatives and friends who'd attended his fake funeral five years earlier.

Big Pete came over and gave Jerry a hug. "I'm so proud of you, Jer," he whispered and that recognition made Jerry gulp down a sob while Joan looked on with a wink and a smile.

Jade hugged her mother who, though now on the rather plump side, beamed in the expensive gown that Jerry and Jade had bought her for the event.

Mrs. Martin was holding Seius who looked adorable in his toddler-sized black tuxedo, though he was constantly pulling at his black bowtie that apparently scratched his neck. He smiled and reached out both his arms to Jade as she approached and shouted, "Mommy!" Jade had promised Jerry that the child would behave during the movie or simply fall asleep. "If he falls asleep," Jerry had remarked with a laugh, "that'll be a bad sign."

Not present, of course, was Holly. She was serving a ten-year sentence for attempted felony murder and second degree false imprisonment at a privately owned women's prison, the Gadsden Correctional Institution in Quincy, Florida, located on the panhandle forty minutes north of Tallahassee. She wouldn't have been invited in any event. Despite Jade's mild protest, Jerry invited her parents and her younger brother, Raymond.

"Why them?" Jade wanted to know when she saw them on the invitation list.

"Holly's parents are good people," Jerry replied. "They treated me great when Holly and I were married. As did her brother. Plus, if not for Holly's Mom, we might be dead."

Jade was cordial when Jerry introduced her to Holly's mother.

"My Holly could be there where you are," Holly's mother said to Jade. "If only she wasn't so selfish."

Jade held her tongue and smiled at Holly's mother, then at Jerry, who quickly pulled her away.

Jerry next found and greeted Jack Fox, Chief Dick Reynolds and Inspector Dan Miller.

"So here's the real anonymous man," Chief Reynolds said. "Or are you Jack Fox's nephew." He looked at Jade, then at Fox. "And you his nephew's fiancé."

"I don't know what you mean," Jade said with a sly smile.

Jerry turned to Fox with a knowing smile, then firmly embraced him during which he whispered in Fox's ear, "Thanks for all you've done for me."

"It was my pleasure," Fox whispered in reply. As he backed away, he told Jerry, "You are now officially, the Notorious Man."

***

An usher tapped on a gong telling those congregating in the lobby that it was time to take their seats. The show was about to start.

"Nervous?" Fox asked Jerry.

"A little," Jerry said.

"No need to be," Fox said. "It's a good story with interesting characters. Isn't that all that matters?"

Jerry shrugged, then grabbed Jade by the elbow and headed for theatre.

They had prime seats in the balcony. With him were the movie's producer, director, and several actors from the film. They patted Jerry on the shoulder and told him he had nothing to worry about. The dailies were great and a couple focus groups had already raved about it.

"It's gonna be a smash hit," was the general opinion.

Finally, the lights went down in the theatre and the audience's chatter and murmuring reduced to silence. Then the screen lit and the movie played.

Chapter Fifty-Three

The Notorious Man

~~~

"The Anonymous Man" grossed eighty-million dollars its first weekend of distribution in theatres and, over the next six months, it closed in on a billion dollars in US and international box office sales. Needless to say, Jerry and Jade and Seius Shaw were financially set for life.

Four months after the movie's release, Jerry and Jade bought a four-bedroom, five-thousand square foot mansion overlooking the Gulf of Mexico, with access to a private beach, on Casey Key Road just south of Sarasota. Their part-time neighbor was none other than Stephen King. One of the upstairs bedrooms with a view of the usual docile, crystal blue Gulf was converted into Jerry's studio where he worked on the screenplay for the sequel to "The Anonymous Man" as well as the continuing comic book adventures of his present superhero, King Midas, that were soon to be subject of another Marvel Entertainment movie.

During his months in prison, Jerry had been visited by several journalists wanting to write either an article or book about his five years of true-life escapades as an anonymous man. Several feature articles were published without his input in celebrity magazines such as *People Magazine, Us Weekly,* and *The National Inquirer.*

It was his agent, Gabe Tivoli, who came up with the idea that he write his own account of those five years. After Jerry enthusiastically agreed, she negotiated a publishing contract with Ransom House for his autobiography tentatively titled, "From Anonymous To Notorious."

Finding time to work on the project was difficult with all his other pursuits but finally, in November, six months after his release from prison, the book was published and quickly vaulted to Number One on the New York Times bestseller lists. At the urging of his comic book publisher, and with permission from Random House, Jerry finished a graphic version of his life story that was published to great acclaim in January of the following year.

Jerry spent his free time, such as there was of it, with Jade and Seius at the beach or driving them around to various attractions throughout the United States. In May, a year after his release from prison, the three of them took a trip to Ireland and visited Jerry's ancestral village on the eastern coast of the Ards Peninsula in County Down.

After the trip, Jerry flew up to Buffalo for a week to visit Jack Fox, Big Pete Shaw and Joan. He even stopped by to pay his respects to Holly's parents.

Fox showed Jerry the latest editions of his King Midas comic books that he had accumulated and wondered, while Jerry was signing them, where the plot was heading. Jerry laughed and told Fox he didn't have a clue. "It's a fluid process. And the good thing is, there are no end to the disasters that befall the human species and individuals from which King Midas is called upon to rescue them."

"You've certainly come a long way, Jerry Shaw," Fox said. "A long, long way. Not many could have pulled off what you have pulled off." With a laugh, he added, "Maybe you really are a superhero."

Jerry nodded as if in agreement with that. "Why not," he replied. "Maybe we all got a little superhero in us."

Fox laughed but then a silence fell between them as if there was nothing left to say or do after all they'd been through over the last now six years. Finally, Fox asked, "So, how's Holly doing? You ever hear from her?"

"No, not a word," Jerry said. "She's stuck in prison for

the next decade."

"Well, you know how I feel about her," Fox said. "It's a good thing she's unable to invade your life again. As I told you before, she's nothing but trouble."

Jerry nodded, trying to look convinced of that, but not really in the mood for another lecture from Fox warning him to stay away from Holly. Of course, he didn't tell Fox that deep down, no matter what their history, he couldn't shake Holly completely out of his mind. He couldn't help missing her. He knew it was ridiculous, but despite her many infidelities and murderous betrayals, he couldn't shake his feelings for her. After all, she'd been his first love.

***

Weeks later, Jerry was alone in his studio, having come to a plot crossroads in the present comic book episode of King Midas. As if sensing this creative impasse, Jade walked in the studio and said, "Come to bed, Jer. You need a break. You're pressing. I can tell." She smiled, raised her eyebrows and said, "I can make it worth your while."

"Yeah, maybe," he said. "But I'm almost there. Give me a few more minutes. Lemme just finish this panel."

After a frustrated sigh and a resigned nod, Jade gave in. She patted the top of Jerry's head and told him, "Don't wait too long. Okay? I might be asleep by the time you come to bed."

Then, she was gone and Jerry was alone with a blank panel and not a clear idea what to draw on it. The story was languishing. Jade was right. He should stop instead of forcing his creative mind to give him something, anything. It would end up being fake and he'd have to write it all over again.

But there was something else bothering him that night, nagging at his mind - Holly.

As if on cue, in the next moment, his laptop chimed, telling him he'd just received an email message. He minimized the comic illustration program and clicked open his email server.

The latest email on it was from a user named, "mstein@hotmail.com."

He frowned. The fictional Anonymous Man's love interest? He laughed, and thought, clever.

He opened the email and upon seeing who had sent it, he let out a gasp.

The author using the name, "mstein," was none other than Holly. Jerry drew in a breath and read what she'd written.

Hi Jerry.

I just got word this afternoon that I'll be getting out of this dump. There were some issues on appeal and looks like I'll be freed within a week. The problem is, I have no where to go. I mean, my parents would take me back, but do I really want that? So, I was wondering, I mean, if you could send me a few bucks to get me started. I'd love to settle down around where you are, and maybe, just maybe, we can see each other now and then. You know, as friends. Have coffee and simply chat about things. Try to figure out how we got to where we got to, that sort of thing. After all, our history goes back fourteen years. And, you were my first and only love.

So what do you say? Is it a deal. You won't have to tell Jade anything. After all, we'll keep it platonic – right? We'd be meeting as friends.

Well, gotta go. Can't wait to get out of this place, get my freedom back.

How's it feel being filthy rich – legally? Must be grand.

Can't wait to hear from you.
I love you,
Holly Shaw

Jerry frowned as he read the message. His frown held when he read it over twice more. The "I love you," valediction gave him a rush. The fact that she signed it using his name, Shaw, despite their divorce, caused a second thrill.

He clicked on the reply link and thought a long time before putting his fingers to the keyboard and...

About the Author

Vincent L. Scarsella is the author of speculative, fantasy, and crime fiction novels, short stories and plays. His published works include the crime novels *The Anonymous Man* and its sequel, *Still Anonymous*, and four novels of the Lawyers Gone Bad Series, *Lawyers Gone Bad, Personal Injuries, Winning Is Everything,* and *Pardon Me.* His stand-alone novels include the urban fantasy thriller, *The Messiah,* the dystopian novel, *Mind Plague,* and the alien invasion story, *InHumane.* He has also authored two young adult fantasy novels, *Escape from the Psi Academy* and *Return to the Psi Academy,* Books 1 and 2 of the *Psi Wars!* Series as well as the YA novella, *Within A Dream.* His novella, *The Walrus Was Paul,* is also available.

Scarsella's pilot script for a dramatic TV series based upon his Lawyers Gone Bad four-novel series is currently in development.

Many of his speculative short fiction have appeared in print magazines such as *The Leading Edge, Aethlon,* and *Fictitious Force,* various anthologies, and in several online zines. His short story, "The Cards of Unknown Players," was nominated for the Pushcart Prize.

In addition to his novels and collections, Scarsella is a prolific contributor to Amazon's Kindle Vella platform of serialized stories told an episode at a time, like a TV series in words. The reader can find Scarsella's stories at the following website: https://linktr.ee/scarsellafiction

Scarsella's plays, "Hate Crime," "Practical Time Travel," "The Penitent," "The Walrus Was Paul – A Beatles Sing-Along," "Land of the Greedy Mouse," and "Last Love," have been staged at colleges and community theatres.

Scarsella has also published non-fiction works, most notably, *The Human Manifesto: A General Plan for Human Survival*, which was favorably reviewed in September 2011 by the Ernest Becker Foundation, and its sequel, *Beyond The Lie*.

Scarsella retired in September 2010 after a long career with the State of New York in the Buffalo area as a prosecutor, attorney disciplinary counsel, and tax attorney and now resides with his wife, Rosanne, in Venice, Florida. He has three children, eight grandchildren with a ninth, and hopefully more, on the way.

Scarsella's writings can be ordered at: https://www.amazon.com/Vincent-L.-Scarsella/e/B002LYOJTQ

Readers may contact Vince Scarsella about this and his other works at vlscarsella@gmail.com

Printed in Great Britain
by Amazon